the EVERBORN CHRONICLES

BOOK 1

THE EVERBORN

BY:

NIXON

CHAPTER ILLUSTRATIONS BY
ISURU SANDEEP

ISBN: 979-8-218-75461-7

Published by House of NIXON Small Press

An Imprint of House of NIXON LLC
Hardcover First Edition 2026
Title In Series: The Everborn
Cover Illustrator: Duy Phan
Cover Designer: Duy Phan
Editor: Tiffany J. Shand
Chapter Title Art Illustrator: Isuru Sandeep
Interior Book Designer: Vladan Sekulić

Printed by IngramSpark, USA & UK, 2025

House of NIXON Small Press is a Veteran Owned and Operated Publisher.

FROM THE AUTHOR

Dedicated to the wonderful city of Malmö, Sweden.

My inspiration for The Everborn Chronicles would not exist without you. I am forever grateful for my time there, the people I met, the kindness, the architecture, and of course...kanelbullar!

A Message for Riley...

"Keep your back against the wind and let your courage carry you forward. Always dream big, adjust your sights when necessary, and continue with one foot in front of the other. Shoot for the Stars, but aim for the Moon, and let the Sun be your beacon that lights the path on your journey toward greatness."

—love, a first time Dad.

PROLOGUE

Cast me out for my rage.

A burning hunger cannot be tamed.

Born of pain, forged in fire, and washed by rain.

I boldly proclaim: the world shall know thy names.

And then I whispered to life—

Tabitha...Drusilla...Agatha...

CHAPTER ONE

MALMÖ

I separated the two men with ease. Their wide eyes and racing heartbeats betrayed their fear, each thud like a war drum in my ears. The silence that followed was deafening.

For five minutes, the two strangers had barked at each other. Loud, arrogant, and flexing their muscles. The kind of men who thrived on chaos and causing a scene wherever they went. Normally, I'd let men like them fight it out—even to the point of death—but I have two rules: no women, and no kids. Tonight, mothers clutched their children tightly, watching the brewing storm among the two men with fear displaying their anxiety. I was tired, hungry, out of patience and the train car provided little room for these two and their juvenile antics.

One of the men's fingers curled into a ball, and his shoulders twitched, but before anyone could blink, I was between the two men, arms outstretched. Both hit the ground hard, backs against the sliding doors. I did not mean to push them so forcefully, but hunger makes control complicated and my strength unpredictable.

"How did you—?" one man stammered.

"You're a monster!" the other shouted, his voice trembling.

The train lights flickered, casting brief shadows over their terrified faces. I took the opportunity to slip into the next car, disappearing before anyone could get a proper look at me. In a snap, I was gone, leaving behind only confusion and silence.

"Välkommen till Malmö Centralstation!" the announcer's voice echoed as the train came to a slow stop.

The train ride from Copenhagen had been uneventful—until the fight. Now, as I stepped into Malmö's crisp night air, the quiet streets and classical Gustavian architecture promised a refuge, though I doubted it would last.

The night was cold, the wind was brisk, the streets were empty except for my footsteps on the cobblestones. Malmö had a peaceful stillness, a quiet contrast to the Dallas chaos I left behind. Midnight approached, and the city seemed fast asleep—all but for one man down the street on Gustav Adolfs Torg.

He turned the corner, walking in my direction. The stench of him hit me first: sweat, cheap cologne, and something more primal. He wore a cheap suit and reeked of lies. A wedding band on his finger spoke of loyalty, but his scent told another story. He'd just left a prostitute.

We brushed shoulders as we passed.

"Ursäkta," he muttered.

I paused, tipping my eight-panel newsboy cap. "Förlåt," I replied.

I extended my hand for a handshake. He hesitated, confusion flickering across his face, but he eventually reached out. In a single motion, I grabbed his shoulder and dragged him into the shadows of a nearby alley. His muffled screams barely escaped through my hand pressed tightly over his mouth.

"This will hurt," I whispered, my voice low, "but only for a minute."

He thrashed, desperation underneath his gaze, but it was useless. My grip held him like a vice, his strength no match for mine. With one hand, I tilted his head, exposing the pulsing vein that betrayed his terror. His body grew limp, surrendering to exhaustion.

I glanced at the moon, the blanket of the night watching me closely. "Forgive me for my sins," I murmured a quiet prayer. Then, without hesitation, I sank my teeth into him.

His life drained away, his blood filling me with warmth and focus. He had been a liar, unfaithful, a man with no honor. In death, his passing had more meaning than it ever did in life.

But as I fed, a watchful feeling crept over me—someone other than the night was watching.

I lifted my head, scanning the alley. The stillness returned, unsettling me. Then, in an instant, something darted past. A blur moving faster than any human could. My instincts roared to life, and before I knew it, I was in pursuit. I followed that elusive shadow down the deserted street, around a corner, and into a clearing nestled in a nearby cemetery.

"Are you following me, mate?"

The voice startled me, cool and self-assured. I turned to see him standing a few paces ahead, his hands casually tucked into his pockets.

He noticed me looking at his chest, the realization hit him. "You're not going to find a heartbeat," he said, smirking.

My stomach dropped. "What?"

He chuckled. "You must be new around here."

I tensed, ready to lunge, but he moved before I could blink. I hit the ground hard, mud splattering my wool trench coat. My hat landed a few feet away.

"You're going to have to do better than that, mate," he taunted, his smirk infuriating.

"Who the hell are you?" I growled, rising to my feet.

He tilted his head, amused. "Jag heter Michael. Och du?"

"I'm Leo," I said, brushing off my coat. "And for the record, you were following me."

Michael laughed again, this time more deeply. "Right. And I suppose you're just wandering around at night, draining the unfaithful in alleys for fun?"

I stiffened, unsure how to respond. "My affairs are no business of yours."

He raised an eyebrow. "That may be true but what you were doing in that alley was rather a rookie move. You're not from here, are you?"

I stayed silent, trying to process his words.

"American?" he asked, with that smirk that seemed to be permanently plastered on his face.

"Yeah," I replied.

"Well," he stepped closer to me, "let me be the first to welcome you to Malmö."

Michael exuded an effortless confidence that was borderline disturbing. He could not have been older than his mid-twenties, early-thirties, tall with an athletic build, olive skin, and hazel eyes that glinted like polished amber. His smile—sharp and knowing—hinted at trouble, the kind that left women breathless and men wary.

He was dressed impeccably: a long tweed coat over a black suit, shirt, and tie, all meticulously coordinated. A silver ring glinted on his finger, its Latin inscription forming an upside-down cross. Each step he took was so light it seemed as though he were floating. I found myself caught in his presence, mesmerized by his movement, a fog settling over my thoughts. Who was this man?

He glanced at his watch, the movement snapping me out of my trance. "Well, mate," he said, "I ought to get going. The crew will be expecting me any minute now. They won't like that you took our catch tonight. You now owe me a favor, not now, but later." He winked at me, then disappeared into thin air behind the late-night bus that drove past us.

The encounter with Michael left me uneasy yet intrigued.

I wondered if we would cross paths again. And this favor, was it a bluff?

Were there others like him?

I sought out Malmö after finding some old photos that belonged to my parents. I figured it was as good a place as any to start my search—my search for answers, and for belonging.

I pulled a Manchester cigarette from my coat pocket, inhaling deeply. The cancerous smoke filled my lungs, grounding me for a moment. The night was still young by my standards, so I wandered the cold streets a little longer, taking in Malmö's quiet charm, passing by 'The Twisting Torso,' tasting the salt off the Baltic Sea that was carried by the cool breeze. Across the city stood Emporia, a sprawling mall in the Hyllie section of Malmö, surrounded by modern corporate buildings, upscale apartments, and Malmö Arena, that gleamed even in the dim moonlight.

It was time to rest, though rest felt intangible with the events of the night replaying in my mind. The lonely moon watched over me, and I returned its gaze before lighting another cigarette and slipping the rest into my pocket.

CHAPTER TWO

QUALITY VIEW HOTEL

The Quality View Hotel loomed ahead, its gold-plated revolving doors gleaming. I stepped inside, immediately noticing the receptionist at the desk. She glanced up from the book she was reading, her blonde hair spilling over her shoulders like molten gold. Her pale skin seemed to glow under the dim lights, but her gaze lingered on me a beat too long, her smile strained. Something in me disturbed her—I could see it in the slight tremor of her hand before she abruptly disappeared into the back office. I frowned. It was late—maybe she was tired. Or maybe it was something else.

"Good evening," I said, my voice low and steady.

"God kväll," a man said, stepping into her place. His thin smile wavered as he glanced between me and the empty doorway she'd fled through. "Hur kan jag hjälpa dig?"

"English," I said curtly.

He straightened, dialing back his false cheer. "How may I assist you tonight?"

As he booked my room, I scanned the lobby. Off to the right, a bar called 'The Social' connected to the hotel, housed a group of five men. I was surprised they were still nursing drinks this late.

A muted television broadcast in the distance of the lobby caught my eye, its English subtitles scrolling:

"...the fourth violent attack in the city in the last two weeks. Police warn residents to avoid walking alone at night. No names have been released, but two suspects remain at large. If possible, travel during peak hours and in groups..."

"Wild times these days," the manager said, sliding the room keys across the counter. "Best to heed the warnings."

I squinted, scanning his lips for trouble. "Warnings?" I asked.

He hesitated, his smile faltering. "The police warnings. We wouldn't want anything to happen to our newcomer, now would we?"

My jaw tightened, anger stirring beneath the surface. It took effort to keep my tone level. "No, we wouldn't," I replied, matching his smile with one of my own.

The contrast between those first few seconds and now felt amplified. He seemed almost reserved, as though he was studying my every movement and word. I couldn't shake the feeling that he was hiding or protecting something—perhaps the young woman who never returned to her desk.

"The elevator is down the hall to the right, seventh floor. If you need—"

I was already walking away, his voice trailing off behind me. *Weird little fucker,* I thought. This city was filled with questions, and I'd barely scratched the surface.

Up in my room, I opted for a long, hot shower to clear my head and reflect on my journey thus far. I had left Dallas behind because it had nothing more to offer me. I'd partied at the best clubs, tasted the finest cuisine, sipped the richest wines, and drained the most worthless souls. Unmotivated, unfaithful, dishonorable. I wouldn't call myself a vigilante; I simply preyed on those who preyed on the weak. Humans are flawed creatures, yet I still find myself feeling sympathy for them. In those moments where I hold a life in my hands, I pray not only for their forgiveness but for my own.

It's always been a struggle, this push and pull between sparing a soul and claiming it. I've learned to make adjustments, feeding only when necessary and intervening when provoked. Without guidance, I stumbled through this existence alone. I often questioned what I was and why I'd never encountered another like me. I've read the books, heard the myths, and absorbed the stories, but none of them ring true. The sun provides a warmth in the cold, I enter homes as I please, and I'm quite fond of garlic.

The real tragedy? History's details change depending on who tells it.

I remember how it all started, back in that orphanage. Changes came over me: unnatural strength and insatiable hunger. Not for food, but for human flesh. After my first victim vanished, I knew I'd strike again. And again, until I killed the very couple who had sheltered me. It was accidental, or so I tell myself, but my hunger didn't leave room for mercy. I hid their bodies and fled under the cover of the night.

That was twenty years ago. Yet here I am, still looking no older than thirty. Time slowing to a pace in which I don't seem to grow older.

After the shower, I sprawled out on the bed, air-drying while staring at the dark ceiling. The city's murmurs seeped through my window—a few cars in the distance, a muffled laugh on the street below, and the ruffle of dried dead leaves. Dallas was far behind me, and yet old ghosts lingered at the edges of my mind. I closed my eyes, forcing myself to rest, though sleep came in fitful waves.

By the time the morning light crept through the curtains, my head felt clearer. I dressed quickly and went out for a walk, the air cool against my face. Malmö was awake now. Shops opened, people rushed from the metro to their offices, baby strollers passed by, and horns honked. I was ready to see what secrets the city might reveal in daylight.

I grabbed a newspaper and sipped my coffee on a bench, reading about the recent violent attacks plaguing the city. Some blamed the steady influx of migrants in the country. Others argued mismanagement of law enforcement. But judging by the groups of people passing by, it seemed everyone was taking the last night's warnings seriously. Two young men caught my eye—something about their demeanor felt off. I watched them quicken their pace behind a woman walking alone in the distance. Folding my newspaper, I had a hunch, so I decided to investigate.

They led me behind a restaurant, in an alley where the trash bins were lined up. As I drew closer, I realized they were grappling with that young woman. Without hesitation, I stepped between them and her. These men were noticeably stronger than the pair I'd separated on the train, their fists clenched and ready. Yet they didn't budge. I reached down to help the woman up, and to my surprise, it was the receptionist from last night.

"Get your hands off me, you filthy Everborn!" she hissed. Before I could react, she slashed at my cheek, drawing blood.

I stumbled back, shocked on two counts: why had she struck me, and how had she managed it so quickly?

Just then, Michael appeared. He leveled a cool gaze at the two men and calmly recommended that they leave. They didn't protest and they bolted without a word.

With the men gone, Michael turned his attention to the woman. "You sure you want to do this mate?" he asked, voice almost playful but underscored by challenge.

She lowered into a defensive stance, eyes burning red, nails elongating, fangs bared. "You and your friend are on the wrong side of town," she snarled.

Her transformation and quick shift was one I recognized instantly. We were all one and the same.

Before Michael could respond, a police officer's voice rang out behind us. "What's going on back there? Come out slowly, hands up!" He had one hand on his holstered pistol, another on his radio.

Caught between them, I looked at Michael, who looked at her, who looked at me. In a heartbeat, the woman fled. The officer shouted for her to stop, then charged toward us. Michael grabbed my arm.

"Follow me, now!" he ordered. We ran, the officer's shouts and radio crackle fading behind.

We raced through alleys, vaulted over fences, even scrambled across rooftops. Strangely, the chase exhilarated me. I felt more alive than I had in years. When we finally stopped, we doubled over, laughing and catching our breath.

"Glad you can keep up, mate," Michael said, impressed. "You might even be faster than me. You didn't miss a step."

"Funny enough," I said, still panting, "I've never ran from the police before."

He chuckled, and I found myself relaxing. Something about his presence made it easy to lower my guard, like we were friends. He asked if I had family in this part of town, and I explained why I'd come to Malmö, summing up my past as best I could.

"That's one hell of a story, mate. Quite odd you don't know what you are."

I bit my lip unsure of what to say.

"Where did you stay last night?" he asked.

I began, "The Quality View Hotel—"

Michael's expression hardened. "Either you're clueless or you're plain foolish. I'll assume the former. Anyway, you can't go back there, mate."

I stood upright, matching his serious tone, but mocking, "and why not...mate?"

His lips pressed tightly together, holding back a retort before he spoke plainly, "You, me—our kind isn't welcome there."

But I pressed for clarity.

"Our kind? What do you mean?"

He sighed and shook his head as if I were a naïve child.

"There's an entire world you know nothing about, Leo. You feed in the open, you sleep where you shouldn't, and you meddle in things that don't need to be meddled with. Stay away from her and that place."

I pointed to my cheek, the wound already nearly healed.

"That woman called me an Everborn. She acted like my touch disgusted her. Why is that?"

Michael smirked, baffled. "God, you really have no idea, do you?" He patted me on my back. Strong but strangely soothing. "I don't think I'm the one to explain it, but there's a divide, and fate has chosen your side. Come with me. You have a lot to learn."

I hesitated. "Where are we going?"

"Two stops, mate," he said, flashing a grin. "First, you need a new suit. Then, I need to introduce you to someone. Someone who can explain better than I can. Dare I say your future boss?"

"My boss?"

He smiled. "The leader of the Everborns, Jericho."

CHAPTER THREE

MORISON'S

Michael had the gift of gab. I hadn't known him for more than twenty-four hours, yet his flair for the dramatics was impossible to miss. Admittedly, I was drawn to his words, even if they sometimes felt like half-truths wrapped in a performance. Still, I couldn't shake the feeling that this "leader of the Everborns" might have the answers I'd been searching for. Everything about this—about them—was new and strangely exciting.

Michael led me into the heart of the "Old City," Gamla Staden, just a block or two from where we'd first met that night. The area buzzed with life, far more vibrant than the quieter and refined Hyllie district we'd left behind. The streets were packed with people from every corner of the city. Vendors lined the sidewalks, their stalls bursting with trinkets and street food, while the air carried the irresistible aroma of freshly baked cinnamon rolls. Clothing stores, cafés, and chatter filled the scene. It was vastly different to the Malmö I'd met on my arrival. Night and day in every sense of the phrase. And yet, weirdly enough, I felt connected to it. For reasons I couldn't quite grasp, this place felt like it was where I belonged.

I glanced at Michael. He stood tall, shoulders back, head high, scanning the crowd with purpose. After a moment, he nudged my shoulder and pointed ahead. "You see that?" he asked.

I followed his gaze across the street, where a group of men was disappearing into a shop with a sign that read *Morison's.*

"That's where we're headed," he said with a curt nod, as if sealing the decision. He started to take a step, but curiosity got the better of me.

"Why a new suit?" I asked.

His answer was as casual as I expected, but the words themselves caught me off guard.

"Because we're not thugs, Leo." he smirked while plucking his suspenders. He winked at me. "They don't dress this nice."

I smiled at his theatrics while he continued.

"Plus, you've been seen with me, so like it or not, you're associated with us now and that means dressing the part. Although, to be fair, your birthright made sure of that."

My birthright, the leader of the Everborns, suits, and police pursuits. Riddles seemed to be the rule, not the exception. I rolled my eyes, and Michael caught it. He flashed a knowing smile, the kind that suggested I hadn't seen anything yet.

"You say my birthright like my future is already written."

"Mate, you're one of us. An outsider no doubt, but you're certainly not one of them."

I paused, studying his expression, and mediating on his words.

"You seem a bit beside yourself," he said with an air of amusement. "Things will never go back to how they were. You want answers, and you'll get them. But first—" He spun around, arms spread like wings, gesturing at the bustling streets. "Look around you, Leo. Tell me, what do you see?"

I sighed, glancing around to humor him. "Are you serious? I see shops. People. Like any other city—"

"No, no," he interrupted, his voice suddenly sharp with eagerness. "Tell me what you see."

I looked harder—harder than I ever imagined I'd have to. Then, a veil lifted, and clarity washed over me. I noticed something strange: people moving in slow motion, their steps deliberate and sluggish. Others darted through the crowds with a speed and precision I recognized instantly. They were like Michael and me. Before vanishing into the shadows, I could see them, but it dawned on me that the humans around us could not keep up with the speed in which our kind moved. We were invisible to them and only showed our faces when we allowed it.

"Use your undead gift of vision and, see all that the world is trying to show you," Michael said, his voice a whisper, his performance significant.

What unfolded before me was like stepping into a world within a world. There was the surface—the here and now, where humans bustled, unaware—and then there was the other layer. A hidden realm, unnoticed by mere mortals. Time moved both slowly and quickly, a paradox unraveling before me. In that moment, I saw them clearly: two separate worlds between man and other worldly beings, separated by the invisible curtain.

A wave of anxiety washed over me, and I felt the dampness under my arms as sweat began to bead.

Michael pointed to a homeless man across the street. "That old geezer over there, cast away by the world, isn't just any homeless man."

I looked at the man, his hunched figure wrapped in layers of tattered clothing. Something about his stillness felt heavy, almost deliberate. I glanced at Michael, his words lingering in my head, and felt a pang of pity.

"He's one of us," Michael continued, his tone neutral but firm. "Also cast away by people like the woman you naïvely tried to help earlier."

My head snapped back to him. Michael had my full attention now. "Tell me more."

"There'll be time for that soon enough." He winked, a grin tugging at the corner of his mouth. "Just know the people at the top are so high that they can't see the ones at the bottom."

Without another word, Michael motioned toward Morison's. "You're going to like old Morty," he said, his grin widening. "It's where we all go to get our digs and there's a bar in the back. That's our hangout. This is our side of town, mate."

I pulled a cigarette from my jacket pocket and lit it, hoping the smoke would steady my nerves. The way Michael talked about Morison, he must be important to the group, I thought as we crossed the street. The cigarette was almost down to the filter when Michael plucked it from my mouth with a casual swipe, extinguishing it with a flick of his fingers.

"Come on," he said, nodding toward the man sitting on the front steps of the boutique. Michael gave the man a small nod, and I copied him, uncertain of the gesture's meaning. Without missing a beat, Michael opened the door, and we stepped inside.

"Lieutenant!" The man behind the counter greeted us with a booming, cheerful voice.

I glanced around, confused. He couldn't be talking to me, and I didn't see a militant order in Michael.

Michael smiled and clasped the man's hand in a firm shake.

"Adopting stray animals again, are we?" the man joked, looking over his half moon spectacles with a glint of amusement.

They both laughed, while I bit the tip of my tongue, swallowing every razor-sharp word that formed.

"This is Leo," Michael said, nudging me forward. "He comes from across the ocean."

The older man's brow lifted as his gaze swept over me, then darted back to Michael. "An American?" he said, his tone laced with curiosity, as if a puzzle piece had fallen into place. "Well then." He stepped forward with a flourish. "Allow me to introduce myself. My name is Morison. I'm the owner of this fine establishment, trusted advisor, retired fighter, whiskey connoisseur, and maker of the best damn suits you'll find in this town. And yes, I am an Everborn."

I met Morison's gaze and extended my hand. As I did, a dagger displayed on the shelf behind him diverted my attention. It was not just a weapon—it looked like an artifact, well-worn but lovingly maintained. Morison kept his shop filled with items like that, each one an unspoken story, hidden behind the golden crest of a family's heirloom. Morison's words replayed in my ear, a retired fighter. *A man who holds onto his past.*

Under the dim light, a photo on the wall was displayed proudly. It showed a younger Morison standing with another man, both grinning with a sense of mischief. I opened my mouth to ask about it, but before I could, Morison ushered us through a set of double French doors.

"Francis," he called out to the bartender as we entered, "three gin and tonics, if you please!"

The bar we stepped into felt worlds apart from the refined order of the shop. Dim, warm lighting illuminated a space filled with low murmurs and quiet intensity. The scent of aged wood and smoke lingered in the air, mingling with faint traces of spiced gin. A chandelier, its crystals dulled by time, hung crookedly from the ceiling, casting flickering shadows over the room.

At first glance, it looked like any other questionable hole in the wall tucked away in the city. But as my vision adjusted, I noticed the details—the way the patrons carried themselves, with a predatory grace that was impossible to ignore. Some had an almost human quality, blending seamlessly into the world outside, while others emanated a quiet, otherworldly menace. Questionable indeed.

The moment Michael stepped inside, the room's energy shifted. Conversations dipped, heads turned, and the quiet power of attention followed him as we walked through. A few offered slight nods of acknowledgment, gestures I could only assume were signs of respect. It was clear: Michael was someone important here.

Morison led us to a table in the far corner, away from prying eyes. He gestured for us to sit, pulling out a chair for himself with practiced ease and tucking his glasses into his shirt pocket.

The drinks arrived swiftly, Francis placing the glasses with care before retreating back to the bar. Morison leaned forward, his expression growing serious. "So, tell me, Leo—what brings you to Malmö?"

As I raised the glass to my lips, the subtle burn of gin and a hint of citrus hit my senses. I hesitated, but his gaze held steady, and I found myself recounting my story—the first time I felt the hunger, my first kill, and the night that changed everything with my foster parents. "That was the night I knew I was different," I finished quietly.

The French doors swung open, and the two men from the alley entered. My fists clenched instinctively, but before I could react, Michael stood and strode toward them. The men straightened as he approached, one of them glanced toward me briefly—a look of curiosity. Michael spoke to them in hushed tones, too quiet for me to catch. The exchange lasted only a few seconds before the three of them turned and left the bar together.

Morison's voice cut through my thoughts, pulling me back to the present. "And you've never met another like you?" The tone in his voice held disbelief.

"No," I said, frustration rising in my own voice. "I've been questioning 'why' my entire existence." I turned to him, my voice flat, neutral, and asked simply, "Have you ever stayed awake at night looking for a reason—any reason to live?"

He diverted his gaze from mine, as if he were ashamed of my words.

"No, I do not dabble in such thoughts. You would not be here if you were not a warrior." He took a sip from his glass before finishing, "You're stronger than you may think."

He dismissed my question like they were frivolous words, but I pressed on, caught in my emotion. "Strong or not, I think of death often, more times than not wanting nothing more than to end this curse."

He rose one eyebrow while running his fingers through his hair.

"Curse?" Morison leaned closer, the faint scent of gin on his breath. "You think this life is a curse?"

I did not answer, and his voice dropped to a near whisper. "Let me tell you something, Leo. We are not cursed. This," he gestured to himself, to me, "is a gift to be cherished. If you ask me, we should not only walk freely on this earth—we should rule it."

His eyes darkened, the black of them swallowing the light, and his voice grew harsher. "But not everyone sees things that way." His thousand-yard stare made the hair on the back of my neck rise. Then, just as quickly, his expression softened, and he sighed. He adjusted his seat, fingers drumming lightly on the table as if steadying himself.

"I'd take it you don't know the story about the fight on Fox Retreat Hill?" He downed the last of his gin in one swift motion, setting the glass on the table with a deliberate clink. "Better known as the First Battle."

He gestured for Francis to bring another round, his gaze growing distant.

"A long time ago, the title 'Everborn' was nothing but a slur for those without pure blood. The Night Walkers treated us as second-class citizens."

He paused; his fingers brushed the rim of his empty glass. "We wanted unity. We believed we could walk this earth freely, living and ruling as one. But the Night Walkers only saw us as a stain on their purity."

His voice dropped lower, the weight of the memory seeping into his words. "They came for us in the dead of night. Ambush. No warning. They butchered anyone who wouldn't kneel—men, women, even children. The blood-soaked Fox Retreat Hill, and for a moment, it felt like we'd lost everything."

Morison straightened in his chair, his gaze hardening. "But we didn't fall. We rallied. I was there, calling on every ounce of fury and strength we had left. I told them we couldn't let the Night Walkers treat us like filth—not anymore. That night, we stood together and said, 'No more.' We drove them back, made them retreat, and made that hill a no trespassing zone for both groups." He sighed, leaning back in his chair. "It's been nothing but petty fights and senseless deaths ever since. I'm too old to stand on the front lines now, but I don't think we'll ever find peace. The Night Walkers don't want peace. They want to cower and hide among the humans, acting as their footstool, hoarding their power while we strive for something greater."

Silence surrounded us, and the pain in Morison's story echoed in my mind. For the first time in my life, I was sitting among others like me—people who, despite their hardened nature, had shown me a measure of hospitality. Yet, to think there was another group out there, one that despised the likes of me simply for my blood, was almost too much to comprehend.

The lines were blurred.

The thought of the young woman from the hotel crossed my mind, her sharp words cutting me deep like the mark she left on my cheek. At first, she'd seemed harmless—a typical receptionist. But in that alley, she'd fought fiercely, as if she needed no saving.

Speaking of those two men, one thought canceled the other as the French doors creaked open and Michael stormed back into the bar, his expression unreadable but his movements sharp.

"We need to leave," he said, striding toward our table.

Morison raised an eyebrow. "So soon?"

Michael didn't answer, his focus shifting to me. "Let's go. Now."

I pushed back my chair. "What's going on?"

Michael was already heading for the door, offering no response.

I hesitated, glancing at Morison. His expression remained calm, but his words carried weight. "Be careful," he said simply.

Michael smirked, calling over his shoulder, "Don't worry, Morty. I'm always careful."

I nodded and hurried after him, the cool night air brushing my face as we stepped outside. The fresh air did little to clear my head.

I quickened my pace to match his. "Do I have time to burn a cigarette?" I asked, already reaching for my pack.

Michael didn't look at me, his focus fixed ahead. "You know, if it were possible, those things would've put you in an early grave by now."

I gave him a large smile. "Yeah, well, given my certain...circumstance, I don't think that's a problem I'll need to deal with anytime soon."

He shook his head. "Hurry up, mate," Michael said, his tone sharp but vague. "We've got something important to take care of."

His words left no room for argument, and I didn't press further. Instead, I followed him into the shadows, feeling like I was being pulled deeper into something I wasn't truly ready for. But whatever it was, there was no turning back now.

Excitement and the combination of fearing the unknown created a whirlwind of anxiety I couldn't extinguish.

I guess I am an Everborn.

CHAPTER FOUR

INTERROGATION

The road narrowed as we moved further from the heart of the town, the pavement giving way to a rough gravel path. Around us, the trees grew thicker, their bare, gnarled branches stretching like skeletal fingers toward the darkening sky. Even without leaves, they cloaked the area in shadows, obscuring the outline of the abandoned house that loomed ahead. The structure was sagging, weathered by time, with its wooden panels splintered and warped. A crooked chimney jutted from the roof, and the few remaining windowpanes reflected the faint glow of the moon, fractured like shards of a broken mirror. The air was heavy with damp earth and the faint, acrid scent of decay, making it clear—this was a place forgotten by the world.

Michael slowed his pace, his sharp gaze scanning the surroundings. "We're here," he said, his voice edged with finality. He turned to me, squinting as he studied my posture. "Are you with us?"

The question hung in the cool air between us, lost in context without any meaning.

"What do you mean?" I asked, my confusion growing.

Michael took a slow step back, his gaze sweeping over me from head to toe. "Before we go in there, I need to know I can trust you. That you will have my back. Just like I had yours in that alley."

The weight of his words settled in my chest. Was this my chance to walk away?

Michael's question felt less like an invitation and more like a challenge. My curiosity surged again, pulling me toward the unknown.

What was inside that crumbling house?

Was this a test?

I extended my hand, meeting his gaze with as much conviction as I could muster. "You can count on me. I'm with you."

Michael's lips twitched—whether it was a smirk or a grimace, I could not tell. "Good," he said, his voice low and clipped. "Follow me."

He led me to the back of the house and down the steps of an old cellar. The air grew colder with each step, and the damp walls glistened with dew. As we rounded a corner, a faint, flickering light came into view. The scent hit me next—a mix of sweat, blood, and something more distinct: false bravery. It was a smell I knew too well from the dishonored humans I had fed on. Only this time, it was coming from another undead being.

My attention landed on the source. He was slumped in a wooden chair; arms tied tightly behind him. His hair was a matted mess, his face was bloodied and swollen, and his labored breaths rasped against the silence. He was not an Everborn and that was clear.

"I need you to watch the door," Michael said, pointing behind me. His gaze never wavered. "Alert us if someone shows up."

I glanced at the prisoner again, but it was too dark, and his face was covered in his own blood, too much to make out his features. Who was he? And what had he done to end up here? I took a quick inventory around the room. That is when I saw them—two figures lingering in the shadows.

"You brought him here?" one of the men said, stepping into the light.

"That's Michael for you," the second man chimed in, his tone laced with sarcasm. "Let's hope this one works out."

My pulse quickened, and my fists clenched. Recognition surged through me. It was the two men Michael had left with at Morison's. Rage overtook me, and before I knew it, I was charging toward them.

I did not get far. Michael's arm shot out, thudding my chest with incredible strength. "Hold on there, cowboy. They're with us."

I froze, glaring at the two men. "Who are they? And why are they here?"

Michael sighed, his patience wearing thin. "We'll get to introductions later. For now, I need you to watch that door. We don't have much time. They will be searching high and low for this piece of scum here," he said, nodding toward the prisoner.

His gaze hardened. "The door," he commanded again.

I took my position near the door, scanning the dark field for any sign of danger. The moon hung high in the sky, its pale light bathing the earth below. Once again, I found myself alone with it, leaning on its cold comfort. From my vantage point, I could see just enough of the room to catch the outskirts of the action while keeping my distance. From the corner of my peripheral, I saw Michael seated, his posture relaxed—too relaxed. Then came the sound of a hard thud, sharp and reverberating.

"Tell me where you took it. Now!" one of the men snarled, punctuating his demand with another punch. The blow landed with a sickening crack, and the sound made me wince.

Violence was not new to me, but I used it only when necessary. These guys on the other hand seemed very adept at using it as a default action. Whatever they wanted from this man, it was clear they considered it worth crossing every line.

Another strike. Another thud. "We know you handed it off to someone in your camp," the man snarled. "However you managed to obtain it is beyond me, but don't think for a second we won't find it."

The prisoner spat, the sound of thick blood hitting the floor made my face curl into a disgusted grin.

The prisoner's defiance was radiating through the cellar. "Kill me if you must!"

I couldn't help but to step inside to get a better view of the interrogation. Michael rose from his seat slowly. He approached the prisoner with the kind of calm demeanor that somehow made the air seem heavier. He crouched in front of the man, running his thumb across his bruised cheek.

His voice low with a twisted comforting tone, “And die you must.” Then, louder, “but not before you tell me where she took it.”

He pulled a small object from his pocket. Unlatched it, and a blade caught the overhead light. For a moment, I thought I saw hesitation in the prisoner’s demeanor. The cellar fell quiet enough to hear the lump in his throat make its way to his chest. Michael handed the pocketknife to one of the men at his side, his movements precise, his expression devoid of emotion.

Michael straightened, dusting off his hands as if the act of holding the knife sullied them.

“Stretch out his hand,” he commanded.

One of the men loosened the restraint enough to grab the prisoner’s wrist, slamming his arm onto the wooden table in front of him. The prisoner struggled, but the man’s strength was unyielding, pinning him in place.

Michael leaned in and was casual as discussing the weather. “Every time you give me the wrong answer, we will take a finger. But to show you I’m not one for idle threats...” He motioned toward the man with the knife. “Start with one.”

The prisoner’s defiance faltered for the first time. His head darted between Michael and the blade as the man holding it lined up the cut.

“No, wait...” the prisoner stammered.

Too late.

The man drove the knife down in one swift motion. The metallic scrape of the knife against the table confirmed Michael’s promise, and a scream ripped through the air, raw and echoing off the damp cellar walls.

The scent of fresh blood hit me like a wave, sharp and metallic, mingling with the cold, damp air. I reached in my pocket and put a cigarette to my lips, the sound of agony ringing in my ears as I fired it up and inhaled deeply.

Michael stepped closer, his expression unchanging as he stared down at the prisoner. “Now,” he said, his voice like ice, “let’s try this again. Where is it? Where is she?”

The prisoner tried to gather his thoughts, his cold, blackened finger lying lifeless on the table before him, a grim testament to Michael’s resolve. I found myself silently hoping he would give Michael the answers he wanted. Yet, deep down, I knew this room would be his final resting place. Whatever he was willing to die for must have been significant, but I could not help wondering how it tied back to Michael and the Everborns.

The prisoner raised his head, his eyes on Michael, his face hidden behind the shadows, but his voice streaked with tears and desperation. His trembled as he began to speak. "For centuries, you Everborns have walked this earth as if you owned it, no regard for us Night Walkers, the original blood, no respect for our way of life. This mission you're on—it's futile, a second battle is coming."

His gaze shifted to me, and though a bloody mess his expression was sharp. It was as though he saw through me, past the hunger and confusion, down to my very core. "You," he hissed, his voice juggling the seriousness and the pain in the back of his throat. "You have no idea what you've gotten yourself into. You think you're on the right side? You think you're one of them? In time, the truth will reveal itself."

The prisoner started laughing and it was bitter and hollow as his attention returned to Michael. "You won't get a word from me. Do as you must! We both know I'm not saying anything."

He leaned forward and let his head rest into his chest. "But tell me, Michael—is any of it really worth it?"

Michael glanced at me, a smirk tugging at his lips—a fleeting expression that masked something deeper. Regret, maybe. Whatever it was, it passed quickly, leaving behind only his usual air of detachment.

"Let's go, mate," he said, making his way toward the door.

As I followed him out, his voice echoed coldly over his shoulder. "Finish it."

The cellar door creaked shut behind us, muffling the prisoner's desperate cries. They grew sharper, angrier, then abruptly cut off. I forced myself to focus on the crunch of the gravel under my foot as we made our way back to the main road.

"What was all that was about?" I asked, unable to keep the edge out of my voice.

Michael didn't break stride.

"Our world is better without him, Leo."

I was not satisfied. "What is it you're looking for?" I pressed.

He stopped abruptly, turning to face me. His hazel eyes caught the moonlight, their usual glint replaced by black coals. "Jericho gives the orders, and I follow. But it's not your concern," he said flatly.

"I thought we had each other's backs. At least that is what it was made out to be," I said.

We were in a standoff, neither of us willing to back down. I asked again, steady but unrelenting. "What are we looking for?"

Michael sighed, and said two simple words, "a diary." The words clipped and dismissive.

Frustrated by my persistence and without another word, he turned and kept walking, leaving me to follow, his voice cutting through the night air one last time.

"A diary."

CHAPTER FIVE

FOX RETREAT HILL

I watched Michael's shadow fade into the night, his movements as silent as the shifting clouds above. He stopped, his figure outlined by the faint glow of a distant streetlamp.

"Lay low for a bit," he said without looking back. "I'll meet you at Morison's in a day or two." His voice was calm, but the air shifted as if the night itself was listening.

As he disappeared, I noticed the shifting colors glow on the horizon, the deep blue of the night sky slowly giving way to hints of dawn. I whispered 'rest well, my friend' under my breath to the moon as time was slipping away. The city stretched out before me, its dark alleys and dimly lit streets still hiding secrets I could not yet grasp. If Michael wanted me to keep a low profile, it meant there were eyes watching, ears listening. Malmö still had its stories to tell.

I searched for new living quarters, keeping Michael's warning in mind. Returning to the Quality View Hotel was not an option. Like the other Everborns, I was not welcome there. My footsteps echoed against the cobblestones as

I wandered through Malmö's quieter streets, scanning the signs for vacancies, a discreet place where I could lay low for a few days. A neon light advertising a modest boarding house caught my eye. Tucked between a shuttered café and a hardware store, its brick exterior was worn and unremarkable—perfect for staying off the radar.

The flat I rented was small, with peeling wallpaper and a single low lamp casting shadows into the corners. A faint smell of mildew and mold lingered in the air, and the mattress creaked under its own weight. It wasn't luxurious, but it would do. Sitting in a rickety chair near the window, I stared out at the empty streets below, my thoughts holding on tight to the events of the night.

Michael had his reasons for what he did earlier. Of that, I was sure. But two things stuck with me: the diary and Jericho. What could be in this diary to make it worth killing for? Secrets and maybe details hidden from everyone except the one who wrote it. And Jericho; the man Michael was to introduce me too. Was he as ruthless as Michael's actions? My suspicions leaned that way, but there were too many unanswered questions.

I leaned back, the chair groaning under my weight. I couldn't ignore the feeling that I was getting pulled deeper into something far more complicated than I'd realized. The diary, Jericho, the Night Walkers—it was a complex network of secret designed to mislead and protect itself. Michael mentioned fate, and I wondered if fate brought me here. The photos I found, the pull and the attraction to city—was it all a coincidence?

That next morning when the sun was well above in the sky, I decided that I needed to see Fox Retreat Hill for myself. The location was perfectly in the middle of the city, dividing one territory from the next. Aware that the location was off-limits to everyone, I needed to at least walk by the area and get a feel for the place.

I gathered my things, coat, leather gloves, threw on my hat, and headed out the door down the street and followed the road to Main Street. Just off in the distance there was a road that seemed forgotten by society. I knew that was the road I needed to be on. I followed the path, and the number of people got slimmer with each footstep, until no one was around. The street had an eerie feeling to it. It was broad daylight, yet it was quiet and untouched. I think this place could only be seen by the undead ones like me. Or at least no one seemed to notice it.

As I continued down the road, I could see this large green hill, now surrounded by gates, and beyond that, tombstones of the falling laid to rest, covering the fields. I looked around once more, scanning the area making sure I was not being watched.

The closer I got to the gates surrounding the hill, the heavier the air felt, like the weight of history pressing down on my chest. I stopped a few feet from the wrought iron fence, scanning the area one last time. Nothing moved, but the stillness felt unnatural. A soft rustling sound broke the silence—a gust of wind. My instincts prickled, the same way they always do when I feel like I'm being watched.

I stepped closer, my gloved hand brushing against the cold iron bars. As I peered through the gaps, taking in the rows of tombstones stretching endlessly, the hairs on the back of my neck rose.

I was not alone.

Before I could turn, a coarse bag was yanked over my head, the sudden darkness disorienting me. Strong hands grabbed my arms, forcing them behind my back. I struggled, but their grip was relentless. I heard a gruff voice mutter, "You should've stayed away, Everborn."

My captors didn't speak again as they dragged me forward. The sound of boots crunching against the crisp winter grass filled the air, accompanied by the distant caw of a crow. Despite the bag obscuring my vision, I could feel the path winding downward, the air growing colder with each step. They were taking me somewhere isolated, but we didn't walk far from the hill.

The bag was ripped off my head, and I blinked against the lights of a flickering lantern. I was in a stone chamber, the walls damp and lined with moss. My captors stood before me, their faces pale and sharp, eyes glowing faintly in the low light.

Night Walkers.

"Unlike your new friends," one of them said, his voice low and menacing, "we're not that ruthless. We won't kill you—at least, not yet."

The other men in the room chuckled.

"Leo is it?" the man asked, his voice dripping with mock civility as he twisted the cap off a fresh bottle of bourbon. He poured himself and the other men a glass, savoring a sip before turning his sharp gaze back to me. "Had fun last night?" His tone was rhetorical, but the venom in his words was unmistakable.

I kept my expression neutral, my silence unwavering. I quickly scanned around the room, cataloging every detail. The sunlight streaming through a small, grimy window told me we were close to where I had been taken. The stale air carried the faint scent of damp earth and old wood. Five men surrounded me, including the interrogator and two giants who had likely dragged me here. They loomed nearby, muscles tense, watching my every move. My survivor instincts kicked in and two things were certain; I would not give them much information, and when the chance came, I would kill them.

"You know," the man continued, swirling the amber liquid in his glass, "that man you killed last night was one of our brothers."

Before I could respond, a fist drove into my gut with the force of a freight train. Pain erupted through my core, and I doubled over as far as my restraints allowed, coughing but refusing to cry out.

"I had nothing to do with that," I rasped, forcing my breath to steady.

"Oh?" His sarcasm was thick, the grin on his face smug. "My apologies, then. I must be mistaken. Maybe that wasn't you with Michael and his goons last night."

He leaned closer, his breath sour with bourbon as he whispered, "The dead of the night talks, Leo. The nightfall is always watching, and the darkness speaks to those who care enough to listen."

Another punch landed, sharper this time, knocking the air from my lungs. My vision blurred briefly, but I held onto my composure, even as I gasped for breath. My rage burned hotter with every strike. I memorized each face in the room, picturing their deaths, my voice, the last sound they'd hear.

The door slammed open with a deafening crash, rattling the walls and nearly rebounding into the figure striding in.

The room froze.

Every head turned as the woman stepped into view, her presence commanding and undeniable.

My vision steadied, my breath leveled, and my gaze focused.

It was her.

CHAPTER SIX

HER

My heart raced, pounding against my chest as I raced down the street. Each breath hung in the air, a cloud of warmth against the cold. Rage simmered in my veins, confusion tangled my thoughts, and though I hated to admit it—a faint, nagging sense of gratitude lingered.

I went from "filthy Everborn" to being released from captivity. She commanded the room with an undeniable presence, her mere entrance silencing every voice. All eyes focused on her, and every movement purposeful. Before she walked in, I was paying for Michael's sins—the cost of association, I guess.

The Night Walkers did not hold back, their fists driving home the blame for actions I witnessed but did not take. They didn't care. She could have stood by, watching me get beaten to a pulp. But she didn't. She stopped them. Had them release me. The question now was, why?

I sat tied to the wooden chair, catching my breath between blows, while they huddled in the corner, voices low but urgent. I strained to catch fragments of their conversation, each word sharpening my focus. Something about a prophecy—it was enough to suck the air out of the room. The energy shifted, tension thickening like smoke.

One of the men turned to me, his face twisted with disgust. He bore into mine, as if trying to unearth some hidden truth. "Are you sure?" he asked. For a moment, I thought he would strike me again, his fists curling at his sides.

She grabbed his arm.

She didn't raise her voice but when she spoke, she froze the room in place. Calm, commanding, final.

"Enough," she said, and the chaos stopped before things went further.

She returned to the corner, resuming her conversation with the man who had been questioning me earlier. This time, they pulled out what looked like a map, unrolled it, and spread it across the table. Their voices were low, but few words floated toward me, prophecy... leader... future... diary.

My ears latched onto that one word—diary.

It was clear this was not just something only Jericho was after. The Night Walkers wanted it too. This diary must hold more than personal reflections. It had to contain something important. Maybe it held secrets about this new world I'd stumbled into, or even the key to ending the war between the two factions. Whatever it was, it had become a point of obsession for both sides.

And somehow, I was caught in the middle.

When their conversation ended, she turned and walked toward me. As she stepped into the light, I got my first good look at her. The faint glow cast soft shadows across her sharp features, accentuating her piercing eyes and flawless skin. There was a glowing shimmer to her gold hair, and her scent—a sweet, floral perfume—hung in the air, both alluring and distracting.

She stopped just short of me, her gaze cutting into me with disdain. Slowly, she shook her head, the motion filled with disappointment. Leaning in, she whispered, "This is the first and last time I will save you."

Her words were nearly drowned out by the intoxicating scent of her perfume. My gaze drifted to her lips, painted in a dark red lipstick that only added to her presence. The way they moved as she spoke was almost hypnotic. The rhythm of her speech seducing me in ways it shouldn't. She was a beautiful rose surrounded by deadly thorns.

The forbidden fruit.

The enemy.

"You have no idea what you are getting yourself into," she warned, her tone sharp and laced with pity. "Leave now and don't come back. Because if we meet again, the next time, it will not end like this."

With a swift motion, she cut the ropes binding my wrists, the blade barely grazing my skin. Without another word, she grabbed my arm and pulled me to my feet. The force of her grip was firm as she hurried me toward the door.

"Run," she said, her voice low and commanding. "And don't look back."

I stumbled out into the cold air, her scent lingering in my senses as I fled. My mind swirled with unanswered questions. I feel like I'm being pulled in two directions. Should I dig deeper into this world? Or should I turn my back on it entirely and remain the outsider I clearly been? But what if this was my destiny? Walking away isn't an option.

I finally reached the block where Morison's was located and noticed Michael and his crew surrounding an old man like a pack of hunting wolves. As I approached, one of the men glanced up, then gave a subtle nod in my direction. Michael turned, his smirk as sharp as ever.

"Leo, hur mår du, mate?" he called out, his voice nonchalant as ever.

I raised my chin, keeping my stride. "I'm good, tack." I looked briefly at the man they were circling, careful not to linger. From the scent he gave off and the heat radiating from his body, I could tell he was human.

One of the men leaned close to the old man, whispering something I couldn't make out, before giving him a firm pat on the cheek and shoving him aside. The man stumbled but did not look back as he hurried away.

Michael's smirk widened. "Hungry?" he asked, his tone playful yet laced with something darker. "And I mean hungry for real food, mate. Not the farm animals you scavenge on." The two men with him laughed, their voices obnoxious and agitating.

Michael turned toward the door. "Come on, let's go inside, grab a bite, and talk."

CHAPTER SEVEN

A SHARED MEAL

I followed Michael through the front door of Morison's, and truthfully, a meal was something I deeply needed. My mind raced, debating whether to tell Michael what I had endured that morning or to let it die in the shadows, unspoken.

But then the smell hit me.

My nose flared, my eyes teared, and the world slowed to a crawl. Every detail around me sharpened, playing to my senses. The hardwood floor beneath my feet felt as though the wood had been freshly chopped, its texture alive beneath my soles.

My shirt held to my skin, and I felt every fiber, as if it had never been woven but still grew in its raw natural state.

The lights blazed, brighter than the sun, momentarily leaving me blind. My skin was hot to the touch, as a wave of heat surged through me, predatory and undeniable. My body reacted on instinct, bloodlust mingling with something more intimate, more consuming.

Michael glanced over his shoulder and his smile said it all. A silent invitation floated in the space between us. A challenge that I lost before I even realized. No words were needed. He knew what I was feeling.

It was feeding time.

We stepped into the bar area, but this was not the Morison's I had visited before. Plastic sheets covered the furniture, their glossy surfaces reflecting the lights above. The air was thick with the scent of blood—sweet, metallic, and fear. It clung to my skin, invaded my lungs, and drowned out every other thought.

The bar was crowded with Everborns, their faces showing excitement, their lips stained crimson. They moved as if time was a concept that they created. Their laughter and smiles flowed above the sounds of weak, shallow breaths.

In the corners and across the tables were bodies—naked, vulnerable, and barely alive. Their pale skin, untouched by the hidden Nordic sun, glazed with sweat and cooling blood. Some were women, their lips a delicate pink, breasts full and exposed, hips curving gracefully even in weakness. Others were young men, their chests sculpted, muscles taut beneath translucent skin, their eyes a hollow, haunting grave.

The Everborns moved casually, displaying a carelessness I'd never seen, and sinking their fangs in wherever they pleased. One knelt beside a broad-shouldered man, her lips brushing his neck before breaking skin.

Across the room, a woman's emotionless face stared at the ceiling, accepting her fate. Her once rosy skin had turned grey and blue, and her body shivered faintly as life slipped away by the minute.

The heartbeat of the room had a sinister energy, and a dark reverence for the act unfolding. The bodies could see and hear everything, their eyes tearing in silent horror, but their limbs barely moved. Their blood was being drained, drop by drop.

No doubt in my mind, I have found the corners of hell. A burning inferno reserved for those marked with our curse, being born of this sin.

Michael gestured to a seat at the far end of the room. "Welcome to dinner, mate," he said, his voice showing amusement. He motioned toward the bodies. "Help yourself. Or do you prefer to watch?"

I swallowed hard, my throat dry despite the suffocating humidity in the room. I had no idea what these poor souls have done to deserve this. Normally, I reserve such acts for the dishonored. The smell, the sight, the sheer eroticism of it all was almost too much.

Michael leaned closer, gleaming with mischief, and wiping blood from his lips. "You'll enjoy it more than you think," he said. "Trust me."

I grabbed the closet victim next to me. I licked my lips and stared at her, as if trying to seduce her on a random Friday night—or maybe I tried to convince myself this was necessary. My will to not indulge started to chip away as the hunger pains grew. I said my little prayer, asking for the strength to rebuke my nature, what I am, and who I was becoming.

Sometimes we fall in too deep.

My instincts clawed at me, demanding I join.

Then the animal in me took over.

I lost the battle.

I stretched her head to the side with one hand and caressed her throat gently with the other, foreplay like we were about to make love. My fingers wrapped around her throat tightly, pinning her in place. In her last moments she moaned under my grip—welcoming my touch.

Finally, I sank my teeth slowly into her soft flesh. Her lukewarm blood hit my tongue, coating my throat and sending a rush of energy through me. She tasted sweet, fresh, and untouched like a virgin. It made me feel weirdly alive, the kind of raw vitality I only get when I feed. And though I hate to admit it, in that moment, I felt awake.

I felt powerful.

"Must have been starving, mate," Michael said, his words snapping me out of my trance. He held her limp arm in his hand and let it drop—thudding against the ground. "You nearly sucked her dry. Honestly, I didn't think you were going to stop."

I blinked and the world around me came back into focus. The bar was already transformed back into the polished establishment of before. The plastic sheets were gone, and the muffled hum of voices replaced the earlier sounds of death. The scent of burned flesh lingered faintly in the air, coming from the furnace in the basement.

I thought it was a dream, but when I looked down, the woman I had been feeding on was draped across my lap, lifeless, and her snow-white body heavy as bricks. I hadn't even realized how much time had passed. Michael laid a hand on my shoulder; he was beaming with amusement. "You act as if you've never done this before, mate."

I stared at what was nothing more but a corpse, regret and disgust slowly bubbling to the surface. *What have I done?* The high wore off, leaving behind a hollowness. Her existence was gone forever. I held onto her, ashamed to let her go, for only that will make the act real.

"You can let go of her anytime you want. We have business to discuss, Leo," Michael said.

I released my grip and let her body fall like a potato sack hitting a kitchen floor. I watched, emotionless, as two men in muck boots, gloves, and aprons loaded her onto a green litter. Their efficiency suggested this was routine for them. *'What's done is done,'* I told myself, forcing the thoughts aside. Dwelling on it wouldn't change a thing.

"You'll need this." Morison's voice broke the silence as he entered the room, a black suit draped neatly over a hanger. "I think I got your measurements right. I'm usually spot on, and you and Michael are about the same build."

He placed the suit on the table beside me, his smile warm and expectant—just another ordinary fitting for a special occasion. "Go try it on, why don't you?" he said, his tone almost parental.

"Get dressed and meet us back here when you're finished. Don't take too long," Michael added, his words sharp, already turning his attention to something else.

I got dressed in the nearest restroom, carefully slipping into the suit Morison had provided. The fit was immaculate, each Italian piece tailored as if he had done this a hundred times before. As I straightened the jacket and adjusted the cuffs, I could not help but glance in the mirror.

The reflection staring back at me was sharper, more defined. The suit gave me a certain edge, a polished veneer of confidence that felt foreign yet empowering. I wasn't sure what I was stepping into, but there was no turning back and I was committed.

Sure, I wasn't fully on board with the way the Everborns did things—their casual disregard unsettled me. But when given only two choices, Everborns or the Night Walkers, you have to choose a side. I also couldn't deny the pull I felt toward them. Being around others like me, despite their transgressions, was a comfort I, only now realized I craved.

I straightened my black tie and posed before opting to take it off, folding it and leaving it on the edge of the sink before heading back into the room to meet Michael.

I hope I'm making the right call, I thought.

The woman back at Fox Retreat Hill had warned me I didn't understand what I was walking into. The Night Walker prisoner at the abandoned house had echoed those same sentiments and made threats of a second battle. That's two for three and normally they say that signs come in threes.

Their words replayed in my mind like a haunting melody. But so did Morison's story and the hurt in his eyes as he spoke of the Everborns' struggles. If you asked me now, I'd say the Everborns got the short end of the stick, and for now, I'll follow Michael until I have firm reason to believe otherwise.

I slipped on my black newsboy cap, threw open the door and stepped out—a brand new man.

CHAPTER EIGHT

GÅ MED ÄRA, MAY YOUR ENEMIES TREMBLE

"Well damn, Leo," Michael said. He nodded his head in approval. "You almost look as good as me."

I adjusted the lapels of my new jacket, smirking.

"Almost, huh? That's high praise coming from you."

Michael chuckled, almost forcing a smile. "Don't let it go to your head mate." He gestured toward one of the wooden chairs. "We've got a lot of ground to cover tonight." He pulled the chair out. "Rake a seat."

I sat and he handed me a knife, with in a black leather sheath. The smell of new leather made my nose tingle as I grabbed to examine the weapon.

"What's this?" I asked.

"For you," he said, as he opened his suit jacket to reveal the knife weaved tightly on his hip. "It's insurance for when the ol' fangs and claws don't do the trick."

I tucked the knife in the back of my waistband, concealing it, hoping I would never have to use it. Without going into further details he turned toward the bar, raising his voice just enough to be heard.

"Old Fashions—a round for the boys at the table."

The round table I sat at was filled with Everborns, every seat taken, with more standing silently behind us. Each of them wore a story written on their faces. Some were scarred and battle tested, their hardened exterior, a testament to lives lived on the edge. Others looked young and deceptively innocent, yet underneath their baby face there was a chaotic malice. There were 'soldiers,' men who followed orders without question, and there were predators, their menace as cold as the steel of a blade.

Collectively, they radiated a shared truth; these were not men to cross. And yet, here I was seated at the table among them, unchallenged by the seating arrangement. For all our differences, we were united by one undeniable fact; we were Everborns.

And as Everborns the name meant something. Something deeper than just a clan or faction you belong to. Our blood made us different than the Night Walkers. Their society was run differently. The ideologies were different and their views on the world shaped their everyday lives. Two different parties with two different ideas on how this world should operate.

A man near the door ushered out the last of the women, locking the door with a heavy click before nodding to Michael. The room fell silent as Michael turned toward us, raising his glass.

"Before we start," he began, "I'd like to introduce this fine gent here." He gestured toward me. "This is Leo. My new right-hand."

A ripple of unease swept through the room—shuffling feet, men shifting in their seats. Whispers rose from the standing Everborns behind us. My throat tightened as I tried to process his words. His new right-hand? What does that mean? And what does it mean for me? For the rest of them?

Michael's gaze hardened.

"If anyone has a problem with it," he said, his tone daring anyone to challenge him, "you know the rules. Extend the challenge if you don't like it."

His words left an unspoken unease. He scanned the room, his grin widening. "But I'll bet my only two fangs on Leo."

The murmurs stopped instantly. The room fell back into tense silence, every eye on Michael. I glanced left and right, acutely aware of the weight of their stares and the sudden target Michael had painted on my back. Despite the tension, none of them dared to meet me head on. The power I commanded needed no words, but I could feel its gravitational pull.

"Skål!" Michael roared, raising his glass one more.

"Skål!" the room echoed, fists and glasses raised in unison. The energy was electric, a war cry in the making.

Michael set his glass down with deliberate care, the sound of the glass clink silencing the room. His cool confidence radiated through the space, demanding our attention.

"You all know who we are. What we stand for. Every one of you is here today because of the fallen who came before us." He nodded toward Morison. "And those who survived."

Morison raised his glass in acknowledgment, his expression somber. Behind his glasses you could see him lost in time, reliving moments too hurtful to speak of.

Michael's voice rose, passion igniting his words. "Across the city, there are those who wish to keep us in chains. They want us to cower in the shadows, to submit to a world order that was never meant for us. They call us tainted, evil—" his gaze locked onto mine, his tone biting as he continued— "or filthy Everborns. But I say, no more!" He paused, letting the weight of his words settle over the room. "This world is ours for the taking!"

The room erupted in cheers, a collective roar of agreement. I found myself swept up in the moment, my voice joining theirs without hesitation.

"And tonight," Michael continued, his voice sharp and piercing through the chaos, "we take the first step toward reclaiming the throne. Jericho has issued his orders. And I chose each one of you because of your loyalty and unwavering commitment to the cause!"

The men erupted again, and one thing was for certain; they would be willing to die for their cause. Michael raised his hand in the air to silent the crowd, "You've already been given your marching orders from Morison earlier. Be at the docks and in position no later than midnight. The shipment is expected to arrive fifteen minutes after."

The men started placing their glasses down on the table, and Michael placed his right hand over his heart and said, "gå med ära" which means 'go with honor.' Then raised his right hand to his right brow, saluting the men. "And may your enemies tremble!"

In unison, each of the men, placed their right hand over their hearts and saluting in the same manner, replying, "med ära! And may our enemies tremble!"

As the men filed out of the room, Michael motioned for me to stay behind. I wasn't surprised—there was unfinished business to discuss. I hadn't received anything from Morison but a suit, and this whole "right-hand man" announcement needed clarity.

"What's this mission you have planned for the night?" I asked, keeping my tone casual. "Right-hand man? What exactly does that mean?"

Michael leaned back, his gaze floating toward the door, double taking to ensuring we were alone. "I'll shoot it straight with you, mate," he said, his voice carrying an edge of seriousness. His eyes, however, told a different story—caution.

He scanned the room like he could feel the walls were listening. "There aren't too many people here I can trust completely. I think there's a crack in the faction, and I fear we're growing weak." He paused, throwing a sharp glance at the bartender and motioning silently for another drink.

His words were surprising giving the battle call he just hosted a few moments ago. I found myself watching him more closely. The ever-present smirk was gone, replaced by a tension that seemed to unravel his usual confident demeanor.

"You're new here," he continued. "You don't have a dog in this fight yet, and that is exactly why I chose you. You are not tangled up in the messy politics or petty alliances. Your intentions are pure." He stopped; his pupils locked onto mine. "I can't explain it, Leo, but I trust you."

As I stared back at Michael, I could tell every word he said was true. There was an undeniable force connecting us, something I could not ignore even if I wanted to. At times, it felt like we were one—different yet intertwined. Yin and Yang, bound by forces neither of us fully understood.

But even as I felt the pull, questions still lingered.

I pressed him, shifting the conversation. "So, about tonight—"

Michael cut me off, his smirk making its return. "Tonight, you'll be by my side. There's precious cargo arriving. Jericho wants us to retrieve it."

He leaned closer, his voice dropping almost to a whisper. "I need you to keep watch—not just over me while I'm working the shipments but keep an eye on the guys...particularly Morison."

I raised an eyebrow. "Morison?" I asked.

"Let's just say—not everyone knows their place."

"So, I'm playing bodyguard now? Is that it?"

"No, no. It's not like that, mate," Michael said, shaking his head. "In the brief time I've known you, I've noticed you have got a knack for hand-to-hand combat. You can fight and fight well." His smirk widened, "and I meant it when I said I'd place my bet on you."

Just then, Morison walked back into the bar, heading toward us.

"You fill the new recruit in on the plan already? It's almost time," he said, his eyes darting between Michael and me. His tone was casual, but the way his focus lingered on me suggested something was off. I could not tell if he overheard the conversation or was just on edge about the mission.

Michael leaned back in his chair, meeting Morison's gaze with a questionable smirk. "Most of it, anyway," he replied coolly.

The tension between them was palpable, and it made sitting there silently as a bystander awkward. They wore the masks of camaraderie, but the animosity underneath was starting to show. I could feel it building, a storm waiting to strike. There was something unspoken between the two but before the tension grew heavier, I interjected.

Big mistake.

"So, what's in this shipment, and why is it so important?" I asked, trying to steer the conversation to safer ground.

Michael shook his head; his expression filled with irritation. "Mate, if I knew, I'd tell you. But Jericho doesn't think it's necessary for me to know that detail—just like that bloody diary we're still on the hunt for."

Morison stepped toward us. "Still bitching about your job, Lieutenant? Give it a rest already," Morison snapped, no longer hiding the irrationality in his voice. This was something they must have talked about before.

Michael's smirk vanished instantly, replaced by a fiery stare. He slammed his fist down on the polished table, rattling the glasses. "That's exactly right!" he barked. "I am the lieutenant, aren't I? But you know all the details. So, tell me what that makes you, Morison?"

Morison didn't flinch. He met Michael's heated gaze with a bored expression, brushing a speck of lint off his sleeve. "We're not having this conversation again. Your time will come when he's ready."

Michael stared him down for a moment longer before taking a slow sip of his Old Fashioned, his hand steady despite the anger simmering beneath the surface. He rolled his eyes and let out a sarcastic chuckle. "Ha, when he's ready." With that, Michael shifted his focus back to me, his temper seemingly cooling.

"Anyway, mate," he said, his tone shifting to something more businesslike. "Here's the plan. Tonight, a cargo ship will be arriving at approximately 12:15. We'll have two of our guys stationed at the entrance, another two at the weigh station, and a few men positioned on the docked ships nearby. One man will be monitoring the radio for any chatter. The alarms at the port will be disabled, so the police shouldn't be an issue. But in case we missed something, we'll need to be in and out within five minutes."

I nodded, listening closely as he continued.

"When the ship docks, two of my men, dressed as police officers, will direct the crew to disembark. While they're distracted, you and I will board the cargo ship with these." He slid a pair of fake IDs across the table toward me. "Once we're inside, we'll head straight to the holding area and retrieve four suitcases. They're light enough for us to carry on our own."

"Four suitcases?" I asked, scratching my head.

"Yes," Michael replied, his tone casual.

"And what about the crew members? They're just going to let us walk off with their cargo. No paperwork or nothing?"

Like a subway, Michael had mischief written all over him. "The guys at the docks will handle it. That's where Morison comes in. He will make sure the bodies are properly harvested for the next buffet." He winked.

"Sounds like you've got it all planned out," I said, keeping my tone neutral.

"Of course," Michael replied, a proud smile tugging at his lips. He rose from his chair, and I followed suit. He paused, fixing his gaze on me. "And, Leo, if things go sideways, I trust you'll handle it." His head tilted toward Morison in a barely noticeable nod; a silent message meant only for me.

Michael turned his attention back to Morison. "Morison, we'll be taking our leave now. Remember, be there on time. No mistakes." His tone was calm, but the authority in his voice left no room for argument.

Without waiting for a reply, Michael motioned for me to follow him, his coat sweeping behind him as he floated toward the door. I hesitated for a moment, glancing at Morison, who was already wiping down the bar, his face unreadable. I walked out the front door where Michael stood waiting.

"Do I have time?" I asked Michael, holding up a single Manchester.

Michael smirked, his tone light but knowing. "Of course, mate. After tonight, time's the one thing we'll have plenty of."

I hesitated, unsure of how to respond. Instead, I lit my cigarette, letting the smoke curl between us. Off in the distance, the faint outline of the Öresund Bridge loomed over the Baltic Sea, its lights shone like a string of fireflies against the horizon, the city lights of Copenhagen, Denmark just beyond the distance. I glanced at it briefly before Michael started walking, his coat catching the wind as he led the way toward the city docks.

I followed, the scent of saltwater growing stronger with each step.

CHAPTER NINE

MALMÖ CITY DOCKS

The clock struck midnight, the faint echoes of church bells carrying over the distance. Their beautiful sounds, carried by the wind and bouncing off the Baltic Sea, whispered in my ear like a gentle melody. The moon sat perfectly in the sky, nestled between the stars above, watching over me as usual, comforting me in the darkness.

But this time, I was not alone.

I stood by Michael's side, feeling an unexpectedly strong, brotherly connection. It was like we were two brothers who shared the same mother but different fathers—observing the same scenery but each having a different view. I felt at ease and ready for our mission together.

The crackling sound of static came to life. "Everyone in position?" Michael whispered into the radio he'd pulled from the inside of his jacket pocket. The static crackle after his query seemed to hang in the chilled night air, almost as tense as the silence that followed.

I glanced at my watch; the time was now 00:13.

Peering into the darkness, I tried to make out the shape of a ship on the horizon. The open waters of the Baltic Sea stretched endlessly before us, its surface a dark mirror reflecting the sparse starlight. Beside me, Michael shifted, scanning the docks with a predator's vigilance.

I tapped him on his shoulder alerting him of the ship now in my focus. Its silhouette against the fog rolling off the water, gave me silent chills of the Grim Reaper, here to escort us down to Davy Jones Locker.

"Is that the ship we're looking for?"

He peered into the darkness where I pointed.

"That's it," he said, leaping to his feet and keying the radio. "All right, boys, it's here. Let's move!"

Seconds later, a police car sped toward the dock's entryway, its lights slicing through the night. Two men jumped out—Michael's usual two. He nodded at me, signaling to follow. My heart pounded.

No turning back now.

As the boat docked, two of Michael's men approached, brandishing papers. I overheard one ask a crew member, "Who's the captain of this vessel?" The crew member's words stuttered, the scent of his anxiety was thick as the sea air—perplexed by the line of questioning.

The officer, impatient, demanded everyone off the ship.

"What's the meaning of this?" demanded the captain, his tone pronounced with authority.

As we approached, Michael took the lead, exuding his usual cool confidence. He addressed the captain directly. "Svenska eller engelska?" his voice smooth and commanding.

The captain clearly furious confirmed, "Engelska!"

"English it is then," Michael said with a smirk. "I am Lead Detective Michael Jönsson from the Swedish Coast Guard and we have reason to believe you have illegal goods aboard this ship."

The way he talked and flashed his fake badge was unnerving with how rehearsed he was. Michael had that same ease, that same unnerving confidence. I was told how this would end, so I shook the thought from my mind and followed his lead. Flashing my badge, I pushed past the captain and onto the steps leading into the ship's cargo hold.

"That's for authorized personnel only, Officer!" the captain barked, stepping forward as if to block our path.

Michael didn't break stride.

"And what business do you have arriving after hours?" he shot back, his tone sharp and cutting. Before the captain could respond, Michael flexed his authority further. "As an officer of the Swedish Coast Guard, I have every right to search every...single meter of this ship if I feel so inclined to." He flashed his smirk, knowing he had the upper hand, "now, step aside."

The captain hesitated for a moment before reluctantly giving way, his jaw tightening as Michael and I moved past him. I met his eyes briefly, and a wave of pity swept over me, as I thought, *Tonight would be his last.* The gold band on his left hand caught the light, and I thought of his wife and maybe he had kids, but I shoved the thought to the far end of my mind. His death was currency for whatever he was carrying onboard. Pointless death but nothing I could do it about it.

Following Michael into the dim cargo hold, our flashlights flooded the darkness. "Do you even know what it looks like?" I whispered.

"Jericho doesn't give straight answers, so no, I don't." His frustration was evident, and his annoyance of Jericho seemed to be more frequent. Michael didn't strike me as someone who liked to follow orders blindly. He added, "All I know is there'll be four suitcases. We just need to open these—"

"Over there," I interrupted, my beam catching four silver suitcases tucked into a shadowy corner. They weren't well hidden—it felt almost too easy. Either careless or a set up I thought. "I think I found them, Mike."

Michael strode over briskly, his voice smooth as ever. "It's Michael, mate," he corrected, patting my cheek like some old mafioso. I recoiled, annoyance bubbling up, but before I could respond he crouched to examine the suitcases.

Laying them side by side, he tried to open each one, his frustration growing with each failed attempt. Finally, he slammed his fist against a nearby box, the thud echoing in the tight cargo hold.

"Dammit," he hissed under his breath.

"Should you even be trying to open those?" I asked minding my tone in a delicate situation.

Michael shot me a rhetorical look, his voice dripping with sarcasm.

"What do you think?"

At times Michael came off as an older brother shouting orders at his younger sibling. In those moments I wrestled with the idea of taking off on my own again, but loneliness was a demon I wrestled with for far too long.

I held my breath; it was none of my business. I was only there to be his "right-hand man" and watch for anything that may lead this mission to hell.

Michael ran a hand through his hair, his faced looked defeated, and his voice anchored with irritation as he muttered, "That damn Jericho is going to be the death of me, mate. I need to know what is in here that he wants so damn—"

Before he could finish, a deafening explosion ripped through the night, shaking the ship. The vessel swayed violently, waves slamming against its sides. Distant shouts echoed from the deck, mixing with the sounds of the Baltic Sea slamming against the ship's frame.

And then, silence.

The muffled cries of the crew were cut off, their fates sealed long before we got here. My attention was on full alert, and Michael was already grabbing his radio.

"What the hell is going on out there?" he barked.

A voice crackled back, thick with panic.

"Michael, something's out here. We can't see it—too much smoke. We have to get out of here, but we might be locked in!"

Michael grabbed two of the suitcases with determination, the metal latches catching faint glimmers of light. He glanced at me, his voice low but firm. "No matter what's waiting out there—we get these to Jericho."

"And your men?" I asked, curiously.

Michael's croaked, his laugh sinister. Shaking his head, he replied, "There are casualties in every war, Leo. Let's move."

He said it so casually, like he didn't care one way or another if his men didn't make it out alive. But I didn't argue. I grabbed the other two suitcases and followed him toward the chaos waiting on the other side of the door.

As we stepped over the lifeless bodies of the ship's crew members, Michael paused to examine one of the men, his expression filled with curiosity. Then anger flickered across his face.

"We need to leave now," he muttered over his shoulder. "Night Walkers are here, but these cuts—I recognize them."

The docks had grown unnervingly silent. I set the suitcases down beside me, scanning the shadows. My voice dropped to a whisper, "We're being watched."

Instinctively, I felt the change within me. My fangs began to lengthen, my nails sharpened, and the glowing red glimmer flickered in my eyes. In the distance, through the clearing smoke, the outlines of numerous figures appeared, Night Walkers. Their presence radiated malice, their silhouettes cutting through the haze like fog lights.

And then, just as quickly as they had appeared, the lights went out.

Sound of bodies hitting the ground nearby and, in the distance, and at the entrance could be heard. Some Everborns took cover, others boldly jumped into battle. The world slowed to a crawl, as the Night Walkers got closer to us two.

Michael shrugged off his coat, letting it fall to the ground with a deliberate motion. His body began to shift, his form mirroring the transformation taking place within me. He looked my direction and gave me the cue with a simple wink.

Before I could fully process what was happening, I was in fight or flight, and running was not an option.

A surge of adrenaline rushed through me, and in an instant, I was charging forward, heading straight for a group of Night Walkers. *It's funny how a time can change everything.* Two weeks ago, I was a lone wolf—stranded, searching for answers about who I am and why I am what I am. Now, here I was, risking my life for a common goal, and for a group of people I just met not long ago

But none of that mattered.

The only thing that did was leave this place alive—body fully intact—and with those suitcases.

One of the Night Walkers stood toe to toe in front of me. I recognized him from Fox Retreat Hill. He laughed under his breath and sneered, "How did I know her letting you go would be a mistake?"

Tugging at the ends of his black leather gloves, he made them snap tighter. "This time, Everborn, there's no one to save you. No one to stop what I should have finished!"

He sprinted toward me, giving me little time to react. It was time to make good on my promise. I caught him by the throat with one hand, my nails piercing his thick exterior like claws through fabric. His face contorted in shock, but my back was kicked in from another Night Walker.

He slipped from my grip, falling to the ground, and scurried off while I turned to catch the other. I threw him to the ground, snapping his neck with one quick motion. The sound echoed briefly before vanishing into the chaos.

I looked up and the first Night Walker was gone.

Another Everborn locked in a desperate brawl nearby, caught my attention. His movements were frantic, his breaths ragged. I grabbed the Night Walker he was fighting from behind, his strength no match for mine. I slammed him down and then with a savage twist, I ripped his jaw apart like Samson did the lion, leaving him lifeless on the freezing dock.

The Night Walkers were relentless, but they were uncoordinated against me. As more of them charged, they began to swarm, attacking in groups now. My anger surged, fueling every strike, every defensive move. The mission was clear: we could not leave without those suitcases.

Out of the corner of my eye, I saw Michael finish off an opponent. He turned to me, his chest heaving trying to catch his breath. His gaze lingered on the bodies piling at my feet. Was he shocked? Or impressed? I couldn't tell. Before he could speak, a shadow darted behind him, striking him on the head.

Michael collapsed at once, his body hitting the ground with a heavy thud.

I rushed to his defense, my fangs baring as I sank them into the neck of his attacker. Blood sprayed in a fountain, covering both Michael and me as I finished him off. The smell of regret in the air was unforgiving. Michael lay motionless, hardly breathing but alive.

The sounds of footsteps echoed closer, steady, and deliberate. Shadows emerged from the smoke, forming a grim outline of menacing figures. The rage inside me burned but was starting to deplete my energy. *I don't know how long I can last.* The Night Walkers wanted us gone, and they would stop at nothing to get what's in those suitcases.

The fight drew on longer than expected. Their numbers felt endless.

For every, one I struck down, two more appeared. *Something is wrong.* This wasn't a random ambush. This had to be planned, calculated. The realization interrupted my focus.

But who?

We were right where they wanted us to be with no escape.

My brief mental collapse didn't allow me to see the blade in my earlier attacker's hand until it tore into my side. Pain radiated from the wound, hot and sharp, the warmth of my blood soaking through my shirt. A scream ripped from my throat as I stumbled, tripping over Michael's unconscious body, knife firmly planted into my side.

Another Night Walker knelt beside Michael, checking his pulse. He raised his boot over Michael's head, ready to finish him. Adrenaline surged, and I lunged forward, using what little strength I had left. With a growl, I pulled the knife from my side and turned it against him, driving it deep into his chest.

His body crumpled to the ground, lifeless—I dropped too.

I tried to steady myself, but my vision blurred. My legs felt weak, and my breathing grew shallow. Then, through the haze, I saw a black car idling just outside the dock gates. It hadn't been there before. A woman stood beside it, her figure barely illuminated by the glow of a streetlamp.

In my disoriented state, I was certain that it was her. The one who warned me to stay out of this. Rage flared, briefly overpowering the pain. I wanted to rip her apart, to demand answers. But I was losing blood quickly and couldn't move.

Through the smoke, three men approached the car. Two carried suitcases.

The man in the center threw the suitcases into the car, then turned to scan the carnage they left behind. The glow of the streetlights caught his face just enough for me to see him clearly. A bitter mix of anger and disbelief flooded my chest.

I struggled to get on my feet, and then I took a step forward, aching to confront him, but the distant sounds of police sirens snapped me back to reality.

We have to get out of here.

Now.

I turned to the few Everborns still standing, motioning to Michael's unconscious body. Pain lanced through my side as I moved. Gritting my teeth, I ripped a strip from my shirt, tying it tightly around the gash to slow the bleeding.

"We have to leave him and get out of here," one of the Everborns said, his voice trembling and desperation oozing from his pores.

I froze and fixated on him with a glare sharp enough to sign his death papers. "You two, grab Michael," I pointed, my voice growing weaker by the minute. "Don't ever suggest something like that again." I pulled him close enough to my face to feel the warmth of my breath.

They hesitated for a moment, their heads hanging low, defeat etched into their face.

"I said let's go!" The force of my voice jolting them into action.

They moved quickly, hoisting Michael between them, his limp body dragging as we made our way toward the dock gates.

"The cargo..." one of them muttered, glancing back toward the ship.

"I'll fix it," I replied sharply, though my voice wavered under the weight of the betrayal that now burned in my mind.

As we approached the gates, the image of the man with the suitcases resurfaced, his face clear as day. My hands clenched, the makeshift bandage around my side slick with fresh blood. Anger simmered, boiling just beneath the surface.

The puzzle pieces clicked into place with clarity. He had orchestrated this, manipulated everything to ensure we'd walk straight into this trap. In that moment I realized that this was a much bigger game that was being played than I realized. The depths at which one will go for perceived power and control was something I wanted nothing to do with.

"I wonder how they knew we were going to be here?" one of the Everborns asked, his voice tinged with suspicion.

I looked up to the lonely moon, its silver glow casting a spotlight over the chaos we left behind. It had always been there for me, a silent companion, a comforting watcher in my lonely moments.

But now, under this blood-soaked night, it felt different—distant.

Betraying.

I let out a slow, frustrated breath, my jaw tightening as the name slipped through my clenched teeth.

"Morison."

CHAPTER TEN

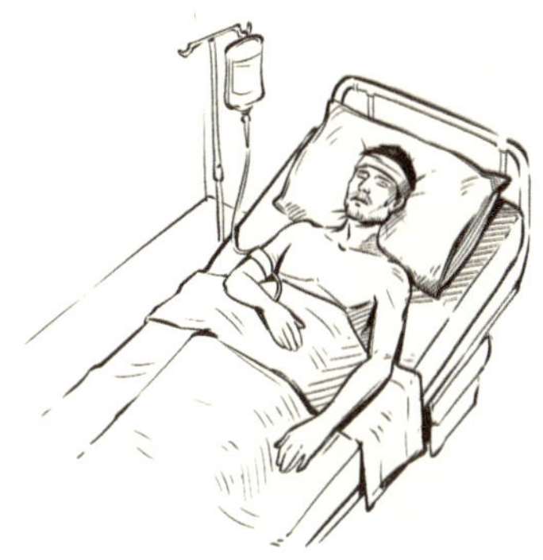

RUMOR HAS IT

Monotone beeping sounds rang in my ears at a steady rhythm while the sharp smell of antiseptic alcohol filled the air, and the faint pain from the stab wound lingered like a nagging ache. My back protested against the firm mattress beneath me, and the veins in my outstretched arms throbbed from the needles delivering fluids to my motionless body.

My eyes struggled to open, the blinding white light above searing through my disoriented thoughts.

Where am I, I wondered.

"Five days," calm and purposeful, a voice called out.

The sudden appearance of someone in the room with me caught me by surprise. I removed the oxygen mask that was filling my lungs with air, my fangs started to bare, then the man placed a single hand across my chest, and with ease my body stopped, no longer able to move from the bed.

"You'll only hurt yourself more if you keep thrashing about." He said calmly.

Knowing I didn't have the energy to properly defend myself, I reluctantly gave in, and eased the tension in my body, but I kept a watchful eye on him, and taking in my surroundings.

"Are we done?" he asked, a smirk gracing his lips, replicating Michael's. He was at ease, and clearly knew he had the upper hand. How did I get here I wandered.

Who is this man?

Am I in danger?

Whatever happened to Michael anyway?

I was confined somewhere I knew nothing about, but it only felt like minutes ago I was watching Morison walk away with the suitcases, betraying us all.

Reluctantly, I nodded, easing the tension in my muscles. The pressure on my chest disappeared as he removed his hand, leaving me to feel free again. He reached down, picking up the discarded oxygen mask, examining it briefly before tossing it onto the tray beside the bed.

"Doesn't look like you need this anymore anyway."

"Where am I?" I said, my voice strained and raspy.

The man tilted his head, considering the question for a moment. "You're safe Leo. No need to worry. All will be answered in due time."

His answer only raised more questions. "Are you the Doctor?" I asked, probing for answers that may hint where I am.

"Doctor?" He repeated, a flicker of amusement crossing his face. He picked up a notepad from a nearby counter, flipping through it lazily before tossing it aside. "No, I wouldn't say that."

"Then who are you?" I shot back, frustration creeping into my tone. "Here to kill me? Night Walker? A male nurse?"

He laughed—a low, casual sound that grated against the seriousness of the moment. His laughter seemed to echo in the sterile room, making the air around him feel heavier. Shaking his head, he moved to turn off the monitors at my bedside and the wires attached to my arms

"That's a new one," he said with a chuckle. "Sure, let's go with that—your male nurse.

"How do you know my name? Who brought me here?" I demanded, leaning forward despite the protests of my aching body.

He stepped closer, his movements sharp but unthreatening. Gently, he helped me sit up so I could face him. There was a quiet strength in the way he handled me, but his calm demeanor felt as if he was hiding his true intentions.

"As for being a Night Walker, well, fear not. Like I said, you're safe. This is Jericho's compound."

His words felt colder than the air in the room.

My journey to meet the leader of the Everborns, Jericho, had been derailed ever since Michael promised to take me to him. It was a cruel twist of fate that I'd finally ended up here—under these circumstances.

The man remained methodical, his focus unwavering as he leaned closer to examine me. The small flashlight in his hand was illuminated as he shined it into each one of my eyes, his movements quick but precise. He then turned his attention to my throat, his fingers brushing over the sides, and finally he worked his hands to the wound below my ribs.

He nodded his head, and his lips curled. "You're healing quickly," the voice of approval. He re-taped and smoothed the bandage over my side, pulling the hospital gown down over the wound.

Slowly he met my gaze, and his movements commanded my attentiveness. "Five days," he repeated. "That's how long you've been out."

A wave of confusion rippled through me, and I resisted the urge to recoil from his stare. My thoughts were a storm of fragmented memories—the docks, the betrayal, Michael's lifeless body, the suitcases. The room felt smaller, suffocating. I longed for a cigarette, something to calm the nerves and make me level again.

The male nurse sat down in the chair in the corner of the room, sunlight streaming through the window and casting long shadows across the floor. He clasped his hands together, leaning forward, his movements like a mob boss.

"So, Leo, what do you remember?" he asked, his voice smooth but with a tone of investigation. It didn't sound like the usual questioning of a nurse—it felt more like an interrogation. My suspicion grew, though I knew I was at a disadvantage.

The hallways echoed faintly with footsteps, and when I focused hard enough, I could feel the subtle cold signatures of two men standing just outside the door. Were they guards, or was this just a precaution?

I shifted, turning to him.

"I remember being at the docks with Michael and the others," I said, deciding honesty—at least partial honesty was the best approach for now. "Then the Night Walkers appeared out of nowhere. We were outnumbered—"

He cut me off briskly, his tone skeptical. "You were outnumbered, yet somehow you survived?"

I paused, his dubious question suggesting he felt there was more to the story.

"Yes, clearly. As Michael would put it, I'm an exceptional fighter."

"Indeed, you must be," he replied, his gaze lingering on the bandage at my side. "To walk away from that kind of ambush with nothing but a stab wound...you could be dead instead"

He drummed his fingers lightly on the armrest, as if piecing a puzzle together.

"Rumor has it, you were taking on Night Walkers alone."

"Yeah, I guess. I don't know. Why does it matter?"

He smiled faintly, leaning back in his chair. "It doesn't. It's just rather... unusual, that's all."

"And why is that?"

"Have you ever noticed that most of us travel in groups of twos?" He asked.

I let his words linger for a moment, processing the information and connecting the dots. "It didn't occur to me at first, but yes, now that you've mentioned it."

"Genetically, we are at a disadvantage," he admitted, his stare piercing into me as if searching for something just beneath the surface. "But what we lack genetically, we make up for with brute force and teamwork." His lips curled into a smirk as he continued, "You, on the other hand, seem to do quite well on your own. Only a few can do that."

He stepped forward, extending a hand. "Shall we?"

I hesitated but took his hand, easing off the bed. He handed me a robe lying nearby and gestured for me to put it on. Once I did, he led me to the door, holding it open as I stepped into the long, cold hallway. The two guards trailing a few paces behind us were a quiet reminder of the compound's vigilance.

"Word around town is you're in, Michael's out," he said with an almost amused tone.

"What does that mean?" I protested.

He pressed the elevator button, motioning for the two men behind us to stay behind. As the door chimed open, he finally answered, "Word's spread about your little performance at the docks—how you saved Michael and got the others out alive. You've won the admiration of the people. Let's just say the walls are talking."

"Rumors are just that," I shot back. I did not have time for the Everborn political game. After a few seconds I continued, "I have an important message for Jericho. Can you take me to him?"

His gaze sharpened, followed by sudden curiosity. "Do you mind me asking what the message is?"

"Yes," I snapped, my voice filled with the simmering anger that slowly made its way to the surface. The memory of Morison's betrayal flashed in my mind, fueling my resolve. "It's for his ears only."

"Fair enough," he replied with a casual shrug. "He's a busy man, but sure he'll make some time for you—especially if it's important."

The elevator doors slid open with a soft ding, and we stepped inside. As the doors closed, sealing us in, I wondered if I was too late to warn Jericho about Morison. I couldn't believe I'd been in a deep slumber for five days. Who knows what Morison and the Night Walkers had been up to in my absence? My anxiety started to creep in—the walls felt like they were closing in, and a wave of nausea swept over me.

The strange nurse glanced at me, his calm demeanor unnerving. "It's the healing process," he said, barely moving, his eyes fixed on the elevator doors. "You heal quickly. The side effects are both a gift and a curse. The nausea will pass."

I shook my head from side to side—a weak attempt of clearing the muck in my head. I cracked my back and straightened up as best as I could. "Where are we going?" I asked, trying to keep my voice steady.

"For a little walk. Fresh air will do you good."

The elevator chimed again, and the doors opened into a dimly lit hallway.

Not again, I thought, my instincts flaring.

The nurse stepped forward, but I hesitated. A firm nudge from his hand on my back propelled me forward, his strength a silent reminder that I was not in charge here.

"Only child?" he asked casually over his shoulder.

I froze mid-step. "Why does that matter?"

"Just trying to get to know you," he replied. His tone was masked with lighthearted small talk, but I sensed he was probing for more.

Something was off, and mentally I started recounting the steps back to the floor we came from. My fists clenched, an itching sensation around my gums like a toddler teething, was my fangs in response to my growing irritation.

"You're wasting my time with useless questions—"

He cut me off, his voice suddenly sharper.

"Where do you come from?"

"Why?" I shot back, my frustration boiling over.

"Who are your parents?" he pressed, his words quick and frantic.

The lights bounced on and off quickly, and before I could respond, everything went dark. Strong hands grabbed me from all sides, pinning my arms and legs. I thrashed, but their grip was unrelenting. I was lifted off my feet, carried like a rag doll, and unceremoniously dropped into a cold metal chair.

Blinding white lights flooded the room, searing my corneas. The nurse stepped forward, his cheerful curiosity replaced by a cold, menacing glare.

"What is this? Where is Jericho?" I demanded, scanning the room in haste.

The laughter of unseen figures echoed through the room, chilling me to the bone. The nurse raised a hand, silencing the unseen crowd.

He perched on the edge of a nearby desk, crossing his arms and legs. His eyes locked onto mine; a grin plastered on his lips.

"You're looking at him."

CHAPTER ELEVEN

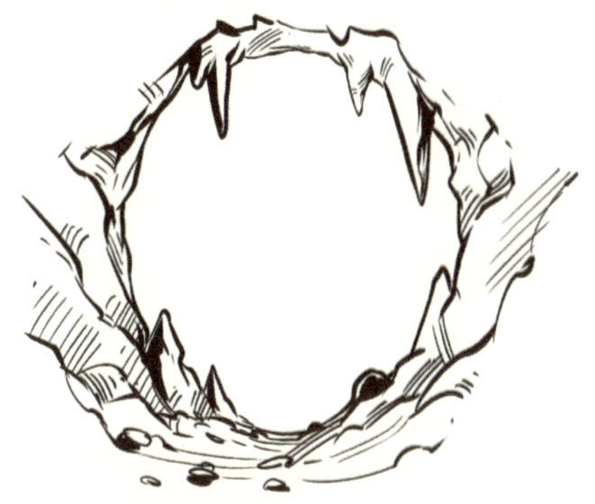

WALLS OF JERICHO

Jericho leaned against the edge of a stainless-steel desk, his fingers drumming lightly against the metal. The lab around us was sterile, bright, and cold. The faint hum of machinery filled the air, punctuated by the occasional hiss of a ventilator. He reached for a glass bottle on the silver tray nearby, the smell of gin fermenting inside, and poured himself a drink.

"In the beginning, there was a fallen star, known as 'The Son of the Morning.'" He swirled the liquid in his glass before taking a slow sip, the low clink of ice against glass echoing in the room. "Anger, envy, pride, greed, sloth, lust, and gluttony became his downfall."

I watched him carefully, almost forgetting the wound on my side. His voice was steady and hypnotic, and his words demanded my attention.

"He was cast to the fiery depths, damned to burn for eternity." The glass was set down with a soft thud. "In his boredom, he created three daughters to keep him company in his eternal agony. They became known as 'Children of the Moon.'"

His studied me, gauging my reaction. "Those daughters, powerful in their own right, were sent above to earth to assist lost souls to their father and maintain balance. One day, a desperate harlot called on them and made a transaction, trading her baby for luxury. They marked him with a kiss, claiming him as theirs forever. The mark made him different, giving him long life, but it also made him bloodthirsty and overly ambitious. Later, he met someone who would be his undoing, and from that betrayal, a history of conflict manifested."

I said nothing, unsure where this was going. The story wove between riddles and cryptic truths, each thread pulling tighter, leaving me uncertain of its destination. I'd never heard this story before, nor of the beings he spoke of, yet I knew deep down that his words mattered. He did not come off as the type to waste his breath over nonsensical conversations.

His eyes lingered on mine, and time stretched into eternity before either of us shifted in our seats, broke eye contact, or spoke.

Jericho rose from the desk, his hands clasped behind his back as he began to pace the room. His voice broke the silence.

"Have you ever wondered where you come from, Leo? How it all started? Surely you didn't think you were the only one."

I blinked, startled by the question.

He flashed a brief smile, disarming the tension in the room.

"You have no need to be afraid, Leo. I promise. Apologies for the earlier theatrics, but recent events reminded me that you can't be too comfortable these days," he added.

The question hung in the air, and I hesitated, debating whether or not to answer. What harm could it do? That question had haunted me my entire life, and maybe Jericho held the answers I'd been searching for.

"More times than I care to admit," I finally said.

"It must be hard," he mused, his voice softening. "Growing up in this world, alone and different. But you've found your way to us, back home like the prodigal son."

"Back home?" I echoed, confused.

"Well, figuratively speaking." He stopped pacing, crouching so he was eye-level with me. He held his focus steady, "Leo, the news of you at the docks wasn't me being coy. I mean this sincerely—I want you to lead my soldiers."

"Just like that?" I asked, the disbelief clear in my voice. "What happens to Michael?"

Jericho shrugged, and a glimpse of frustration crossed his face. "Michael is good at following orders, but his ambition..." He paused, choosing his words carefully. "His ambition blinds him. In the wrong hands, ambition eventually breeds chaos, destruction. It can be the difference between victory and ruin. And there's no reason why he shouldn't have known about that scum, Morison."

I stiffened, my breathing slowing. "You know about Morison, how?"

Jericho straightened, a look of disgust on his face taking shape. "I'll admit, Leo, it took me a bit to realize the diary was missing." He turned back to the desk, tracing a finger along its surface, his voice dropped, low and cold. "Morison was the only person who knew of it before its disappearance."

He paused, lifting the glass of gin to his lips and draining it in one deep sip. The glass hit the desk with a hollow thump. "But none of that matters now. The Everborns got to him, and I need you to retrieve what was taken."

My legs, weak from the injury, finally found their strength again. I stood, stretching stiff muscles before fixing Jericho with a level stare. "What's the deal with this diary?" I asked, my voice steady but firm. "I saw a man lose his head over it. Why is it so important?"

Jericho studied me, his gaze showing internal calculations behind the calm exterior. I could feel it—the careful weighing of what to reveal and what to withhold. My patience was wearing thin. Unlike Michael, I was not another pawn in his game or this war.

He smiled something sinister. "For now, just know Leo," he said, his tone measured, deliberate. "The diary holds the key to all our existence."

I blinked, caught off guard by the sudden information. Before I could form a response, Jericho continued. "The diary belonged to the first Everborn, and within its pages, you'll find its darkest confessions."

"What do you mean?" I eagerly asked.

"The first Everborn was manufactured in a lab, Leo," His voice calm, almost clinical. "Not born or created by some deity."

The confusion hit me like a freight train, leaving my mind in pieces like an unfinished jigsaw puzzle. Manufactured? In a lab? The idea was at odds with everything I'd ever imagined or what little I thought I knew. I could barely process it.

I stared at him, searching his face for any hint of deception. "That's... impossible," I managed to say. "You said that a child was marked and—"

"Yes, yes," he interrupted swiftly, waving a hand as if brushing away an insignificant detail. "That was the original Night Walker. What I am talking about is entirely different. Though alike, they are not the same."

"You mean pure bloods versus those who aren't?" I asked, sitting back down in the chair.

My attention snapped back to Jericho, my mind racing to decipher truth from half-truths and the new revelations.

"Exactly," he said, excitement clear in his voice. It was almost like a story he'd told a thousand times before, each retelling sparking fresh joy. "It's said that the first Night Walker went astray from the values we current Everborns hold dear to our hearts. They squandered the blessings they were gifted."

He leaned forward, his tone softening but his intensity undiminished. "But now it's my job to preserve our legacy forever, and you can help with that mission."

Before I could respond, he added, "We just need to reclaim that book." He paused, his gaze lowering as if lost in thought. With a deep sigh, he said, "There's something else, Leo. Something only a select few know."

He hesitated for just a moment, then continued. "A long time ago, one of those sisters came to me. She delivered a prophecy—more like a warning. She told me that one day, a lost boy would rise. He would either unite the world or tear everything apart."

I sat frozen.

A thousand questions flooded in, but none made it past my lips. Jericho's expression remained unreadable, a mask of control over whatever emotions might be lurking beneath.

Finally, I managed to ask, "And you think that's me?"

Jericho tilted his head, considering me. For the first time, a shadow of doubt crossed his face. "I'm not sure," he admitted. "And that's the great mystery. Many before you have been mistaken." He stood up and motioned to the door. "Follow me."

I trailed behind him as we left the sterile lab and entered a candle-lit corridor. The echoes of our footsteps followed us down the hallway, leading to a staircase. We ascended to a landing that was brighter than the shadows we had just passed through, the shift in light almost throwing me off. The hall resembled more of a boarding house than the pristine laboratory below.

When we stopped in front of a large wooden door, he reached into his pocket and handed me a key.

"This is your room," he said, his voice firm but calm. "But if you stay here, understand this, the price of admission is that diary. That's all I ask from you."

"And Michael?" I asked.

"Don't worry about him. I'll get him caught up. But for now, rest. You'll need your energy."

CHAPTER TWELVE

SHIPS PASSING IN THE NIGHT

Accepting the terms set by Jericho—the price of admission—almost felt like striking a deal with a serpent. Sly and cunning, slithering along its belly, ready to strike at the perfect moment. It was one of those deals where you knew you didn't have the upper hand, and your options were limited, neither truly beneficial over the other. I took the key from him, hoping it would bring me closer to the answers to resolution. But from what I could tell, Jericho liked to keep his cards close to his chest.

Even with Jericho's assurances of my safety, I couldn't afford to let my guard down. I needed to cross my T's and dot my I's. The way he dismissed the topic of Michael made my stomach churn. In some ways, it felt like a betrayal to the one person who brought me in and showed me the ropes. But it was clear that Jericho saw his people as pawns in his chess game. And I couldn't help but wonder what chess piece he saw in me.

I closed the door behind me and flicked on the light. In the center of the room sat a round polished wooden table with a wine glass, a decanter, and a note with my name on it. Of course, Jericho knew I'd stay. Son of a bitch had this waiting for me like a peace offering some sorts.

Approaching the table, I inspected the decanter, its contents thick, dark, and rich, resembling red wine. But the handwritten note held a different confession. It was blood. Human blood.

I popped off the cap and inhaled, letting the scent course through me and stir something up more savage. The heat radiating from it was indeed comforting. Still, I hesitated, the decanter was full and heavy in my hand. Some poor soul was drained dry for this. Jericho's gifts seemed to have strings attached, and this one felt no different. But the ache in my side flared, reminded me of my current situation. Sharp and relentless. I needed this—to feed, and my hunger won.

After pouring a glass, I raised it to my lips.

Paused.

Then, I swirled the liquid slowly watching the blood trace the rim of the glass, creating a tornado of aroma that awoken my senses. The glass pressed firmly to my lips and the warm liquid felt smooth on my tongue, its sweet taste dancing like an electric current. As I swallowed, the pain in my side dissolved, replaced by a rush of energy that left me feeling invincible.

I was hungry for more.

The exhaustion that had dragged at me since the docks was gone. I was ready to find this diary and put an end to all this madness.

With a newfound purpose and energy, I walked to the closet to see if any clothes were there, and of course, a black suit in my size was perfectly hung up waiting for me. As I got dressed, there was a sudden knock on the door. I figured one of Jericho's minions had come to collect me. I threw on the suit jacket and rushed to the door.

"Yeah?" I asked as I opened it, and to my surprise, Michael stood there. A wave of relief and guilt collided, hitting me all at once.

"Mike? You're good!" I said, trying to keep my voice steady.

"I told you, mate," he replied, walking past me into the room. "It's Michael." He had a toothpick between his teeth, rolling it back and forth as he glanced around.

I let out a chuckle. "Michael, right. How are you?"

"I'm good, mate! Why wouldn't I be?" He smirked and walked over to the table, picking up the decanter. He turned it in his hands, inspecting the deep red liquid. "I see you've got your fill of the Kool-Aid. Amazing what the blood does for you, isn't it?" His smirk lingered as he set the decanter down.

I let the door swing shut behind me, turning the lock with a satisfying click as the metal latch settled into the frame.

"I was starving," I said, sinking into the leather chair across from Michael. "What can I say? I'm not exactly used to these...methods."

"You're right! Your method usually involves middle-aged men who hate their marriage, and farm animals of the sort." Michael's grin widened as he leaned back in his chair, the toothpick rolling lazily between his teeth. "Hardly a method—not a dignified one anyway. I think I'll stick to tradition, mate." He winked, the toothpick in his mouth shifting with the motion.

I exhaled deeply, not taking offense to his words. I was thrilled he was up and about, walking around in good spirits, but I was growing curious about his visit.

"What can I do for you, Michael?"

"Can't a friend stop by to say hi?" He jumped out of his chair and began pacing the room, his movements restless and deliberate. "First, I want to say thank you for getting me out of there the other night." Michael stopped by the window, peering behind the curtain as if he needed to remain hidden. "I understand some of my men wanted to leave me behind." He shook his head in disbelief; his gaze fixed on something far beyond the glass. "They've already been dealt with. It's hard to find true loyalty these days, Leo."

His tone sent a chill down my spine. "I don't know if you know this yet, but Morison was behind the attack," I said carefully, watching for his reaction.

Michael nodded, pausing for a moment as though wrapped in his own thoughts. Then a sinister smile spread across his face.

"I know, mate. I knew that as soon as I saw the captain and his crew were bleeding out in front of us that night. Morison has a unique way of biting his victims—keeping them alive but barely mobile. That way, he can harvest them later."

I stared at him, stunned. "Why didn't you say anything?"

Michael turned back to me, letting the curtain fall lightly into place. "Because our dear friend will get what's coming to him. He chose the wrong team." His gaze locked onto mine as he took a step closer. "Speaking of which,

I saw you and Jericho talking earlier," he said, his voice almost casual as he moved toward me. "What were you two talking about?"

The question sent my thoughts racing. Did he already know what was said? Was he testing me? Jericho had promised to fill him in, but to what extent, I didn't know.

"Jericho was just talking about the docks. I told him about Morison," I said, rising from my chair to walk around the room, hoping to hide the discomfort creeping into my expression. The thought of the diary came to mind, but I pushed it aside.

"Nothing else?" Michael pressed.

"And just about living here among you all," I added, trying to sound nonchalant. "He gave me a rundown of the rules of his compound."

Michael squinted, reading my body language, surely searching for cracks in my story. After a moment, he started toward the door, then stopped just in front of me.

"Jericho's great," he said, his voice dropping, "but his way of doing things isn't always in the best interests of those around him." He gave me a friendly punch on the shoulder, his smile returning. "See you soon, mate."

I stood frozen as the door clicked shut behind him. The pressure of guilt did not fade with his exit; instead, it was replaced by a wave of paranoia. I would have to confront Michael about the truth eventually, but not now—not when the tension between us was already simmering.

I grabbed my hat, jacket, and boots, bracing myself as I headed toward the entryway of the compound. The mission was clear: obtain the diary. The Quality View Hotel seemed like the best place to start. The first time I'd been there, I was nothing but an innocent traveler, ignorant of the underworld that existed within its walls. The second time, I'd been cut while trying to help the woman from the front desk who had later saved me from a torturous fate at Fox Retreat Hill.

But this time?

This time, I wasn't going for peace talks. This time, I'd leave no stone unturned.

I started making my way to the Hyllie side of town; a light dusting of snow fell from the sky, and the innocent laughter and chatter of the city marked its ignorance of the darkness that hid within it. My undead senses were open, noticing the scandalous shadows lurking in the corners, hearing the irregular heartbeat of the old man whose days were numbered, spotting Everborns musing about the locals, and the slow rotation of the earth catching the rays of the sun casting in the horizon. I was i tune with my surroundings and the beings around me.

I gathered my thoughts as I approached the hotel, standing just across the street in the shadow of a narrow alley. The building loomed ahead, its polished exterior a sharp contrast to the darkness I knew lurked within. I watched the comings and goings of the patrons—an older couple dragging suitcases, a young man with a hurried gait—but there was no sign of Morison or the young woman from before.

The minutes ticked by, each one chipping away at my resolve.

Was I wasting time here?

The longer I waited, the more it felt like the walls of the city were closing in, and I couldn't shake the thought that someone—something—was watching me.

I need to make my move, I thought. *Sooner rather than later.*

Finally, I gathered the courage to make my way to the front door and get some answers. Just then, I heard something behind me—something so quiet not even a dog would have noticed it.

I quickly spun around, my muscles tense, only to find the woman from the hotel standing there, her figure framed by the falling snow.

The way the snow caught in her golden hair and shimmered against her pale skin made her look like an angel sent from the heavens. But I knew better. Beneath that Swedish exterior lurked a dangerous woman, one whose men left me bleeding out just days ago. But this time, there was no malice in her stance.

No hissing.

No threatening glares.

It was unsettling.

"Figured you'd come after us sooner," she said, her tone casual.

"I would have, but tyvärr, I was healing from a stab wound," I replied, my voice dripping with sarcasm.

She stepped closer, her movements deliberate but not threatening. "I'm sorry about that," she said, her emerald eyes briefly meeting mine. "I did tell you to stay out of this."

I shrugged off my jacket, folding it neatly and placing it on the ground beside me. "I'm glad I didn't. Who knows what you and Morison are up to? Where is that scoundrel anyway? Hiding from the inevitable?"

She shook her head and raised her shoulders slowly. "Perhaps," she said.

I let out a small chuckle, letting my fangs show as I scanned the alleyway, ensuring I wouldn't be taking by surprise again like we were at the docks. "Let's get this on, yea?" I exclaimed, my voice echoing off the brick walls.

"I'm not going to fight you, Leo. There are things you should know."

Her words caught me off guard, but I figured it was one of her tricks—a mind game to throw me off. What information could she possibly have to tell me?

"No," I said sharply, and lunged toward her.

She sidestepped with ease, still showing no signs of aggression.

"Playing hard to get?" I asked, the edge in my voice sharper now. "Where is the diary...?" I paused, searching my mind for her name.

"Natalie," she introduced herself, finishing the question for me. "The name is Natalie, and right now, you don't need to know about the diary. But what I can tell you is—"

I cut her off and lunged again, this time managing to graze her arm with my fingers, drawing blood.

She hissed, clutching her arm tightly as crimson stained her sleeve. "Helvete!" she cussed, glaring at me. "You bloody fool. If only the brains matched the looks!"

I paused, waiting for her to make a move, but she stood there, unmoving, desperation in her voice. Then she said, "Jericho is not your friend, Leo, and neither is Michael."

Her words struck a nerve, and without thought, I lunged. My hands wrapped around her neck, slamming her against the wall. I held her there, my grip tight enough to crush her windpipe.

"I could make it, so you never speak lies again," my voice just above a whisper. I waited for her to speak again; I was waiting for deception.

She choked, gasping for air, but somehow managed to speak between labored breaths. Her hands clawed at my arm, her legs flailing, desperate for solid ground. "Jericho..." she choked, her voice barely audible. "You don't... understand."

I hesitated.

What am I doing?

My grip loosened as doubt crept in.

No women, no children. That had always been my code. And she had spared me once before. I cursed under my breath and released her. She crumpled to the ground like a rag doll, coughing violently as she clutched her throat.

"You have two minutes to speak," I said coldly, stepping back.

Natalie dragged herself upright, wiping snow from her clothes as she struggled to catch her breath.

"Like I said," she croaked, "they're not your friends." She coughed again, wincing, before continuing. "You've been on Jericho's compound, haven't you? Have you seen his lab downstairs?"

"Why?" I asked, my tone sharp, my eyes never leaving her.

"He's..." She hesitated, her expression shifting to something raw and vulnerable. "He's draining Night Walkers of their blood."

Her words carried the power of a freight train. Fury flared in my chest as I demanded, "And why would he do that?" Part of me wanted to dismiss it as a lie, but another part—the part that couldn't trust Jericho—held back. "The Everborns are the ones trying to coexist," I shouted, "even when you all started this war!"

Natalie stared at me like she was looking at a fool.

"Is that what they've been telling you?" she asked, shaking her head in disbelief. "Has it occurred to you that you've only been given one version of the story?"

"And why would they lie?" I shouted, my anger boiling over as my hands moved toward her neck again. But before I could grab her, she spoke.

"Because, Leo," she said, her voice steady now despite the fear in her eyes, "he plans to create an army."

"An army?" I asked hesitantly. "What for?"

"Come back to the hotel, and I'll explain. Something doesn't feel right here. We can't be out in the open."

I double checked her movements unsure of what to believe. I sensed no lying in her but still the muscles in my jaw tightened.

"You must take me for a fool."

"Fine!" she said, throwing her hands up. She glanced at her watch, "we're running out of time as it is." She hesitated, her voice softening as she looked around, cautious. "He wants to use his army to wipe out the Night Walkers first—" She stopped abruptly, her attention darting around us like deer in the wild. Her gaze returned to mine, steady but urgent. "And then enslave the humans. He wants the world for himself and his loyal subjects."

Her revelation twisted something inside me. The logic of it felt warped. I could understand his vendetta against the Night Walkers—that rationale made some sense. But enslaving humans and taking over the world sounded reckless at best. And at worst, a task too large with many variables to control.

"When you were at his compound, did you get a good look around?" she pressed, her tone sharpening with desperation. "The answers may be right under your nose."

"I'm tired of everyone speaking in riddles. And I don't work for you, Natalie," I snapped, my voice rising. "Speak plainly!"

From somewhere behind us came the dull crunch of snow underfoot. My attention shifted immediately, my senses heightening. A figure stood in the shadows, obscured but unmistakably there.

Natalie turned her head sharply, and before I could react, she bolted, her feet barely touching the ground as she vanished into the dark.

"Everything good here, mate?"

The familiar voice pulled my attention back.

Michael stepped into view, his casual stride at odds with the tension that had just filled the air.

I watched Natalie's figure disappear toward the hotel, wanting to chase after her, but Michael's sudden appearance anchored me in place.

"How did you know I was here?" I asked, my tone more accusatory than curious.

Michael strolled closer, his smirk as infuriating as ever, but this time, it felt off. Too deliberate.

Too calculated.

"A few men back at the compound said they saw you heading out in a hurry," he said, taking a quick look toward the direction Natalie had run. "Figured I would check in. Make sure you didn't need any help with." He paused. "Whatever this is."

His suspicion clogged the space between us but despite what he might have heard he remained casual.

He laughed, "you're fast, mate. I tried to catch up, but you were moving like a man on a mission."

"I was looking for the diary," I finally said, my eyes locked on his, unblinking.

Michael rolled his wrist in a slow circle, a gesture that showed his impatience. "And?" he prompted, his tone sharp, probing.

"And... nothing. She doesn't have it."

I didn't know what to say. I was caught off guard and didn't even get that far into our conversation for me to probe her about the diary. I didn't know if she even still had it.

He smirked, shaking his head lightly.

"Mate, that Swedish beauty on her face will eventually fade... even for our kind. Don't get caught up and lose your edge. Keep your mind sharp."

"There's no lust," I said, my voice firm. "All I got from her was something about an army being created at Jericho's compound."

Michael's expression shifted, his usual smirk replaced by a moment of puzzlement.

"An army?" he repeated to himself.

"Guess I'm not the only one out of the loop," I said, studying his reaction carefully.

We began walking back to the compound, our footsteps pressing against the snow was the only sound for a while. Michael was uncharacteristically quiet, lost in his thoughts. But my mind wasn't at ease. I couldn't shake the feeling that Michael's appearance wasn't a coincidence.

How long had he been there?

How much did he hear?

What does he know?

Him coming to my room earlier, was that coincidence?

The questions ate at me, each one digging into my psyche deeper than the last. My paranoia grew with every step we took.

Was I being watched?

CHAPTER THIRTEEN

TWO CAN KEEP A SECRET

We made our way back to the compound, my mind heavy and thick like clouds on a rainy day. Everything was in a haze as I reflected on Natalie, Jericho, and the questions they raised. I had my concerns, just as I was sure Michael did, though following me around town seemed to have taken a back seat to the news of Jericho's hidden army. I could see it in his face, in the way he walked—the lump in his throat, his hands flexing and twitching at his sides. He was less than pleased about critical information being kept from him.

Then again, I was keeping secrets of my own.

As we approached the front gate of the compound, Michael quickened his pace, his steps more purposeful, more urgent. He moved ahead of me, his voice clipped as he said, "Enjoy your day, mate. I've got some pressing issues to attend to."

He didn't look back to see if I'd heard him, didn't wait for a response. The usual confidence that cloaked his insecurities—the smirk, the bravado—was now gone, stripped away like a bandage ripped from a fresh wound. His internal scars were on display, and I almost pitied him. The character he worked so hard to maintain was beginning to crack.

But pity wasn't enough to quiet the doubts chipping away at my mind. Was Michael's appearance at the hotel merely a coincidence, or had he been following me all along? The thought lingered, bitter and unshakable. I needed answers, but first, I needed to find Jericho.

I entered the building a few moments after Michael, giving him space to breathe while I needed space to investigate. The faint hum of activity echoed through the compound, a contrast to the phlegm swirling in my chest. I went straight to Jericho's office, but no one was there. I scanned the garden outside his office window; empty.

Roaming the corridor, I ignored the nods and salutes from Everborns who obviously received the memo that I was in charge going forward—a position I did not embrace.

Finally, I pulled one of the men to the side, gripping the collar of his shirt. "Where is Jericho?"

The man stumbled over his words, his voice shaky as his eyes darted to avoid mine. "It's almost 18:00," he said, glancing at his watch to confirm. "If he's anywhere, he'd be at his lab."

I released him, his shoulders sagging in relief. Just as I turned to leave, he called out, "He doesn't take kindly to interruptions!"

"There's a first for everything," I muttered, quickening my pace toward the elevator at the far end of the corridor.

I rode the elevator down to the last floor, the doors opening to the dark, cold hallway where Jericho once interrogated me. The lightbulbs flickered erratically, casting shadows that danced along the walls like recreational users at a rave. Beads of dew dripped from the damp walls, glistening like sweat on a hot Midsummer Day. The distinct scent of cleaning solution was emanating from the lab, cutting through the stale air. Yet, the hallway was eerily quiet.

I rounded the corner and entered the lab, but it was empty. The computer equipment and machinery were off, and the room was eerily still—except for a half-+finished glass of liquor sitting on the table. I picked it up, the chill of the glass still clinging to my fingertips. Whoever had been here couldn't have left long ago.

I scanned the room, searching for notes, papers, anything that could suggest something afoul was at play. But there was nothing—no evidence, no answers. Could this draining of Night Walkers be a farce? Conflicting thoughts battled for space in my mind. The one thing I knew was that I couldn't trust anyone.

I stood there, silent, longing for a cigarette, when the faint creak of a door echoed in the distance. My breath hitched as I moved quickly, tiptoeing behind the laboratory door. Was my mind playing tricks on me? Through the thin sliver between the door and its hinges, I saw a man in a lab coat appear from what looked like a hidden door, blending seamlessly into the wall.

I watched him make his way to the elevator, his hands empty but his face heavy with defeat. He disappeared, and the hallway returned to silence.

Once the man was out of sight, I moved to the wall he had come from, tracing my fingers over every crack and curve of the stone. Suddenly, there was a low hiss, like air being released, and the door became ajar.

My heart raced.

Whatever lay on the other side had been meant to stay hidden.

I pushed the door open just enough to slip through, not wanting to risk making noise. Beyond the door was a narrow hallway, dimly lit, its silence pressing down on me like a physical weight. My footsteps were light as I followed the corridor to a grated landing where bright lab lights shone through.

I stepped back, ensuring I didn't make any noise on the metal grates. Below, through the gaps, I saw a man standing in front of what appeared to be a cage. The glare of the lights made it hard to see, and I squinted, straining my eyes to make out more.

"Your resilience is something to be admired." The voice was unfamiliar, steady but edged with amusement.

Then, a second voice, this one unmistakable. A devilish laugh followed. "See, I have my own scientist now," Jericho declared. "Once I get my hands on that antidote—" He pressed his hands against the bars of the metal cage, his voice smug and assured. "Your service will no longer be needed."

I shifted, lowering myself closer to the ground. The grated landing beneath me offered an obscured view, and the blinding overhead lights created blind spots against the lab floor. I couldn't see who Jericho was speaking to, but there were no signs of Night Walkers—only a lone figure in a cage.

A weak voice pushed through the sterile air. "And what makes you think..." A ragged cough interrupted her, her strength fading with each breath. "You will find it?"

Jericho remained cool, dismissive. "I had a fool in a position of authority. Nothing more than an errand boy."

His words hit hard.

I tensed, disappointment pounding hard against my chest, but I wasn't entirely surprised. Jericho was playing a different game from everyone else, following his own rules, and disposing of those who had no purpose. Michael had led the failed mission at the docks, but I couldn't lay the blame on him. Maybe Michael should have had scouts recon the area in advance but still a trusted insider had orchestrated the ambush, knowing every single detail. Instead, Jericho pinned the blame on him, shifting pieces around for his next move.

The woman's voice rasped again, quieter this time. "And now?"

Jericho stepped back from the cage, scratching his chin, his tone turning thoughtful. "Now, I have someone stronger. More competent. Someone who wants nothing more than to fit in."

Cold beads of sweat formed on my forehead.

He was talking about me.

The woman, drained but not defeated, used what little strength she had left to cling to the bars of the cage. Her grip was tight, heavy-handed, and when she shook them, the metal rattled violently, sending sharp echoes rippling through the lab.

"He won't help you!" she cried out, her voice hoarse but unwavering.

I stiffened.

She spoke as if she knew exactly who Jericho was talking about, like she knew the man in question. Could she be talking about me? Or someone else?

I was certain Jericho had been referring to me, but her words—her desperation—didn't add up. Who was this woman? I wiped the sweat from my brow with the back of my hand, listening closer to the exchange.

Jericho clapped, an ovation like it was the closing act of a theater show. The other man in the room scrambled to regain his composure, picking up the papers that had slipped from his grasp. Judging by his reaction, he wasn't one of our kind.

"After all these years I'm glad to see you still have some fight in you, darling," Jericho mused, stepping closer to the cage but keeping just outside her reach.

His smirk deepened.

"Angel eyes with a wild side, disguised as a delicate flower, but the thorn that stuck Henrik's hands."

The tiny hairs on my neck rose, my breath hitched, and my ears sharpened. My attention was split between the woman's rasping voice and the sharp hiss of air pressure being released from the hidden door behind me. Someone was coming. I needed a way out.

My gaze darted down the narrow hallway, searching for an escape route, but all I found were locked doors and a dead end. My options were limited. Either lie and say that Jericho wanted to speak with me or take this person out before they alerted him of my presence. I crouched lower, pressing myself into the shadows, waiting for my moment.

The footsteps grew louder, and they were purposeful.

They got closer.

The moment the figure rounded the corner, my hand shot out, clamping tightly around his throat. A strangled gasp escaped him as I hoisted him off the ground, his feet kicked against empty air, and a clipboard fell from his hand.

It was the man from earlier—the one I saw leaving the lab when I first found the door.

His hands clawed at my grip, his face stretched wide with panic, his mouth opening and closing like a fish gasping for air. I walked forward, keeping him suspended, pushing him back toward the door he just came through. I loosened my grip, just enough for him to sputter out words.

"What—what are you doing here?" His voice was hoarse, barely more than a whisper.

"Who is the woman in the cage?" I demanded.

He coughed, struggling to breathe. I needed answers quickly. Slamming him against the cold stone wall, I tightened my hold. "What does she know about me?"

His mouth opened, his lips forming the start of a word, but instead of answering, his trembling hand moved toward his coat pocket. My grip on his throat tightened as a warning, but he still managed to pull something out.

A small black device.

One red button sat in the center, a dull grey antenna jutting out from the top.

I reached to stop him, but I was a second too late.

Click.

A sharp beep filled the air, followed by a low mechanical whine.

His bloodshot eyes slowly rolling up into the back of their sockets, and a twisted smile forming at his lips.

"She's—" he wheezed. "The Everborn."

He choked on his last breath and went limp in my grasp; dead.

I barely had time to process his words before the red warning lights flared to life, alarms blaring through the underground halls.

A sharp crackle burst through the air.

The radio glued to the scientist's dead cold hand came to life. Jericho's voice breaking through, sharp and authoritative, distorted by static.

"Shut the compound down!"

I had to get out of here.

Immediately.

CHAPTER FOURTEEN

ESCAPE ROUTE

The distant crackle of Jericho's voice barking orders over the radio faded as I made my way down the hall toward the elevator. My pace was quick but controlled. I knew running would only create more noise. I scanned the corridor carefully, eyes gauging every shadow, every corner. There was a strange feeling in the air, like a virus entering your system, attacked by a fever, burning hot. It was as if the compound itself knew I did not belong.

Ding.

The elevator doors slid open.

To my surprise, it was empty. No guards, no watchful eyes. Maybe Jericho hadn't caught on to me yet—or maybe this was the calm before the storm. I stepped inside, pressing the button for the main floor, my reflection staring back at me from the polished metal walls.

As the elevator climbed, my thoughts spiraled.

What if Jericho already knew?

What if Michael did?

The encounter in the lab replayed in my mind like a broken record.

She's The Everborn.

The words echoed in my skull, louder than the alarm had been.

Ding.

The doors slid open to a different kind of chaos.

Men rushed through the compound, their movements like a militia. Some were locking doors, others sprinting toward the outer gates. But amidst the tension, they still saluted me as they passed, oblivious to the truth or maybe locking me in. My heart pounded in my chest, but I kept my face neutral, forcing every muscle to remain calm.

And then there was him.

Michael.

Leaning casually in the doorway like he did not have a care in the world, peeling slices from a large red apple with his pocketknife. His posture was relaxed, and his attitude was weirdly calm, just another routine drill.

"Where've you been, mate?" he asked, slipping an apple slice into his mouth. The blade scraped against his teeth as he pulled it free, the metal tang echoing in my ears sending a cold chill down my neck.

"I was walking the compound," I lied, forcing a shrug. "Needed some fresh air."

Michael's eyes drifted up from the apple, locking onto me for just a second, long enough to make me think about making a run for it. But then he looked away, slicing another piece.

"Fresh air, huh?"

He chewed slowly, savoring it.

I didn't respond.

My gaze searched around, making mental notes of the exits, the guards, the narrowing opportunities.

Michael extended the half-eaten apple toward me, his grin widening.

"Hungry?"

I forced a laugh, shaking my head.

"Never took you for an apple kind of guy."

His smirk deepened, but his expression remained cold.

"It's like the Garden of Eden, Leo."

The words coupled with his demeanor added to my confusion.

"Excuse me?" I asked, my voice more questionable than I intended.

Michael chuckled, flicking the knife shut with a quick snap of his wrist. He slid it back into his pocket in one fluid motion, stepping forward as he tossed the apple into a nearby bin.

"This compound," he said, waving his hand around lazily. "We can have anything we want here." He paused, his gaze cutting through me. "But stay away from that tree."

More riddles. What the hell was he talking about?

"I don't get it," I muttered, trying to keep my voice steady. "What does that have to do with anything right now?"

Michael's smile twisted, somewhere between amusement and menace. He leaned in, lowering his voice just enough for only me to hear.

"One day, mate," he whispered. "One day you will."

For a moment, we just stood there, his words like two walls closing in on me. Then he stepped back, clasping me lightly on the shoulder.

"Come on," he said, tilting his head toward the hall. "Let's go."

I forced a nod, falling in step beside him. But inside, my mind was calculating.

I need to get out of here.

Whether Michael knew the truth or was just toying with me was unclear. I couldn't trust him anymore. Too many variables and uncertainty when it came to him and Jericho. Add the strange prisoner trapped into the cage below in the lab was another frightening layer. If I didn't find a way to escape soon, I wouldn't get another chance.

"Where are we going?" I asked as he led me through the front doors and into the snow-covered yard.

"We need to check with the men up front. See if they've noticed anything," he replied, his tone casual, with a slight edge beneath it.

I nodded again, falling just a step behind, my eyes trained on his hands and watched every subtle movement for a threat.

Then he continued, thinking out loud, "It's unusual for anyone to get into this compound who isn't supposed to be here." He shot me a glance, raising an eyebrow. "My suspicions?" He let the question freeze in the cold air for a beat, then smirked. "It's a bastard from within, mate."

The blood in my veins started to race, pulsing so fast my arms began to itch. But I kept my face neutral, playing along.

"You mean like another Morison?" I asked, my voice steady despite the alarm bells ringing in my head.

We reached the front gate where four men stood on guard. Michael paused, turning to face me directly. His voice dropped and, in that moment, I knew I was screwed.

"Yes, mate."

I noticed two of the guards subtly closing in, their steps slow, casual. Michael continued to read me as he finished, "Just like Morison. Is there anything you want to tell me, Leo?"

The guards took another step closer, their movements mimicking a pride of Lions closing in on its prey. I shook my head. Imitating confusion to his question.

"No. Why do you ask?"

The mask he was wearing dropped in an instant. "Do not play games with me!" His voice cutting through the frigid air. "What did you find in that lab?"

Before I could respond, the two guards lunged. I dodged the first, but the second grabbed my arm with a sure grip. The other two rushed in, their hands like iron clamps locking my arms behind my back. A sharp kick to the back of my knees sent me crashing into the snow, the cold cutting deep to my bones.

I barely had time to process before the guard I'd dodged earlier hauled himself up and slammed his fist into my jaw. Pain exploded across my face, my vision blurring at the edges.

Through the haze, I saw Michael step forward, calm and calculated, like a cat toying with a mouse. He loomed over me, his shadow stretching long in the snow. His gaze flicked up to the doorway of the compound, then back to me, his expression unreadable.

"Mate," he said quietly, almost tenderly. "Jericho is no friend of yours. Tell me what he's hiding down there, and we can work this out."

He sounded reassuring—like he wanted to help—but I knew better. Michael was up to something. His own hidden agenda that was separate from Jericho's plans. It was only a matter of time before we came to blows, and the thought left a pit in my stomach, an ache so tight it twisted into nausea. He must have known I was up to something this whole time.

Michael glanced toward the doorway again, his attention split.

What the hell is back there? Whatever it was, it had him more rattled than he wanted to admit.

"Mate," he pressed, his voice dropping into something softer, something more dangerous. "Tell me what's down there."

I stayed silent.

His jaw clenched, and without looking away from me, he pointed for one of the guards.

Crack!

A heavy, gloved fist smashed into my face, snapping my head sideways and driving me into the snow. The sting bloomed across my jaw, my vision blurring from the impact.

"Lift him up," Michael said, almost lazily.

The guards yanked me upright, my arms pinned tight behind my back. Michael crouched so we were eye-to-eye, his breath misting in the frigid air between us.

He stared at me for a long moment, then sighed, as if he were the one burdened by this.

"Tell me, mate," he whispered. "Is she down there?"

I leaned back, my mind racing. *The woman in the cage?* I thought. What does he know about her? She must be important to Michael as well. But how did he know someone was down there?

I turned my head, spat the blood pooling in mouth into the snow, and forced my eyes back to his.

"You know about the woman being held hostage?" I asked, my voice low.

Before Michael could answer, the sound of crunching footsteps echoed from the distance behind us.

"Is that Leo?"

Damn it.

Jericho's voice weaving through the cold, sending a fresh wave of adrenaline pulsing through my veins.

I was outnumbered.

Surrounded.

Michael looked up toward the sound, his frustration clear. But before Jericho reached us, he leaned in close, his voice falling to a whisper, low enough for only my ears.

"You know her too, mate."

Jericho's shadow stretched across the snow as he approached. "Get him on his feet," he barked.

The guards shifted, dragging me upright. Michael was still crouched in front of me, close enough that I could smell the small tang of blood and the sharp bite of his cologne.

Now or never, I said to myself.

I snapped my head forward, driving it into Michael's nose with a sickening crunch.

Boom!

Michael roared, stumbling back, his hands flying to his face as blood gushed down his shirt. The sudden chaos threw the guards off, and I seized my chance. I wrenched one arm free, grabbed the nearest guard, and yanked him in close, our chests colliding.

I wasted no time and with little effort I sank my teeth into his throat.

Hot blood flooded my mouth as I tore back, ripping through flesh and muscle like a medium rare steak. Like a fire hydrant, his blood rapidly sprayed covering my face like war paint.

His body sagged, knees buckling.

He choked on his own blood, the sound thick and wet.

He clutched at the gaping hole now present under his chin, but it was pointless.

The other guards lunged, but I was already moving, my body fueled by raw instinct. The snow was slick beneath my worn boots, the cold biting at my skin, but the fire inside me burned hot.

It was on.

"Seize him, now!" Jericho's voice carried through the chilly air, sharp and commanding.

But they were too slow.

The shift inside me was instant.

My fangs pushed through my gums, my hands curled into claws, and every nerve in my body fired like it was ready to burn the metaphorical bridge that connected us.

The first Everborn lunged, but I dropped low and swept his legs out from under him. He hit the ground hard, searching for his breath.

I didn't give him the chance to find it.

The next one came fast, but I was faster.

I removed my jacket in one motion, twirled it above my head like a lasso, before snaking it around his neck like a noose. I pulled upwards as hard as I could and there was a brief second where I felt his pulse hammering beneath his skin right before he stopped struggling and his neck popped.

His body went limp, collapsing into the snow at my feet.

I straightened, chest rising and falling like rough waves of the sea. I faced Jericho.

"Let me leave," I pleaded. "And I won't come back."

The silence stretched for an agonizing few second. Just the wind cutting through the compound, stirring the snow around our feet.

"Not tonight, mate."

I turned to the voice behind me.

Michael.

He staggered to his feet, his face twisted in fury, blood still dripping from his nose. I turned just as he was pulling himself to his feet. The usual smirk was gone. What replaced it wasn't anger. It was something colder—something personal.

He started toward me, slow with each step quickening.

He sprinted the last few steps, and I met him head on. We collided, fists flying, claws slashing. His strength matched mine, each strike landing with bone-jarring force. Every time I moved, he countered. Every time he struck, I blocked. We rolled through the snow, grappling for control, neither of us gaining the upper hand.

This fight felt different than others.

I almost felt like I was fighting a brother of mine.

Someone close to me.

We broke apart, both of us breathing hard, circling each other in the snow. The others—Jericho and his men—formed in a tight semi-circle around us, cheering us on.

It felt ritualistic.

Jericho tossed two pocketknives at our feet.

"A fight to the death!" He yelled.

The crowd erupted, cheering us on.

"Michael," I said, my voice hoarse. "Let's stop this."

He didn't answer.

He just kept circling, focused on me, like he was waiting for his opportunity. Jericho's shadow loomed behind him, but I kept my focus on Michael.

"Jericho's lying to you," I said, voice steady despite the pounding in my chest. "The woman in the cage? The Night Walkers he's draining? The army he's building? He's using you, Michael. Using all of us."

Michael hesitated.

His steps slowed, just enough for me to see a small trace of doubt adorning his face. His jaw clenched, and the tension in his shoulders returned like a coiled spring.

"Don't say another word mate," he muttered.

The sound in his voice sounded half threatening and half warning. Was he trying to tell me something? I thought about his own agendas and figured anything I kept quiet in front of Jericho was for Michael's reasons and his reasons alone.

Before I could say another word, he lunged again but stopped mid-action.

The compound went pitch black.

The lights went out.

A silence fell upon us.

My mouth was covered, and something dragged me by the back of my collar.

NATALIE

CHAPTER FIFTEEN

A COMMON ENEMY

"We want the same thing you know?" he asked. "I'll do my damnedest to ensure you succeed."

I exhaled deeply, taking note of the closed window shutters in the corner. "Why now?" I asked. "You invited me here under the cloak of the night. We could get caught."

"My establishment is well secured," he replied, taking a measured sip of his dark whiskey.

"The rest of the Night Walkers will undeniably question your involvement." I peaked behind his shoulders; nothing. Then to the quiet blindspots for anything or anyone hidden. I scanned for evidence of listening ears—again nothing. My two men stood at the doors, keeping watch, but when dealing with someone two-faced, it was hard to feel truly safe.

His actions were questionable. "Legend has it that you were there that night at Fox Retreat Hill," I added.

He slammed his hand down on the wooden bar, the sound cracking through the quiet room.

"I only protected myself and those around me. They attacked first. Plus, there's more to the story."

One of my men flinched at the outburst and sprang to my side, fangs bared, claws extended, ready to defend me if needed.

"It's fine," I said, holding up a hand.

My guard hesitated before stepping back, though his glare remained fixed on the man across from me.

The tension hung in the air for a moment before he spoke again, his tone softer now.

"Listen," he began, massaging the back of his neck. "I agree our kind should walk this earth freely," his voice soiled with regret. "But I do not agree with all of Jericho's methods." He swirled the whiskey in his glass before taking another sip, he stared into the distance.

I stayed quiet, dissecting his frustrations, searching for the deceit in his words. His confession was heavy, paired with an undercurrent of remorse. Still, I had to be certain. This task was not going to be easy, and convincing others to trust him would require delicate handling.

I extended my hand, my gaze unwavering.

"Looks like we have a common enemy now."

Time passed briefly, him considering the line he crossed, before shaking my hand.

"Alas, we do," he replied.

I kept scanning the room, the walls whispered horrors I could almost feel. Blood—human blood—was soaked into the very grain of the floorboards, the little metallic particles hung in the air from the last time they must have fed.

It disgusted me.

"So, this is where it all goes down, huh?" I said to Morison, my voice sharp, pushing through the room's oppressive silence. The thought of innocent lives being discarded like garbage made my stomach churn. The Everborns had turned this place into a den of indulgence, a mockery of what we were meant to be.

He didn't turn around; his focus was on the drink he was pouring at the bar. "We're predators, they're prey," he said, his tone so casual it chilled me. "It's nature at its finest, Natalie. The circle of life, some would call it."

The ease with which he dismissed the atrocities tightened a coil of anger in my chest.

But I said nothing.

At this moment there were bigger stakes at play, and Morison was the only way I would be able to get close enough to kill Jericho.

He reached beneath the bar, pulling out a chest and resting it on the counter. From under his shirt, he produced a small, tarnished key dangling on a necklace. With deliberate care, he unlocked the chest and retrieved something wrapped in an old, weathered cloth.

"This," he said, walking back to the table where I sat, his voice heavy, "is the key to all it...well, one third of it, anyway."

He placed the item on the table, his gaze lingering on it with a mixture of reverence and apprehension. Slowly, he unwrapped the cloth, revealing a small, worn book. Its leather cover was dry and cracked with age, the dull scent of parchment wafting from it.

"I retrieved this diary from Jericho," he said, holding it up so the low light in the room illuminated its surface. "It won't be long before he knows it's missing." His voice carried a sense of unease, his hand lingering over the diary as though reluctant to let it go.

Like letting go of a beloved trinket, he admired it one last time before he slid the book across the table.

I caught it with steady hands.

The leather was cool against my skin, and I could feel the history of its significance.

Morison continued, rushing through his words this time.

"There's a ship arriving in two weeks. Onboard are four suitcases containing the second piece of the very thing that started our existence—everything Jericho's been fighting for...But it's incomplete."

His posture gave way to his excitement as he sunk deeper into the wooden chair.

"There's a third piece," he said quietly. "I'm sure it has to do with blood and Night Walkers."

"Ursäkta?!"

I leaped to my feet; a wave of disbelief coursed through me, fueling my outrage. How dare he mention something so vile? My mind raced, torn between dismissing Morison's words or finding out the truth.

"Explain yourself!"

Morison interlocked his fingers and cracked his knuckles as he leaned back casually. Then he put the glass to his lips, his lids shut, and savoring the alcohol as though it would be his last drink. He spoke, his voice measured and deliberate. "Read the diary for yourself," he challenged. "You'll have too eventually. You'll learn what I've learned—the little I know so far. My reading was cut short when Michael came strolling in. I had to hurry up and pack up the diary before he could nose around. Whoever that diary belongs to though I believe is very much alive."

My fingers trembled as I held my fists clenched at my sides. "What are you talking about? Who?"

He focused on me with a stern, unyielding intensity. "I can't say with certainty, but there's a woman locked underneath the compound." He pointed back to the diary, and he continued. "She might be the author of that book."

My lips frowned while I stared at the diary, trying to process the information.

"But what do you think he's been doing with the Night Walkers he catches? He has them dried up, dead and piled in his lab."

My eyes turned away from Morison, unable to stomach any more of what he was saying. The vile of his words, each revelation, twisting a knot in my chest tighter. *But he could be correct.*

"He's draining the blood of Night Walkers. Running tests. That lab is probably the most secure place on his entire compound," Morison said, shaking his head in dismay. "I only saw the place because he allowed me too."

My frustration boiled over.

"If you can't get in without his knowing, then how exactly are you helping us?" I grabbed my jacket and motioned to my men to follow. "This is a waste of my time," I said over my shoulder, my voice cold with dismissal.

"No, wait!" Morison cried, his voice reeked of desperation. He lunged toward me, grabbing my hand.

My reaction was immediate. I yanked my hand back and dropped into a defensive stance, ready to strike back if he tried anything. A low hiss escaped my lips as my fangs bared.

"Don't touch me," I growled.

Morison raised his hands in a placating gesture, his face pale but resolute. "Just read the diary for yourself!" he pleaded. "Be at the docks, two weeks' time, at midnight!"

For a moment, I stood frozen, my mind racing. Morison's words churned in my head, stirring a mix of anger, doubt, and an uncomfortable sense of necessity. The diary, Jericho's lab, defenseless Night Walkers being drained—all of it must end. If there was truth in his claims, then the war we are fighting is bigger than Night Walkers vs Everborns.

I straightened slowly, retracting my fangs back. My voice was cold and absolute. "We may have a common enemy, Morison, but don't think for a second that makes us friends."

I tore into his soul, giving him my one and only warning.

"And don't ever grab my hand like that again."

Morison swallowed hard, then smirked. "Sometimes, Natalie, we find friends in the most unlikely places."

I turned without a word, my coat flowing behind me as I strode toward the door. My men fell into cadence beside me, watchful and vigilant, reconning the shadows for any surprises. The freezing air hit me as we stepped out into the streets, the quiet of the night amplifying every sound. We looked left and right, giving careful attention to the alleyways one last time before heading to our vehicle.

Clear.

Sliding into the back seat, I glanced once more at the doorway. Morison stood there, a silhouette against the lights, his figure fading away as the car pulled off. His words lingered, unsettling, and hard to forget.

I let out a slow breath, recounting every detail of our conversation. Tonight was the easy part, I realized. The hard part—navigating the chaos ahead—was just beginning.

CHAPTER SIXTEEN

PURITAS SANGUINIS

We arrived at the Night Walker compound just as the sun was cresting the horizon, painting the sky in hues of orange and lavender. The building stood inconspicuously along Hyllie Boulevard, blending seamlessly within the business district, nestled between Emporia Shopping Mall and IKEA. Though it appeared like another corporate building to the human eyes, the truth was hidden beneath the levels of secrecy.

As the gates opened, the sound of tires rumbling against the gravel echoed. The large water fountain outside greeted us, its elegant design a reminder of our lineage—our purity. Large, manicured bushes lined the edges of the courtyard, their symmetry guiding the eye toward a broad, marble staircase that led to the building's main entrance.

I took a deep breath as my men opened the tall double doors for me. The familiar scent of polished marble and aged wood filled my senses, grounding me even as my chest tightened with both anticipation and dread. My grip on the leather-bound diary was firm.

What do I tell the council? I thought.

"Natalie," a familiar voice called from behind me.

I turned to find Albin striding toward me, his expression equal parts stern and weary. He was assigned to me as my mentor, but lately he's been more of the council's watchful shadow.

"The council has been waiting for you," he said, his voice calm with a hint of reprimand.

"Yes, Albin, I know," I replied curtly, cutting him off. My patience was already waning.

He sighed, shaking his head in visible disappointment.

"They're not happy. Do you have any idea how this makes the both of us look? The recklessness of it all?"

His words cutting deeper than I cared to admit.

"My apologies," I said flatly, unwilling to waste energy on an argument. There were bigger battles ahead.

I could feel the weight of Albin's disapproval bearing down on me, the unspoken burden of my actions thickening the air between us as we climbed the stone steps, my boots clicking against the polished floor and amplifying my unease.

Inside, the building was a vision of opulence—bright, open spaces with sleek marble floors and walls lined with floor-to-ceiling windows that offered a panoramic view of the city.

Every detail was a statement of superiority.

Albin gestured grandly. "After you, my lady," he said, his voice mixed with sarcasm.

I rolled my eyes. "No need for pleasantries now."

I pushed the doors open, revealing the chamber within.

Seven figures sat at the far end of the room, their presence intimidating. These were the elders of our kind, *Puritas Sanguinis* or Purity of the Blood—a council as old as the Night Walkers themselves. Their gazes bore into me as I entered, and the grip of their scrutiny was suffocating.

I sat down in the leather chair facing the council, the heavy doors slamming shut behind me with a sense of finality. The silence that followed was deafening, broken only by the rustle of robes as the council shifted in their seats.

"Do tell us, where you have been, Natalie?" one of them called out, their voice filled with authority.

I took a deep breath considering the disapproval that would follow my answer.

"I was in Gamla Staden," I said, my tone measured.

"Gamla...Staden?" another elder echoed.

A third elder leaned forward, their eyes narrowing. "She has no respect for the laws that govern us."

"What were you doing in the Old City?" the first elder pressed.

I stood, pacing as I spoke. "I met with one of the Everborns. Morison."

The air in the room shifted. The council froze, their disbelief tangible. For a moment, it felt as if time itself had stopped.

Finally, one of them cleared their throat.

"What news do you bring from Morison?"

"It's information about Jericho," I said with my voice firm despite their scrutiny. "He's running experiments on the Night Walkers who've gone missing. He may know secrets of the first Everborn...and how to create another."

"Another?"

A heavy silence fell over the room, the gravity of my words sinking in.

One elder leaned back, their expression showing skepticism. "Natalie, has it ever occurred to you that Morison may be lying?"

"Yes," I replied, my tone edged with impatience. "But if his claims are true then we must act now."

Another elder shook their head, their voice rising with indignation.

"And you think this justifies entering the Old City without permission? Let alone with zero protection. You reckless little girl!"

One of the elders raised a hand, silencing the murmurs with a single authoritative gesture. Their sharp gaze locked onto Albin. "And what do you say about this Albin? Where were you while she was gallivanting across town, putting us all in jeopardy?"

I caught the faint tremble in Albin's hands as he struggled to find words, his discomfort palpable. Finally, he answered, "I was asleep in my chambers."

"Asleep?" the elder mocked, their tone dripping with disdain. "Pathetic."

Albin straightened, his jaw tightening as he tried to regain composure. "But I think we should hear the rest of what she has to say," he added. His demeanor as he looked at me was filled with a mixture of frustration and warning. "She's already gone this far, so it's only fair—"

"Stop!" the elder barked. "We are on the brink of a civil war. Nothing is fair, but I agree, say your piece, child."

"Morison believes Jericho is draining our people dry of their blood." As the words left my mouth, nausea churned in my stomach. Repeating such a vile truth felt like swallowing glass. "They end up in a lab at his compound. That's where our missing has fallen."

The room fell silent, every elder locked onto my words. For a fleeting moment, I considered mentioning the diary, but the atmosphere was already chaotic. To reveal that the creator of the diary may still be alive would cause even more tension in one setting. They wouldn't hear me out anyway.

I pressed on.

"There's a shipment arriving in two weeks, carrying a serum or antidote of some sort. Michael, one of the Everborn's lieutenants, will be there with a small team. I want to gather a few of our fighters and intercept them. Morison said the contents of that shipment are vital."

"And you trust Morison?" the lead elder asked, his tone sharp.

"For now," I replied confidently, hiding the unease gnawing at me.

The council murmured among themselves, their voices rising and falling like the tides. Finally, one voice broke through, louder and more frustrated than the rest.

"She's going to lead our men to their deaths. We cannot trust Morison...an Everborn!"

Without much thought, I shouted, "I'll go alone then!"

Albin quickly grabbed my arm, desperation clear in his voice.

"Natalie, please—hush!"

I pulled my arm free and stepped forward, standing tall before the council.

"It's true! I'll go alone. If I'm wrong, then it's only my life at stake."

"Wrong again!" one of the elders snapped. "If they know anything about us—our hideout, our defenses—we're all in jeopardy!"

"I assure you; I've told Morison nothing!" I cried.

"Enough!" The lead elder rose from his chair, his gaze sweeping across the room before settling on me. His voice, weary but commanding. "Natalie, I, the others, and the *Puritas Sanguinis* do not agree with your constant defiance."

I swallowed the lump in my throat, unable to respond.

He sighed, shaking his head as though the weight of his decision burdened him deeply. "But if what he says is true, we are all in grave danger—Night Walkers and Everborns alike."

The room murmured like a court waiting for a verdict.

Finally, the elder's voice rose above the whispers, decisive and unyielding. "We hereby grant your request."

The room erupted in protest, but he silenced them with a sharp glance. "The decision is made."

Relief washed over me, but it was short lived. This was a chance to prove myself to the council but if I had been lied too by Morison, this could lead to disaster.

"A mission like this requires the utmost confidentiality," the elder continued. "Tell only those who must know. The last thing we need is Night Walkers roaming the streets and taking matters into their own hands. Do you understand?"

"I understand," I replied, my voice steady. I took a deep breath, willing confidence into my tone. "I won't fail us."

I turned to Albin, whose face betrayed his shock at the council's decision. "I have work to do, Albin." My voice was firm, commanding. "I'm going to my chambers to rest before tonight's shift at the hotel."

Albin hesitated, then gently laid a hand on my shoulder. His whisper was soft but laden with concern. "What mess have you gotten us into?"

I placed my hand over his, a small gesture of reassurance.

"You don't have to join us if you don't want to," I said.

I knew my actions and revelation was too much for him to bear. He was strong but very compliant and followed the law of the council to a T. Going off the beaten path wasn't something he was accustomed to doing, and I knew he greatly disapproved of my motives.

His gaze searched mine for a moment before he nodded and followed me out of the great hall to the elevators.

I pressed the elevator button, the quiet ding breaking the silence. As the doors closed, sealing me in my stillness, I let out a slow breath. I glanced down at the weathered pages of the diary in my hand, their edges frayed but intact. My heart pounded in as I hesitated, fingers hovering over the first page. A mix of dread and curiosity churned within me. Whatever lay within these pages, it could not wait any longer.

I opened it carefully, the scent of aged paper filling the confined space.

My eyes landed on the first line, scrawled in dark ink.

"Dear diary..."

CHAPTER SEVENTEEN

DEAR DIARY

Before I knew it, the elevator doors opened, and I stepped out onto my floor. The hallway buzzed with activity—Night Walkers rushing about, some preparing to head out for their jobs, others herding small children, packing them up for school. The familiar hum of chatter and the occasional burst of laughter filled the air, mingling with the faint scent of coffee brewing in one of the nearby apartments.

A little girl skipped across the hallway, her backpack bouncing on her tiny shoulders. She paused when she saw me, her bright giving way to my tension.

"God morgon, Natalie!" she called out. She was filled with a youthful joy as she made her way toward the elevator. Her innocence washed over me, and I forgot about the horrors that lay ahead. I found myself smiling, a rare and fleeting reprieve.

"God morgon, little one!" I called back, a moment of peace that had been absent from the pass few hours.

She disappeared into the elevator, her laughter lingering in the air, a fragile reminder of what I was fighting for. As the doors slid shut, my smile faded, replaced by the turmoil that settled deeper into my chest. These families—these children—they relied on us to keep them safe. I couldn't fail them. Every step I took toward my room was a reminder of what was at risk, and failure wasn't an option.

As I reached my door, I paused for a moment, the hallway now quieter behind me. I took a deep breath before walking in. I slammed the door shut behind me and quickly ran to my room. I jumped on the bed, and braced myself for whatever information this diary may hold. I turned to the first page and continued where I left off:

"12 June 1948,

Dear Diary,

It's been a week since I arrived in Malmö, and I'm loving it so far! The city and culture are such a contrast from back home in Dallas, and my cowboy boots have been the talk of the class! The students in my work study are friendly, and I already feel like I'm settling in.

This week has been a whirlwind of unpacking, navigating the city, and diving straight into the lab to prepare for our end-of-summer research project. I still can't believe Mom and Dad let me travel this far! From what I can tell, it's going to be a busy summer, but I know it'll be worth it. I just hope I find time to explore more while the weather is warm. The long, bright days here are unreal. It's like the sun never sleeps!

Everyone here talks about midsommar and too bad I didn't arrive here on time to experience it but maybe next year? Gosh, I can't believe I'm already thinking about coming back, but there's something about this place. It's just so lovely and peaceful.

Today for lunch, a few of us girls went out for fika—a coffee break with snacks and lots of laughter. I could get used to this! And tomorrow tonight, we're heading out to explore the city. Maybe I'll even find myself a tall, handsome Swedish husband! Wishful thinking, but still a girl can dream.

Anyway, I have to be up early in the morning tomorrow. I want to get a run in before heading to the lab. Dr. Townsend is a real hard ass, but he is the connection you want in this industry. That guy could literally make or break your career. Best for me to stick on his good side and make a great impression. With that said, good night diary!"

I closed the diary and stared at its worn cover, shaking my head. These words—this carefree life—it was nothing but the fantasies of a schoolgirl blissfully unaware of the real world. My frustration mounted. *What does this book have to do with anything?* My grip on the leather tightened as doubt crept in. *Was the council right about Morison? Did he play me?*

I leaned back against the headboard, aimlessly observing the dim room. The hum of the compound's activity below was faint, but soothing, yet it did nothing to ease the turmoil in my mind. I glanced back at the diary in my lap. There had to be more to it than a naïve young woman's journey to Malmö.

There had to be.

Flipping through the pages, I caught glimpses of scattered phrases—some smudged with time, others scrawled in a hurried hand. The mundane musings of a girl's life. And then, a page caught my eye, the name "Henrik" boldly written across the top, surrounded by a cluster of hearts. My brow furrowed as I traced the name with my finger.

At first glance, it seemed like another entry from a schoolgirl's life—a fleeting infatuation, perhaps. But this was the first name I'd encountered in the diary.

Perhaps a lead or a clue.

Something about it made me pause though.

Who was Henrik?

I leaned closer, focused, and squinting as I began to read. The handwriting seemed more deliberate here, as if the writer wanted these words to live forever. There was a pressure in the ink that had not been present before so I pressed on.

"6 July 1948,

HENRIK

Dear Diary,

I think I've found my future husband!

Two days ago, the school hosted a small 4th of July celebration for us Americans, a little slice of home here in Sweden. It wasn't like the parades and fireworks back in the U.S., but the gesture was still nice. A picnic in the park with flags, music, and a few beers. I think we embarrassed ourselves with our red, white, and blue outfits, though. The Swedes looked at us like we were some kind of spectacle.

As we were laughing and joking, he appeared out of nowhere. His sudden appearance almost made me spill ketchup all over my shirt.

Face-palm!

I swear, it was like magic! A tall guy with long hair, an even skin tone, and the most beautiful hazel eyes I've ever seen. When he smiled, it wasn't just a smile—it was a smirk that said trouble.

Oh, Diary, I was so ready for trouble.

He walked straight up to me and asked my name, and all I could do was stutter, "Susanne," like a fool. My heart was pounding so hard I thought the whole park could hear it. He had this leather jacket that fit him perfectly, and when he spoke, his voice was smooth like honey. If he'd asked to whisk me away right then, I would've said yes.

Of course, we exchanged contact information, and we're going out next week. I have no idea what to wear though, but I'll figure it out. He told me his name is Henrik, and he's lived in Sweden his whole life. His family comes from way up north—near the Arctic, he said. I didn't ask his age, but honestly, who cares? He's perfect.

I know this might just be summer love, but maybe it's more. Part of me doesn't even want to go back to Dallas at the end of this. I'm liking the place more and more each day. The Swedes are just so laid back.

What if I stayed here? Not forever but maybe another year or two?

Okay, I'm getting ahead of myself.

Goodnight, Diary!"

I placed the diary down and rose from my bed, my throat dry and my thoughts swirling. I needed a drink. As I poured a glass of water, the name Henrik played over and over in my mind like an annoying catchy. I'd heard it somewhere before—I was sure of it. A book, a story, perhaps even whispered in passing. Could this be the connection Morison hinted at?

I felt like a detective, secretly piecing together puzzle pieces and fragmented information. The diary belonged to a woman named Susanne, and the name Henrik was important to this woman and ultimately...us.

The thought alone gnawed at me, creating an internal tornado that refused to settle. I had to dig deeper, to uncover the truths buried beneath layers of secrecy and our history. Susanne must have written something about the creation of Everborns for Jericho to hold on to this dusty old book for ages. He couldn't move forward with whatever plans he had in motion though. Something was missing, and it was enough to slow Jericho down.

I glanced at my watch.

Time was slipping away, and my shift at the Quality View Hotel was fast approaching. A job I loathed. Sitting behind a desk, doing nothing while the world drifted away, felt like a waste of who I was and what I could be. I wanted to fight—to lead a platoon against the Everborns, or against whatever threat might one day expose us to the humans. But the council's strict laws demanded that all Night Walkers take normal day jobs, go to school, and hide in plain sight. It was their way of protecting us, of keeping the world ignorant.

In a sick twisted way, I sort of agreed with Morison and the Everborns. That we should be able to walk freely among the humans. I just didn't agree about the taking over part. Though deep down I knew they would never accept us even if we lived segregated and feasted on our own farm grown food supply. It's natural for humans to fear what they don't know, and history has taught us Night Walkers that when people are afraid, they react in inhumane ways.

Tragedy.

And me?

They thought sticking me behind a desk at a hotel's graveyard shift would keep me out of trouble:

One day you'll sit on the council, Natalie.

Do better, Natalie.

Keep your nose clean, Natalie.

Always with the reminders of my destiny. I never asked to be in line for a seat at the council table. All I ever wanted was to be on the frontlines and make a difference out there in the real world. But my bloodline had other plans. With my blood purity level, I was considered too "pristine" to risk in battle. So here I was, hidden away under the guise of normalcy, while the real threats like Jericho, Michael, and the rest of the Everborns snatch us up one by one.

I rolled my shoulders releasing tension in my back and neck. Shaking off the bitterness, I grabbed the diary, settling into the snug leather chair by the window. The day started to grow quiet, transiting into the later part of the evening. The city bathed under the lonesome moonlight and streetlights.

I flipped through the pages, this time venturing further in. My fingers stopped on a longer entry, one that seemed worth the read.

I took a deep breath and began again.

"21 February 1950,

Dear Diary,

I don't know if I'll ever get used to the winters here! The days are short, the nights are long, and the temperatures are frigid. I wake up while the moon is still up, and by the time I leave the lab the moon is up again. My skin is pale, darkish blue, and my lips are dry from the cold. I'm starting to resemble the dead! Never knew I would grow to miss those ridiculous hot Texas summers.

All is not lost though. Henrik did get me a classical Viking animal scarf this past Christmas. Also, he got me a ring. He doesn't know that I know about it hiding in the closet though. But if I'm being completely honest diary, I'm not totally sure how I feel about it, or what I would say if he did ask me to marry him.

I love the man, and we've had nothing but great adventures since we've first met. He's helped me tremendously with securing a job out here working at one of the largest scientific labs in the Scandinavian region. His uncle had put in a great word for me that all but guaranteed I would have a position. I couldn't thank the two anymore!

But lately Henrik and I haven't been agreeing on a few things. I'm not one to judge anyone so I feel bad about talking about his lifestyle, especially since it's not one he can exactly control. And the group of friends he runs with aren't the type of men I feel comfortable being left alone with. One of them seems to always watch me with a careful eye. I've brought this up to Henrik, but he said Jericho is just being protective, and he's like a little brother to him. Whatever, I still can't stand it. Them two and the rest of his crew could get a little rowdy at times. It doesn't put my mind at ease knowing what they are capable of either. I just wish he had more sympathy toward me and others.

Still, I wrestle deeply with this idea of leaving the man I dropped my whole life for. I committed to him by staying in this country, and I invested a lot of time in this man. When he's good he's good. He treats me great, it's just in those moments his jealousy sets in, or his hunger takes control. I wonder sometimes how he would treat me if I pissed him off while he was hungry. I promised to keep his secret hidden and at times I still don't believe this is real life.

Yet, I would climb the highest mountain for him. It's like he has a hold on me, and I can't break free. Every time we lock eyes, the rhythm of my heartbeat forgets how to hold steady, a silent seduction drawing me near, keeping me firmly in place.

Last week he subtly said he wanted me to join him in this life and the next. That's when I thought he was proposing but things became a little more...sinister. I've seen his strength. I've seen his power. I've seen what he could do whenever he wanted. He assured me that I was safe with him, and I trust him. But there's still much to think about.

Hej då Diary."

Well, so much for the perfect love story, I thought. If it weren't for his name playing over and over in my mind, Henrik might have been like any other fleeting college romance. But his name—and now the mention of Jericho—changes everything. I can't believe they knew each other. Surely the answers were deeper in this book.

Maybe Morison wasn't lying after all.

Jericho had aged remarkably well considering the date of this entry. My thoughts spiraled. How was it even possible that he was still alive? Even Night Walkers eventually succumbed to old age. And he's an Everborn. There isn't an Everborn alive with more than forty-five percent pure blood running through their veins—the very essence that connects them to us. But that other fifty-five percent was what made them different. As for the rest of their genetic makeup and why it happened? No one knew.

Their origin remained a mystery even to them.

I peeked at my watch, keeping an eye on the time to ensure I wouldn't miss my midnight duties or give the council another reason to chirp at me. I reached to put the diary down, but a swift breeze from the window made the pages flutter. Rising from the chair, I moved to shut the window, carrying the diary on the way.

My fingers stopped on a peculiar page, the bold title catching my eye: ***Test Subject 101***

"Date: 8 May 1951

Time: 19:31

Test Subject # 101

Findings as follows:

Tonight, I ran my 101st experiment. Results were as expected. Though violent thrashing occurred at first, the test subject showed significant brain activity. Its DNA merged perfectly with the blood sample when administered quickly after initial death and mixed with Compound Green x9.

Henrik continues to press for results, his impatience growing daily. He wants answers, and I'm not sure he should get them.

I put Test Subject 101 down before he could wake. I'm not ready to share my findings, not yet. The isolation here has become unbearable. I write because I have no one else. Friends, family—they are all out of reach. Even my coworkers have been replaced, and the guards outside control every movement in and out. It's just you, this lab, and the growing child in my womb.

Diary, I fear his plans and this army of otherworldly beings he keeps going on about. That he wants me to help create.

No one—man or otherwise—should have that much power.

In three days, when he and his men leave to feast, I'll..."

The loud pounding on my door sent a jolt down my spine, interrupting me mid-thought.

"I'm coming!" I called out, clutching the diary tightly as if protecting it from a thief.

As I was approaching the door, I couldn't help but keep reading, step by step. Susanne's words felt like a desperate cry for help, a warning to anyone who might stumble across her story.

My steps froze as I read the last few sentences.

"I'll take my chance and..."

The knocking grew louder, more insistent.

"Who is it?" I barked, finally tearing my attention from the diary.

I peeled the door open, revealing Albin standing with his stern gaze.

"It would do you good not to get lost in books, fairy tales, and frivolous dreams, Natalie," he said sharply, pushing past me.

He grabbed my coat from the chair and shoved it into my hands.

"It would also be in your interest to not be late for your duties. Let's go!"

His commanding tone left no room for argument. I slipped the diary in my coat pocket and followed him into the hall, my mind swirling with questions about this mysterious Susanne.

What did she intend on doing?

CHAPTER EIGHTEEN

HIM

We arrived at the Quality View Hotel, where I loathed my duties almost as much as I loathed the council for chaining me to this desk.

Menial work.

Filing papers, checking guests in—rinse and repeat. But tonight, despite the redundancy, I felt something I had not in a while, optimism. Getting the green light from the council to carry out this mission was enough to push me through the night.

I sat at the desk, my mind plotting and scheming as I checked a few people in—Night Walkers and unsuspecting humans alike. Across the lobby, the usual group of Night Walker men lounged at the round table near the bar. They were some of my most trusted subjects posing as patrons but serving as my undercover security. Every now and then they would peel themselves from their intense poker game and patrol the area, but we never had any issues here.

The soft clatter of pool balls echoed from the game room, blending with the drone of a local news station on the TV overhead. I grabbed the remote and muted the sound. The newscast was going on again about violent attacks and kidnappings being seen by eyewitnesses. The Everborns were sloppy but most of careless. I blocked it all out. I had business to handle.

I peeked into the office behind the desk, where Albin sat like a mouse—silent and brooding and ruffling through his newspaper.

"My dearest Albin, are you ignoring me?" I called out, my voice syrupy sweet, mustering what sincerity I had left.

He sighed without looking up from the newspaper.

"I'm not ignoring you, Nat. I'm merely avoiding confrontation."

I inhaled slowly.

"There's no confrontation to be had," I said, brushing off his dramatics.

He spun his chair around to face me, hands clasped like he was ready to deliver a lecture. His gaze bored into me, and he paused for a moment.

"You should abandon this mission," he said plainly.

"I can't, sorry," I replied without hesitation.

His lips curled in mild frustration.

"I guess proving you are right triumphs over the safety of everyone else."

He didn't wait for my response—he spun back around, the newspaper rustling as he dove back into it.

I clenched my jaw but said nothing. Was he wrong?

Maybe.

Maybe not.

This situation was bigger than my ego, but maybe ego was the fuel needed to ignite a spark among us Night Walkers. Finally wake us up—stop playing defense and be on the offensive for a change. Albin wouldn't understand that some rules needed to be broken for the betterment of us all and our future.

I turned from the office, and sat back at the front desk, the chair creaking beneath me. Albin's words lingered, but I cast them aside. I had the mission and other things to focus on. Morison wouldn't go behind his faction's back and come to me without good reason. I thought about him having his own motives but that didn't matter, I would deal with that when the issue arrived. For now, the enemy wasn't him, or Michael. Nor were the Everborns as a whole.

It was Jericho.

And his atrocities had to end.

The hands on the clock ticked steadily, each second dragging the night deeper into silence. The hotel traffic thinned, leaving the lobby in a kind of eerie stillness. My mind drifted back to Susanne's diary, her words lingering in the air and whispers like a ghost in the dark. I felt it in my bones—I was getting closer to answers that could finally help thwart Jericho's plans.

Curiosity gnawed at me until I couldn't resist. It was time to dive back into one woman's confessions.

I flipped through the pages, my focus sharp, like a student cramming for an exam. Each word more impactful than the last. I found myself gasping, flinching at the rawness of her entries. Susanne started as just another college girl, full of dreams and ready to change the world.

I pitied her naivety, the way she stumbled into things she couldn't possibly understand. She wouldn't last in today's world. Not with the Everborns and Night Walkers constantly at each other's throats.

But the experiments—the horrors she took part in—left a bitter taste in my mouth. I couldn't forgive that. Her hand in the madness felt like war crimes of those who claimed they were "just following orders." It echoed the darkest chapters of our beginnings. She hid behind obedience—perhaps fear of what Henrik really was.

She should have been brave!

She tried to make amends in the end, but it was too little, too late.

What's still unclear is if she's even alive.

But what fascinates me more is the secret she carried. The one buried beyond her written words. The diary was in Jericho's hands this whole time so surely, he knows the truth. She hid the process of creating an Everborn from Henrik, but I wonder if he has told anyone.

The chime of the clock striking 01:00 pulled me out of Susanne's diary, my fingers still clutching the worn pages. I was piecing together her story, her experiments, her regrets—and the picture was starting to form. But something about it all still felt incomplete, just out of reach. She was pregnant at the time of her 101st experiment entry but no word of the child has been spoken of.

At least not one that I know of.

Before I could dive deeper, the front doors of the Quality View Hotel creaked open, and a gust of cold air followed the man who stepped inside.

He wasn't like the usual late-night guests.

No luggage, no rushed demeanor. Just a newsboy cap pulled low over his brow and a long tweed overcoat that brushed his knees. His presence hit the room like the cold draft—imposing but magnetic.

And then I smelled him.

Undead as ever.

Not fully masked by the strong cologne clinging to his skin, but distinct enough to make my hands tremble ever so on the desk. It wasn't unpleasant, but it was familiar in a way that sent a ripple of unease through me.

One of us? I questioned. Or one of them?

He approached the front desk, his strides confident. My mind raced, teetering the line of fight or flight. Should I make the first move, or wait to see his intentions?

My body tensed.

"Good evening," he said, his voice deep, steady, and unmistakably foreign.

An American.

He stood tall, chest out, and had an athletic built. His brown eyes glowed bright under the hotel lobby lights, but they hid a story behind them. One of someone trying to escape their past.

I gazed at the stranger a second too long. I was trying to place a face I couldn't quite remember. I swallowed hard, forcing my feet to stay rooted behind the desk but something about his presence threw me off.

Without a word, I turned and disappeared into the back office, needing space to clear my head and process who just walked through our door.

Albin wiped the sleep from his face and jumped up from his seat.

"What's wrong with you?"

"Nothing...I..."

I struggled to get the words out, but instead I pointed to the door.

"Just handle it—without care Albin."

He nodded and made his way without question.

From the safety of the office, I listened as Albin's voice floated through the thin walls.

"God kväll," Albin greeted, his tone polite but distant.

I peeked between the crack in the door, watching the exchange. The stranger's shoulders were broad, his posture relaxed. Albin's fake charm only stretched the tension tighter. But still neither one attacked.

Instead, the man took the room key with a quiet approval and disappeared down the hall before Albin could even finish his sentence.

The moment he rounded the corner, Albin reentered the office, his expression sharp with unanswered questions.

"What was that about?" he asked, closing the door behind him.

I stared at him, my thoughts a tangled mess. Finally, I managed to mutter, "He's an Everborn—I believe."

Albin's brow furrowed, skepticism clouding his features.

"Nat," he sighed, rubbing the back of his neck, "he may be an Everborn, but he's not *an Everborn*. Not one I've ever seen anyway, and I've come across a few in my time."

"Well, he's not one of us. Couldn't you smell him? Don't it."

Albin's feet shuffled, clearly distraught over the newcomer's presence. "I'll admit," he started. "I've never known our kind to exist anywhere else but here so yes, it's rather odd that he comes from across the ocean. I'll let the council deal with it."

"No need to report him yet," I protested.

"Why not?" Albin asked.

I thought about telling Albin about the contents of the diary and that Susanne had a child that wasn't not accounted for. The whole idea felt connected somehow.

"I will meet with them myself and report him once I'm done with the docks."

Albin sighed but didn't argue.

This stranger—whoever he was—wasn't just passing through.

Coincidence? I think not. Fate maybe.

I decided to keep my eye on him, follow him around town, and learn what business he had here. Of course, this would have to be a side mission—one I'd keep from Albin and the others. Whatever his purpose, it left my instincts buzzing like bees in a hive.

The rest of the night was uneventful, the hotel falling into its usual quiet lull. I sat back at the front desk, the glow of the lobby lights radiating across the polished floor. Between checking in a guest here and there, I flipped through the fragile pages of Susanne's diary, her confessions pulling me deeper with every word.

But her story came to an abrupt end.

Her final entry was written in hurried, shaky handwriting, the ink smudged as if the pen trembled in her grip:

"...the echoes of footsteps are ascending upon me. Should this be my last words, I only wish for my child to be set free."

A chill crept down my spine, and I found myself staring at the page long after I'd finished reading. My chest tightened with emotions I couldn't untangle—pity for her fear, resentment for her role, anger at the cruelty toward her, and, beneath it all, an unexpected thread of empathy.

By all accounts, she was an ordinary woman caught in extraordinary circumstances, forced to make impossible choices to survive. *The choices we make,* I thought, running my thumb along the brittle edge of the page. After that final entry, she vanished into history—forgotten, only to now be resurrected.

But two questions puzzled me: who was Henrik and why did he break the cardinal rule of not telling humans about our kind?

The clock ticked steadily, the tranquility of the night broken only by Albin's soft snoring in the office behind me. We hadn't spoken since our last exchange. I knew he meant well, always trying to protect me, even when my stubbornness got in the way. I was headstrong but he'd understand when this was all over. When Jericho was gone, and the truth was laid bare, Albin would see that I'd been right all along.

I glanced at my watch, the distant glow of dawn creeping over Emporia Mall and the surrounding buildings. Time to feed. But I wasn't hungry. I needed to meet Morison before the city was awake. We had to go over plans for the upcoming dock heist.

I stood, not wanting to disturb Albin. For a moment, I lingered at the office door, watching him sleep. His face, even while he slept, was masked with worry. I considered waking him—just to say something, anything—but he would only try to stop me.

I grabbed my coat and slipped the diary into my bag, holding it close to my chest like a precious family heirloom. As I approached the front doors, I paused, my reflection on the glass showed a determined woman—a reminder of what was at stake, and the events to come.

With one last glance over my shoulder, I stepped outside, the crisp morning air biting against my skin. The city was still, caught between the last whispers of night and the first breath of the day.

CHAPTER NINETEEN

LINES CROSSED

"The moon hangs in the sky like an all-seeing eye, judging us in silence, holding our secrets until we die. The stars gossip, and the dark sky whispers stories of our evil deeds. For every action, there's a reaction—and excuses are plenty. The cost of survival sometimes is the lives of many."

I thought of Albin, and the poem he used to recite to me when I was a little girl. I didn't know what it meant then, but I do now. The gravity of those words are as true today as they were the night of the first battle. My heart felt heavy, my mind raced, and suspicion hung in the air like smoke—thick and suffocating.

Morison sat beside me as we made our way to Malmö City Docks. It's been a few days since we worked out the details of the plan. The silence between us vibrated with unspoken tension, a quiet reminder of two enemies with a common goal.

Finally, Morison broke the silence.

"Is there something on your mind?" he asked, unbuckling his seatbelt and shifting to face me. "You seem loaded with guilt."

I kept my gaze on the road ahead, swallowing the lump in my throat. My fingers drummed on my thigh as I fought back the sting in my eyes.

"Albin is missing," I said. I turned to him, my expression sharp, voice low but firm. "If you have anything to do with his disappearance, I promise you—"

"I have nothing to do with that." He was firm but not defensive. "Honestly."

I held my stance, searching through his eyes in the dark, but I did not push the matter further. I would figure out Albin's disappearance as soon as I could but for now, we had Michael and the docks to worry about.

I turned my head back to the tinted window, watching the city blur past—buildings stacked like silent witnesses, indifferent to what we were about to do. Each one felt like a marker, counting down to the inevitable.

I shifted in my seat, breaking the silence.

"Michael," I said, "You're sure Jericho's sending him?"

Morison nodded without hesitation.

"I'm positive. I sat beside him as he rallied the troops."

I allowed a small, amused smile to curl at the corner of my lips.

"Just a reminder, Morison—there's no going back after this." I said it lightheartedly, but the truth of my words settled between us. He would never be able to return to the Everborns. Whether he liked it or not, he belonged to us now. A small victory, but a satisfying one.

Unimpressed, he exhaled deeply.

"I'm aware."

Silence crept in again, thick, and uneasy, until he spoke once more. "And Leo?" he asked, his curiosity barely masked. "What do we do with him?"

I kept my gaze fixed on the dark stretch of the Baltic Sea ahead, my expression unreadable. "My men have their orders," I said quietly. "Hurt him enough to avoid suspicion—but keep him alive."

Morison let out a dry chuckle, turning to the window, watching the city lights flash past.

"And they paint us as the bad guys," he muttered under his breath, shaking his head with a mix of disbelief and resentment, maybe regret. "You still think he's a filthy Everborn?" He asked sarcastically.

I bit my lip, aggravated at the stupidity of his question. "No, I don't," I said. "I actually think he's an ignorant Everborn who's going to get himself killed. Do I need to go over his importance again?"

We arrived at our designated location, just a few blocks from the docks. The black car slid to a quiet stop, blending seamlessly with the shadows that draped the empty streets. The hum of the engine faded, leaving only the distant ruffles of leaves in the background.

From the front seat, my guard looked over his shoulder.

"It's 00:10, Natalie."

In the distance, I spotted Michael and Leo slipping through the gates of the docks—like thieves in the night.

"Right on time," I murmured, a faint smile tugging at the corner of my mouth. I extended my hand without looking.

"The radio."

The guard passed it back, the cold metal fitting perfectly into my palm. I glanced at my watch, the seconds ticking away with surgical precision. The anticipation in the car was honest, but Morison remained silent beside me, his expression stoic, his posture rigid.

Our eyes met briefly.

"This is it," I said, low and steady.

He gave a curt nod, staring out the window.

"Indeed, it is. Let's get this over with."

I checked my watch one more time.

00:20.

I raised the radio to my lips, pressing the button. The soft hiss of static filled the silence.

Then, with a single breath, I gave the order.

"Now."

And just like that, chaos erupted.

I rolled the windows down, letting the cool night air rush in, trying to steady my nerves. The calm was gone, replaced by the sounds of hissing, growls, and flesh meeting bone—Night Walkers clashing with Everborns. A mini civil war unfolding in the shadows, hidden from unsuspecting humans.

I sat quietly, the radio inches from my lips, my grip tightening with every passing second. My stomach twisted into knots; a nauseating chill crept over me. Sweat pooled in my palms, my breathing rhythm, thrown off by the distant screams and battle cries.

Was this worth it?

The question surfaced like an uninvited guest, eating at my resolve. I knew the answer. The ends justified the means. If any of my men died tonight, they understood the risk. This was bigger than any one person—bigger than all of us.

The breeze carried the smell of fresh drawn blood, sharp and undeniable. My nostrils flared as the scent of death followed, lingering in the air and weaving itself into the fabric of the night.

We sat in tense silence, waiting.

Then...static.

A brief pause.

And a voice, panicked and breathless, crackled through the radio.

"Leo's been stabbed, Nat!"

My blood boiled instantly. I snatched the radio, pressing the button hard enough to crack the plastic.

"Who did it?" I growled, my voice low and venomous.

Morison jolted upright, looking at me, waiting for answers.

The voice on the other end stuttered, "It—it was Bjorn. An honest accident, I think."

My jaw clenched tightly.

"Pull the car around," I snapped at the driver, my tone leaving no room for argument.

As the car lurched forward, I turned to Morison, my anger steaming underneath the surface.

"Bjorn's had it out for Leo ever since I turned him loose."

Morison glanced at me, suspicion on his face. "You think he meant to do it?"

I let out a bitter laugh. "I guess you're not the only backstabber, huh?"

The words hit their mark, and silence settled between us like a third passenger in the car.

When we reached the gates, I stepped out, the wintry night air biting against my skin. I signaled to my men for them to move quickly. I watched from my seat as they hauled the suitcases from the chaos beyond.

The scent of death grew stronger, seeping through the crack of the car window.

Morison stood just outside the gates, his eyes darting nervously as he helped collect the suitcases. His hands trembled, whether from the cold or from the lines he crossed, I couldn't tell.

"I think Leo saw me," he whispered, his voice laced with panic.

I met his gaze, unflinching.

"Like I said, Morison—there's no going back." I shrugged my shoulders, dismissive of the fact he was now known as a traitor.

Without another word, he hurriedly threw the suitcases into the car, slamming the door shut as he disappeared behind the dark tint of the windows.

I stayed behind, motioning for Bjorn to approach. He swaggered over, his arrogance oozing with each step.

"Thanks for all you've done tonight," I said, my voice calm, even sincere.

He smirked, the bravado in his response disgusted me. "Just doing my job, Nat."

Arrogant bastard.

Without warning, I buried two fingers into his eye sockets right before twisting his neck.

Crunch!

His body crumpled to the ground, limp and now useless. I stood over him, calmer than I have felt that night.

"Leo better make it out alive," I muttered, my voice low and venomous.

Leo would be the key to finding Susanne. My gut tells me she's still alive. From what I've read in the diary and puzzling the pieces—she must be the one and true Everborn.

The distant wail of police sirens broke the moment. I turned and made my way back to the car, my steps quick but measured. Morison stared at me from the window, his face pale, his eyes wide with fear.

He slowly rolled the window up, disappearing behind the glass, hiding the coward that he was.

I didn't look back.

We drove to a hidden location east of the city, an abandoned warehouse tucked between rolling hills and long pastures—isolated, long forgotten, and perfect. The four suitcases sat stacked between Morison and me, a silent barrier reflecting the one growing between us.

"This is it," Morison muttered, tapping the driver's shoulder. "Pull around the back."

The building loomed ahead, weathered but standing strong—a testament to its resilience. The car rolled to a stop, tires crunching over gravel. As we stepped out, the night air wrapped around me, thick with the scent of damp earth and rusted metal. The place reeked of history; the kind built on secrets.

Morison led the way through a rusted side door, my men following close, carrying the suitcases with guarded precision. I stayed alert. This could still be a trap—I wouldn't put it past him.

Inside, stale air settled over us like a suffocating blanket. Morison found the fuse box, flipping a switch. The old lights flickered, buzzing like harmless rumors before holding steady.

"Over here," he said, his voice echoing off the concrete walls.

He moved to the center of the warehouse, kicking aside debris until he cleared a space. Reaching into his coat pocket, he pulled out a match, striking it with a quick flick. The flame danced for a heartbeat before he set it to a pile of old logs and dried papers. A small fire crackled to life, casting shadows that seemed to lean in, listening attentively.

"This should keep us warm," he muttered, more to himself than to me.

He pointed to a makeshift table, little more than a slab of wood on rusted barrels. "Put the suitcases there."

I grabbed one, setting it down gently, my fingers lingering on the latches. Morison was gleaming, fingers twitching with anticipation, drumming together like a child waiting to unwrap a gift.

"Shall we?" I said, arching a brow.

Morison knelt, glancing up at me once before flipping the locks. An air release escaped as the case unsealed, releasing a rush of cold air that billowed like mist. Instinctively, we both stepped back.

When the vapor cleared, four large silver capsules gleamed under the flickering lights, sleek and ominous. Stamped across each capsule in bold silver lettering: "Università degli Studi del Salento."

I read it to myself, my voice low, the words confusing as they left my mouth. The out loud looking over to Morison, "University of Salento?"

We were dumbfounded.

"What the hell?"

Morison's brows knitted together, confused as I was.

"Italy?" He questioned.

The question hung in the air, unanswered—just another piece of a puzzle growing more complex with every revelation.

I reached for one of the capsules when Morison's voice snapped through the silence.

"Careful!"

His tone was sharp, laced with caution.

"We don't know exactly what it is yet."

I paused; I let his warning lingering in the stale air between us. Time was slipping through our fingers.

"We don't have much time," I replied, my voice steady, masking my growing curiosity.

With a firm twist and pull, the capsule came free from the snug foam encasing it. Cold to the touch, its smooth metal surface reflected the flickering firelight.

I didn't waste a breath.

Without speaking, I shot Morison a look, my fingers subtly flicking in a silent command. He understood, digging into his pocket and tossing me his lighter.

I flicked it open, the small flame flaring to life with a soft sizzle. I held it close to the capsule, letting the light expose its contents.

A glass vial nestled inside, suspended in place like a fragile artifact. The liquid within shimmered—a vibrant, shade of evergreen needles, thick like mercury but with an eerie luminescence that seemed to pulse quietly with its own life.

My stomach twisted.

What the hell is this?

I swirled the capsule gently, watching the green liquid shift like a small ocean trapped in glass. Without a word, I handed it to Morison.

He held the capsule carefully, rolling it his hands, and smiling with intrigue. Silence stretched between us until his lips parted, his voice low and cautious.

"In your readings," he paused, glancing up from the capsule, "did you come across anything about... an antidote? A serum?" His words grew sharper, layered with eagerness. "Injections—anything?"

And then it hit me.

Thinking back to a brief mention of a substance binding DNA and blood, something called Compound Green x9.

A half-finished entry in Susanne's diary flashed through my mind, fragments of words now stitching themselves into clarity. My stomach dropped with the weight of realization. But it wasn't just what I'd discovered that rattled me—it was the second, colder realization that followed. If I'd connected the dots, then Jericho must have known this for a while.

Morison's voice grew faint, fading into the background.

"What is it? What do you know?" he pressed, but his words were distant, like echoes in a tunnel.

My chest tightened, heat spreading under my skin, the scarf around my neck suddenly suffocating. Then, slicing through the haze, the radio crackled to life—its sharp vibration rattling against the table, jolting me back to the present.

"Nat—are you there?" an urgent voice cut through the static.

I rushed to the table, my footsteps heavy, the sound of my heels echoing off the warehouse walls. I grabbed the radio, my grip firm.

"Go ahead," I commanded.

"Leo's alive," the voice reported, breathless and tense. "Him and the rest of the Everborns are fleeing the docks."

My heart skipped.

Relief surged like a sudden current, and my gaze shot to Morison. Leo was alive. That meant he'd make it back to Jericho—and Jericho would realize exactly who he is.

"Leo's going to make it," I said, but loud enough for Morison to hear.

Skepticism creeping into Morison's voice, "and how do you know Jericho won't kill him?"

I placed the radio back on the table, the faint hum of static filling the silence. A slow, knowing smirk curled at the corners of my lips as I turned to face Morison.

"Because" I said, breathing easily now.

I locked eyes with him and smiled like discovering a long-lost language.

"He's the boy in the prophecy."

MORISON

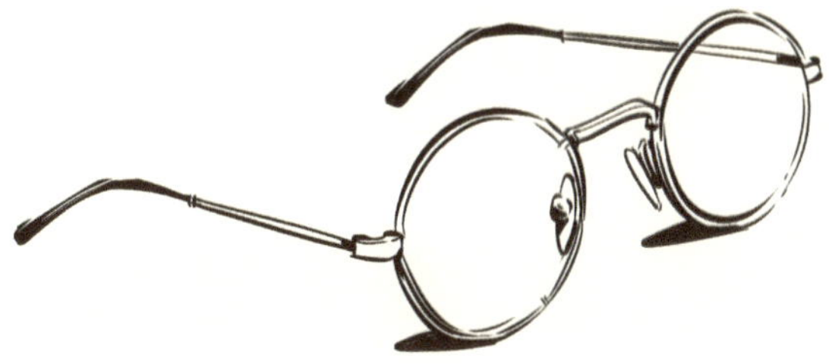

CHAPTER TWENTY

COLLECTOR OF FINE THINGS

"Michael will destroy everything that has been built over the years." Jericho sat deep in his emotions, fidgeting, and rubbing his palms together with a slow, anxious rhythm. His eyes were closed, locked in a trance or deep meditation. The old leather chair creaked beneath him, the sound amplifying the tension in his office.

His eyes shot open as he spoke his deepest fears.

"His ambition is dangerous, and it puts us all at risk."

I watched Jericho.

The wrinkles on his forehead were deep, and the veins along the side of his head pulsed with pressure, the anger simmering just beneath his composed exterior. He looked ready to explode like a volcano that had laid dormant for years, now trembling and awake. The pressure had been building, and it was ready to wreak havoc at any moment.

He made no mystery of his feelings toward Michael, yet it was clear he was conflicted—caught between practicality and a deeper, paternal bond. I feared to ask what his plans were, but knowing Jericho, he never left things up to chance. He would eliminate any threat to his legacy, but something was holding him back.

I stood there, arms crossed, unsure of what to say.

I'd met Michael when he was just a boy, and though I hadn't intended to, I'd grown fond of him, even come to love him like a grandson in some ways. He'd stood toe to toe with the best of the Night Walkers, holding his own in situations where most Everborns would've folded. He was powerful, a skilled fighter and he stood apart from the rest. No doubt that's why Jericho kept him under his wing all these years.

"There was a time," I said, my thoughts slipping into speech, breaking the silence, "when you believed him to be the boy of the future. What did you mean by that?"

That got Jericho's attention.

He rose from his chair and walked toward the bookcase on the far wall.

"Legends of a prophecy," he said, waving one hand dismissively. "He's not the boy, but we'll get to that later."

I thought for a moment, vaguely recalling whispers of a prophecy but they were nothing more than campfire stories, really.

Myths.

Old wives' tales told in passing. I'd never paid them much mind. I was just a child then, but the talks were mostly lost to time and buried with history.

"I wanted to share something with you," Jericho said as he returned from the bookcase with a book under his arm.

"You're a collector of fine things, yes?" he asked.

A smile swept across my face. "Well, yes, I like to think so. If it holds any significant value, I have it or I can find it."

"That you can." Jericho returned a smile and pointed, but his grin held something sinister behind it. He fixated on me with surgical precision.

He pulled out his chair and dropped into it with a heavy thud. Then, with deliberate care, he placed the book on the table. It was bound in black, worn leather— thinner than a Bible, but its presence felt sacred.

"This," he said, voice low and steady, "is a diary—a special diary. I've never shown it to anyone. Never spoken of it."

For reasons I could not explain, the book called to me. A quiet power radiated from between its covers, drawing me in, a moth to the light. My eyes latched onto it, unable to look away. I could feel its history, unspoken, but lingering in the air. And instinctively, I knew, that whatever was inside those pages was never meant for our eyes.

He looked up at me and continued, "I share this with you because of your loyalty for all these years. One day soon it will all pay off."

I peeled my eyes from the old, tattered book.

"Do you mind me asking what makes the book so special?" I asked.

Jericho's smile stretched from ear to ear, and his excitement sent an uneasy wave from across the table. The way he shook his head while rocking back and forth in his chair made me realize he was enjoying this moment. Something up his sleeves that he's been dying to share.

"You're asking the wrong question, Morison. It's not the 'what' that makes it special." He paused, letting the tension build before he continued. "It's special because of the 'who'."

My mind was racing to stitch Jericho's cryptic words together. My thoughts were nothing more than a meaningless jigsaw puzzle with pieces missing.

"The...who?" I asked.

The words didn't seem to make sense to me as they rolled off my tongue. Nonetheless, the situation piqued my interest far more than I led on.

"Yes, Morison. The who. The diary is special because of who the writer is."

His smile went cold as quickly as it came.

"A damn nagging ache in my side I would say."

Each word he uttered was spewed with disgust, a disdain for the writer. His nose twisted, as he recalled the bitterness he had never let go. Whoever the author was, they were living rent free in his mind, and they left their history all over his sour face.

I'd never seen Jericho so distraught.

The author had a hold of him.

... And the diary had a hold of me.

As Jericho spoke, his words faded into a distant blur. My mind was occupied on the potential contents hidden between those covers. If it could shake the most powerful being I had ever known, then it must hold secrets worth uncovering—the kind of truths that could reshape our world as we know it.

The office door creaked open, and Jericho, startled, quickly shoved the diary into one of the desk drawers, burying it from view.

One of his lap dogs entered, the stench of his humanity offending me at once.

"Pardon me, Jericho," he said, cautiously.

Jericho didn't hide his annoyance from the interruption.

"What?!" He said.

"There's been..." his voice faltered as he noticed me sitting there. "Significant progress."

"I'll be there in a moment," Jericho said, already rising from his chair.

He barely waited for me to stand before ushering me out of the office with a casual flick of the wrist.

"Morison," he added, "we'll talk again shortly. For now, keep the leash tight on Michael, will ya?"

He scurried off in one direction, his pristine boots striking against the marble floors echoed throughout the hall.

I went in the other direction, silently, but the scent of the diary's leather clung to my senses like a smell I could not shake. The thought of it invaded my mind persistently while I made my way to the shop.

I entered through the back entrance, the bell above the door clanged as I stepped into the shop. The scent of old parchment and bronze polish greeted me with a quiet invitation of a homeowner welcoming a long-lost guest.

I moved through the narrow aisles, brushing pass shelves cluttered with relics: cracked medallions, a Knights Templar dagger, ancient Roman coins stamped with Caesar, and old books covered in dust.

My hands moved from habit—sorting, dusting, adjusting displays. From the other side of the wall, the sound of ice mixing in a glass and the low hum of laughter from the bar reminded me that everything was, at least on the surface, back to normal.

I smiled, grabbed my handkerchief from the polished counter, gave it one final wipe, and tucked it into my pocket as I made my way to the bar to enjoy the usual Everborn commotion.

"Francis, any kanelbullar left?" I called out as I stepped through the doors.

He glanced behind the glass counter before answering, "Jaja!"

I moved behind the bar and poured two cups of coffee—one for myself, one for Francis. I scanned the floor. Everyone seemed occupied: conversations buzzing, a card game in one corner, an argument about handball in another.

Perfect.

"Francis," I said, gesturing to the kanelbullar with a nod. "Grab one and come talk with me. Rest your feet a bit."

We chose our usual corner table with the wall bench. Sat kitty-corner, just like always—positioned so we could cover each other's blind spots while keeping a full view of the bar.

Old habits from our time together in the field.

We sat, sipping our coffee, letting the moment breathe.

Francis bumped his shoulder lightly into mine before breaking the silence. "We're almost at count for the upcoming harvest," he said with a grin. "Should have a few more bodies soon."

I took a sip but didn't acknowledge the report. Instead, I traced the brim of my mug with a finger, letting the silence speak for me. Then, in a low murmur, careful no one would hear, I asked, "Do you remember what it was like..."

I finally looked up and met his eyes.

"Before we opened this bar?"

He studied me for a second, trying to read between the lines.

"Yes," he said with a chuckle. "You were a hoarder. Still are. You call them valuables—I called them crap and scrap metal."

We both laughed, but for different reasons.

I pressed further.

"No, I mean before even then."

His smile faded.

He looked around the room, scanned the action, then leaned in.

"If you mean..."

He paused. Suspicion in his eyes.

"I...thought that was a time buried. Never to be spoken of again?"

I raised one hand in protest. "I know—I know. I just—"

Caught between fantasy and reality, I struggled to get the words out.

"You just what?" he shot back.

"Just... you ever think about what life might've been like if... you know?"

Francis sighed, finishing the last of his coffee before standing.

He faced me directly; his lips angled away from the room behind us.

He didn't have to say it, but I could see it in his expression, the past we both worked so hard to erase.

"No," he said firmly. "I value the life we've built."

He reached down, grabbed my empty mug, and paused.

"But those kinds of questions..."

His voice dropped.

"...are the ones that get the fangs plucked from the mouths of men."

He turned and made his way to the bar, carrying on, making drinks for customers as usual like this moment didn't happen.

I reclined back in my seat and knew he was nothing short of correct in his sentiments.

I took a bite from my kanelbulle, and focused on preparing for my next meeting with Jericho and Michael. Jericho was expecting a shipment of some goods and needed Michael to fetch it for him.

I had two days before that meeting and started to feel anxious because spending time alone sometimes let the mind drift to places it shouldn't.

The thoughts rapidly coming and going were dangerous.

I took my final bite.

Swallowed.

And as hard as I tried, I could not break free from the moment.

Once you think about something you can't unthink it. The thought is forever.

I had work to do.

CHAPTER TWENTY-ONE

A NEW THREAT

Michael stormed out the door, fists clenched tight to his sides. His boots struck the marble floors with a force that sent low vibrations through the stone, each step echoing his frustration. Anger and resentment carved sharp lines across his face, and with every stride, his ambition burned more brightly—a fire I'd grown weary of.

"Follow him," Jericho commanded, his voice low but firm, dismissing Michael's outburst without a second glance.

I gave a silent nod and followed, the heavy door closing behind me with a soft thud. My pace was brisk, quicker than a walk but measured, my steps controlled as I navigated the gravel path leading toward the compound gates. The crunch beneath my boots was the only sound that filled the tense space between us.

I closed the distance, my voice cutting through the night.

"You let him get under your skin too easily, you know?"

Michael didn't slow, didn't even turn his head.

"I just don't appreciate his games," he muttered, his words stiff with irritation. His gaze stayed locked ahead, sharp with determination, his stride unbroken. After a beat, he added under his breath, "I need a drink."

I shook my head, offering a steady, almost indifferent tone.

"In due time. You'll get your chance."

As we neared the gates, I reached out, placing a firm hand on his shoulder, halting him just before the guards. His body tensed beneath my grip, the fire in his eyes burned bright when he finally turned to face me.

"Go to my shop. Get what you need," I said evenly, holding his gaze. "I've got more to discuss with Jericho."

Michael shrugged my hand off, his jaw tight.

"I'm sure you do."

With a curt nod to the guards, he signaled to them to open the gates and strode out without looking back.

He disappeared into the night, swallowed by the darkness beyond the gates, while I turned back heading toward my quarters—using Jericho as an excuse, nothing more. My steps were brisk, but it wasn't the cold biting at my heels. It was the weight of an earlier conversation with Jericho, his words looping in my mind like a curse I couldn't shake.

Something about it left me uneasy, like a splinter buried too deep to pull out. Michael's frustrations weren't baseless. His feelings of insignificance were valid, and I'd only managed to play along for so long, pretending it didn't bother me too. He was right—Jericho kept him in the dark on purpose.

Jericho was powerful, his influence stitched into every corner of our world. To question him was dangerous. To defy him would be suicidal. And yet, the seed of doubt had been planted, growing roots, I couldn't ignore. I knew one thing for certain; I couldn't take on Jericho alone. Not unless I had help from an outsider.

I quickened my pace, my thoughts racing just as fast, Jericho's voice a shadow in my mind.

"Michael will destroy the Everborns."

"Michael is not the boy."

The words echoed louder now, like I'd missed something crucial hiding in plain sight.

I made my way to my room, slamming the door shut with a force that echoed through the empty space. The lock clicked into place beneath my palm, but it did little to ease the tension coiling in my chest.

Paranoia crept in like an unwelcome guest.

I moved to the windows, yanking the curtains closed with quick, sharp tugs. Shadows flickered against the thin fabric, and for a moment, I thought I saw movement outside. I shook it off, pacing the room, my steps uneven. I checked every door, every corner, even the closet—empty, of course.

No one's here.

I exhaled, a shaky breath I hadn't realized I'd been holding.

Of course no one was here.

In the middle of the living room, my gaze fell on the old, dusty floor mat. I stared at it for a minute or two, then crouched down, peeling it back to reveal the loose floorboard beneath. My fingers found the familiar groove, pressing one side until the opposite end popped up with a soft creak.

Reaching into the hidden compartment, I pulled out a dusty, worn notebook—its cover cracked, the leather faded with time. Jericho called it a diary. Said it was important, though he never shared why. He told me many things, but not where this came from. Not what was inside. Only that it was the key to our survival.

I turned the diary over in my hands, feeling the power of it—both literally and figuratively. The leather cover was worn; its edges frayed from years of handling. I flipped it open, and there, scrawled across the first page in faded ink, was a name.

Susanne.

I stared at it for a moment, rolling the name around in my mind. It meant nothing to me—no face, no memory, just a name. I wondered briefly if I'd ever known someone called that, but nothing surfaced.

I settled into the old chair by the small table, adjusting my spectacles and reaching for the lamp. The dim light boomed to life, casting an awkward spotlight across the room.

This was it.

Whatever secrets Jericho kept locked away were now in my hands.

I pried open the brittle cover, running my fingers over the cool, cracked leather, admiring its resilience. I was a collector of fine, old things—and this diary would've made an excellent addition to my collection. But this wasn't about sentiment. I was on the clock, and Jericho would soon realize it was missing. When that happens, my head might very well find itself on a silver platter.

According to him, I was the only one who knew about this diary. Not even Michael.

I started with the first page—nonsense.

Scribbled words, mundane thoughts, reflections about a move to Malmö, as if she were writing to pass the time.

A few more pages in—more of the same.

Sentimental drivel about school, the weather, a boy named Henrik she fancied. I flipped faster now, my patience thinning with each turn. Page after page filled with the details of an ordinary life.

I shook my head, "humans" I muttered in disappointment.

Frustration bloomed in my chest. Was this some elaborate game Jericho was playing? A test? Or worse—was I being used as a pawn in one of his endless manipulations?

I slammed the diary shut, its brittle spine groaning under the force. My fingers trembled —not from fear, but from the realization that I'd risked everything for what seemed to be nothing more than the ramblings of a young woman.

I tucked the diary back beneath the floorboard, the wood creaking as I slid it into place.

I needed air.

I left my room, the door clicking shut behind me. My footsteps echoed down the dimly lit corridor, the faint scent of damp stone lingering in the air. As I rounded the corner, I heard footsteps approaching from the opposite direction.

Jericho.

I straightened subconsciously, tipping my hat as we crossed paths.

"Jericho," I greeted, my voice steady, masking the unease rumbling in my gut.

"Morison," he replied. "Just the man I was coming to see."

Shit.

Without another word, he clasped me behind my neck. His grip was deceptively casual, but beneath it, I felt power and control—a hunter guiding his prey.

"Come with me," he said, steering me down the hall. "We need to talk."

My mind raced as we descended deeper into the compound, the corridors growing colder with each step.

Did he know?

Had he discovered the diary was missing?

Was this the moment I'd meet my final resting place?

He led me to a door few were ever allowed to pass through—his private lab.

The sterile smell hit me at once, sharp, and metallic. The undertones of chemicals mixed with something more primal—blood, faint but present.

Human, most likely.

Jericho kept them alive for their usefulness, but I would have harvested them long ago. Their existence offended me.

Jericho motioned to one of the scientists to unlock the door, and the heavy glass groaned open. The cold mist hit my face like a light slap.

I stepped inside, masking my apprehension. But beneath my calm exterior, my pulse steady quickened.

"This is Scientist Luca Moretti," Jericho introduced. "He is the one who has cracked the code on the very thing I—" he cleared his throat, correcting himself before he continued, "We need."

Luca approached me, hand extended, and a smile on his face that said he thought he was the smartest man in the room. I stared at him, *nothing but food* I thought. I didn't bother shaking his hand. Instead, I had more pressing questions to get to, and no time for networking.

"Sorry," I started. "When you say, 'crack the code' what are you referring to?"

Jericho flashed a wide smile, his teeth white as snow, arms folding across his chest with the stance of someone who was about to call checkmate.

"Morison," he began, his tone warm. "We've known each other for some time and right before the first battle. You've been a trusted advisor; someone I've relied on through the many storms we Everborns faced."

He paused, his smile fading, and the mask removed but replaced by a colder threat. His eyes narrowed, sharp and observant, and his voice dropped into more serious tones.

"But I need to know one thing."

The oxygen between us vanished.

"Can I trust you?"

I didn't flinch. Didn't allow myself to.

"Yes," I replied quickly. "Of course."

His gaze lingered, he observed me like I was a specimen under glass. My heart rate stuttered, I froze beneath his stare. I could not breathe—would not dare break eye contact. He was looking for cracks.

After what felt like an eternity, Jericho's mouth curved.

"Good," he said simply. "Follow me."

I exhaled silently, my chest tight with the breath I'd been holding.

Luca trailed behind us, his face glowing with anticipation for our journey. Jericho led the way down the corridor, stopping near a blank stretch of stone wall. He ran his fingers along the surface, pressing into a spot that seemed no different from the rest. A soft click and a pop, and then part of the wall shifted, revealing a hidden door—seamless, undetectable to anyone who didn't know where to look.

My jaw tightened, but I kept my expression neutral.

Where the hell are we going?

"Many, many years ago, Morison," Jericho began, his voice taking on the rhythm of a storyteller. There was some passion behind his words like a man who'd rehearsed this tale far too often. "Before you came to us, before Fox Retreat Hill, there was a woman named Susanne."

Susanne.

The name hit me hard.

I kept my face blank, but my mind raced. The diary hidden beneath my floorboards. Her name screaming out to me. Reaching for my arm like she needed help.

"And there was a man named Henrik," he continued, his voice steady as we descended a narrow metal bridge suspended above a vast, well-lit space.

And the name *Henrik* was our history.

Beneath us, a sterile white glow spilled across the floor of an underground lab—far larger than anything I'd expected. It was pristine, clinical, filled with equipment, chains, shackles, and torture devices.

I gathered no one knew about this.

Jericho's footsteps pressed against the metal grating.

"And there was a prophecy," he added, glancing over his shoulder at me. The harsh lights caught the evil his eyes just on time. "The one you were talking about?"

I gave a small nod, unsure if the question required a verbal answer.

Jericho began, "It is said that a boy would unite or destroy." His voice low, like the words themselves were sacred—or cursed.

"When I was young—much younger than I am now—I worked for Henrik." His footsteps pressed forward as we moved deeper into the sterile corridor, past Night Walkers sprawled on surgical tables, their bodies limp, tubes snaking from their veins, faces frozen in eternal stillness. "We thought Henrik was the boy. He believed it himself, right until his death."

His words floated in the air, brittle and sharp.

Jericho's jaw clenched as he continued.

"After Henrik's death, I found and raised Michael. Trained him. Shaped him." He exhaled sharply, almost a laugh, but devoid of humor

"I learned Michael isn't the boy either."

The further we walked, the heavier the air grew—suffocating with chemicals, blood, and something else.

Something ancient.

"At one point," Jericho muttered, "I thought the prophecy was just the ramblings of Henrik's fevered mind. A fantasy." His eyes grew darker with a truth he hadn't spoken yet. "But after years of searching I finally found my answer."

We reached the end of the corridor, where a massive iron cage stood like an executioner's monument. Chains clinked from within.

I froze.

Inside the cage was a woman—battered, bruised, yet defiant.

Her wrists were shackled to the bars, dried blood streaked along her arms, but her posture remained upright.

Strong.

Her stare was sharper than daggers, fixated on Jericho like he was the only one there.

I was struck silent.

My breath caught in my throat.

There was something about her.

I could smell her.

Not human but not like us either.

Stronger.

Finally, my voice found its way through the haze.

"And who is this?"

Jericho stepped closer, resting his hands on the cold metal bars and pressing his face as close as he could to her—but the woman's gaze never wavered. The tension in the air was thick enough to grab with both hands. She was patient, but she wanted Jericho's heart in the center of her palm.

"This," he said, mockingly, "is the woman who killed Henrik."

He gripped the bars tighter, his knuckles whitening, and a sneer crept across his face.

"This is Susanne."

CHAPTER TWENTY-TWO

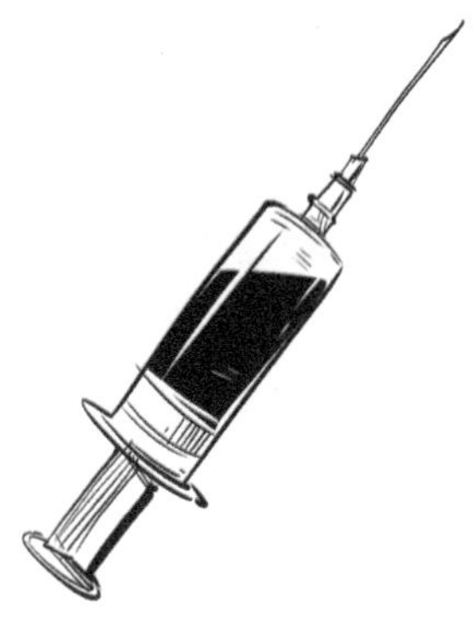

US

I stood there, frozen—caught between fear and fascination.

The concept of time was frozen, and I could not help but to calculate how long she had endured?

Exhausted, battered, worn—yet defeat was not present, and hope was not lost.

Her frame was slim, her skin pale beneath layers of grime. Eyes like amber tree sap glinted with defiance, lips cracked and dark as if stained by her own blood. She stood as tall as the shackles around her ankles allowed, spine straight despite the weight of her chains. In a way she was a beauty to admire.

Here she stood—the supposed Everborn—face to face with Jericho, a man whose presence usually meant certain death.

Luca approached the cage, a large syringe trembling in his hand. Its contents were unmistakable, blood. He hesitated, looking at Jericho for reassurance before continuing.

Susanne's body snapped into motion, twisting and thrashing like a wild serpent. She hissed, lunging as far as the chains would allow, teeth bared in raw fury. Luca stumbled back, pale, and breathless.

"Go ahead and stick her," Jericho commanded, his voice sharp with disappointment. He shook his head slowly, taunting Susanne. "All these years... and you still haven't learned?"

Luca approached again, this time more cautious.

Susanne's gaze never left Jericho. Her hate was palpable—enough, it seemed, to burn through the iron and set her free to claim her revenge.

I finally broke the silence, my legs weak as I sank into the nearest chair. I needed to ground myself and process the impossible.

"How long has she been down here?" I asked, forcing myself to sound neutral, careful not to anger Jericho.

Jericho did not hesitate.

"She's been here as long as I've held leadership, Morison."

I did the math in my head. That would make her—

"As old as you?" The question slipped out, low and disbelieving.

Jericho chuckled, stepping away from the cage, his confidence filling the room like smoke.

"Older, actually," he corrected. "She was older than me when she met Henrik."

"Ah... I see," I murmured.

I didn't press for more answers, my fist to my lips as I watched Luca draw the needle from her arm. The effect was immediate—a tranquilizer flooding her veins. Susanne's body sagged, knees buckling, her eyes rolling shut, lids heavy. Her head bobbed, slow and detached, as she slipped away from this world—her own existence finally too much to bear.

Nothing like that first hit, I thought. The rush of blood after going too long without it.

Still, the sight was unsettling to see, her body crumbling to the ground, powerless to the substance. Yet the rush she felt was really no different than the bodies I would harvest.

I changed the subject, leaning in, masking my curiosity with casual interest. "What are the dead bodies for?"

Jericho reached for a nearby lab chair, dragged it over with a soft screech, and sank into it beside me. His posture relaxed, but his eyes stayed sharp—calculating.

"Our blood, Morison," he began, fingers drumming against the armrest, "is less than half of what the Night Walkers carry." He flicked two fingers toward Luca, who promptly retrieved two glasses of gin like a trained dog.

"Something about her blood, mixed with this special serum, and thanks to him," Jericho continued, tilting his head toward Luca. "We've got it figured out." He smiled. "This is how we create true Everborns."

He took a slow sip of his drink, letting the words settle in. "I'm building an army, Morison. To take over—not just over Night Walkers. Everything." He leaned back, casual as ever, like he was pleased with his work. "You could be the first to be turned if you want. A gift for your loyalty."

I forced a thin smile, standing up as if the conversation hadn't just shifted the ground beneath my feet.

"Appreciate the offer," I said, brushing imaginary dust from my coat. "But I should get back to my shop. Can't leave it unattended for too long."

Before I could step away, Jericho moved—fast. Suddenly he was in front of me, close enough to rip my throat out if he wanted. His grin was gone, replaced by a stern, cold look.

"Speak to no one about this," he said, while playing with the bright silver cuff links on his shirt.

No threats.

No theatrics.

Just the simple, crushing weight of authority.

I held his gaze, steady despite the pulse pounding in my ears. "You have my word."

I left without another glance, walking through the sterile hallway, back through the hidden door, and up to my room—to the diary beneath the floorboard. My feet moved on autopilot, but my mind raced.

Susanne. Henrik. Jericho.

Of all the things I witnessed that day, two truths clung to me like shadows I couldn't shake. One—Jericho has been lying to us this whole time. *Ignorance is bliss,* I thought. For years, I believed Jericho was the only true Everborn, his blood the key to immortality. But the truth had been locked in a cage beneath our feet all along—a truth powerful enough to shatter everything we've ever known. Night Walkers are the one and only true bloods. Everborns are tainted blood; defects with a twisted ideology, but they can be created.

And two—an army. The idea sank deeper, threading through my thoughts like a nagging whisper. I've always believed we should walk among the humans, not only exist from the shadows, but take our rightful place in the world rulers.

But an army of true Everborns?

That kind of power isn't just dangerous to humans.

It's dangerous to us.

With that much strength—who would lead who?

MICHAEL

CHAPTER TWENTY-THREE

CABIN IN THE WOODS

Morison was blabbering to Leo, spinning the same old war stories I'd heard a hundred times before. The classic tale of a has been, middle-aged man clinging to the fading glory of his so called "prime." Sure, their stand against the Night Walkers at Fox Retreat Hill was admirable—encouraging even—but the significance of that battle died with the men who fought it. Now it was just another story, retold to inflate egos and drown regrets in imported gin.

The creaking swing of the bar doors snapped me from my focus on Morison. Two of my men walked in, their expressions sharp and urgent. *This better be good,* I thought, my jaw tightened. I caught Leo's subtle shift, the faint tension in his shoulders as their presence registered.

Before he could make a move, I was already on my feet, striding toward them. One of the men let his gaze linger on Leo—a flicker of curiosity better yet resentment from that sloppy alley encounter.

Amateurs.

They had one simple task—kidnap Natalie. If they'd done their job right, we wouldn't be cleaning up messes now.

I shot him a look—a silent warning—and both of them straightened instantly, their postures snapping into disciplined rigidity. Without a word, I motioned toward the door, leading them outside. The cool air refreshing against my face as we stepped out, the gossiping chatter of the bar fading behind us.

Out here, there were no wandering eyes or listening ears.

I turned to face them, my patience already thin.

"So, did you find it?"

One of them shifted his weight, hesitant.

"No—not exactly."

I exhaled sharply through my nose, fighting the urge to reach for his neck.

"Are you going to make me drag it out of you, or are you going to spit it out, mate?"

He glanced at his companion, then back at me, finally speaking.

"We didn't get the diary, but..." His voice trailed off, riddled with nervousness.

I tapped my foot to the rhythm of the seconds crawling.

"But what?"

The other man, the quieter one, kept watch on the street, his gaze twitching rapidly. The first man swallowed hard, then said, "We have something rather someone better."

I tilted my head, the tension in the air growing thicker.

"Go on."

He hesitated, then blurted, "We have Albin."

For a moment, the words hung there, suspended between us. Then a slow, amused smirk crept onto my face. I placed my hands behind my back, pacing on the slick cobblestone sidewalk, letting the news settle.

"Well," I said, my voice low, measured, "if we can't get her, then she'll have to come to us."

I clapped him on the shoulder, both of us sharing a brief, dark laugh.

"Where is he?" I asked, the amusement fading from my tone, replaced by cold efficiency.

The quieter one spoke up this time.

"We've got him holed up in a cabin outside the city. Can you believe it? The idiot came to us. Rambled on about Natalie, something about the diary, and needing to stop her before she made a mistake. That's when we bagged him."

I let out a soft chuckle, shaking my head to a tale that was old as time.

"Desperation turns men into fools."

But in the back of my mind, gears were turning.

Albin would never come to my men willingly. Not in secret, not ever. Something didn't add up. With the diary in Natalie's position, she must have read something that shifted the tides of this bubbling war. Jericho wouldn't tell me much, but maybe Albin knew something that could tell me about what Jericho had up his sleeves.

Maybe I was closer to the truth than I'd realized.

I gathered Leo.

Him, me, and my men made our way to the cabin just off the beaten path outside the city. When we arrived, Albin was already tied to a wooden chair, sitting like he was expecting us. His face was a swollen mess, blood crusted along his temple, bruises bloomed like dark ink across his skin. His fear showed behind his defiance—coming to us a mistake he surely regretted.

I approached, pulled the gag from his mouth. He gasped, sucking in the stale air, the false bravery trying and failing to surface beneath his labored breaths.

"I don't understand why you're doing this," he rasped, spitting blood onto the floor once he found his composure.

I didn't answer. Instead, I turned to Leo.

"Watch the door."

Simple instructions.

I wanted to see if he could follow them without question—a test. I liked Leo. Something about him drew me closer to him. I couldn't deny the bond that was growing between us but still he was an outsider first. His strength could be an asset to the Everborns, but only if I could mold him. Control him before Jericho gets to him and brainwash that naïve brain of his.

I didn't flinch.

I waited until he sat back up, his breathing ragged. Then I gave a simple nod.

"Tell me where you took it. Now!"

A closed hand punch landed with a sickening crunch, his cheekbone fracturing under the force. I could hear it—the brittle snap of bone giving way. I was certain Leo could hear it too.

Punch after punch, Albin's defiance chipped away like old paint. Eventually, he spat blood and met my gaze, his swollen eye barely able to stay open.

And he smiled.

"Kill me if you must," he whispered, the words slurred from the swelling.

I leaned forward, crouching until we were eye-to-eye. I reached out, wiping a smear of blood from his face with my thumb, then looked at him—like he was nothing more than the dirt under my boot.

"And die you must," I whispered back.

I reached into the inside of my suit jacket, retrieved and handed a pocketknife to one of the men. I remember one time when I was young, I watched Jericho torture a man until he got the answers he was looking for. No matter how strong one claims to be, they all have their breaking point—and I was ready to explore his.

The knife flashed under the dim light and then a finger severed clean. His screams filled the small space, bouncing off the walls, filling the gaps in the air like static.

He was desperately holding on, but he was most certainly breaking.

I could see it in the way his breath hitched between sobs.

Finally, he couldn't fight it anymore. He croaked, "She'll be at the docks waiting to ambush you all."

His voice was weak, but the words were truthful.

I arched an eyebrow.

"How does she know about the docks?"

"One of your men came to her in the middle of the night," he gasped, wincing with every syllable.

I tilted my head, trying to process it.

"If what you say is true," I murmured, standing to my full height, "then I must let her think she has the upper hand."

Albin coughed out a laugh, shaking his blood-soaked head.

"Seriously?"

I smiled down at him, a smile without warmth.

"I'll let her win the battle," I said, stepping closer, "but I'm fighting a war mate."

For the first time, I felt like a monster. But...I didn't feel bad about it.

Leo returned, standing silently, his eyes caught between me and the bloody mess that used to be Albin.

Albin's gaze met mine one last time, and in that moment, I could see him accepting the fact that he was not leaving this cabin alive.

I asked one final time, lowering my voice.

"Where's the diary?"

Silence.

Then, with the last of his strength, he whispered, "Is any of it really worth it?"

I didn't answer.

The question was pointless.

I smirked at Leo, patted him on the shoulder, and turned to leave.

As we stepped into the freezing night I gave my final command— "finish it."

The door creaked shut behind us, muffling the last sounds Albin would ever make.

We walked outside, the snow crunched beneath our boots, each step punctuating the silence between us.

Leo was restless.

I could feel it—the tension rolling off him in waves. Questions burned behind that nonchalant mask he wore, but his hesitation coiled around him like a shadow he couldn't shake.

My mind, however, was elsewhere. Bogged down, trying to stitch together the pieces of what was to come and how I would navigate the pickup. I would let Natalie believe her ambush at the docks worked, and let Jericho start to lose trust in me.

It was the perfect misdirection.

All the focus would be off me.

Leo would be painted as the savior of the night. A hero in the making. They would thrust him into the spotlight, replacing me as the lieutenant, and while everyone watched him, I would be free to move in the dark.

His voice broke through my thoughts, sharp and persistent.

"What are we looking for?"

I clenched my jaw tight enough to crack my fangs. *How many times was he going to ask me the same damn question?*

Eagerly I answered, "a diary," dismissing any conversation he may have wanted to carry on.

I needed space. Time alone to process, to maneuver the next steps without Leo breathing down my neck.

"I'll meet you at Morison's in a day or two," I said, already turning away, leaving him standing there with his questions and doubts.

I didn't look back.

The snow swallowed my footsteps as I disappeared into the night, heading back to Jericho's compound.

CHAPTER TWENTY-FOUR

LOOSE ENDS

The night grew colder as I made my way back to Jericho's compound. With Leo gone, I could finally hear the whispers of the dark—the sounds that were drowned out by his relentless questions. The night was quieter than I had ever heard it. The moon hung high, casting a pale, indifferent glow. An owl perched in a nearby tree watched me silently, its mirror for eyes reflecting a judgment I refused to acknowledge. A cool breeze slipped past, brushing my cheek, and a haunting feeling followed like the lost soul that was Albin.

What have I done? I just killed a man tonight.

Not in battle.

Not in the heat of survival.

Just a man tied to a chair, defenseless, hopeless. I was becoming the very man that I secretly loathed. His last words echoed in my mind like a cracked record, refusing to be silenced.

Is it all worth it?

His question danced around my head like a long-winded ballet dancer—graceful in their maneuver but refusing to leave the stage. Guilt crept in, slow but persistent, an unwelcome guest that knew they could not be turned away.

If it had been in battle, it would've felt different—cleaner, even. *I didn't physically commit the act;* therefore, my hands are clean.

Did they blame Pontius Pilate? Or were his actions necessary for the eternal forgiveness of sins?

My mind danced on both sides of the coin until I finally pushed the guilt aside, burying it under layers of justification. This was a battle. A war. And in war, every man must come face to face with his maker—even us, the undead.

A bitter irony, really. Stronger than the humans yet cursed with their one defining flaw—death.

Albin, *the poor bastard,* even spoke of a second battle. Not as a threat, but as a warning—like the date was already written. A fight I want no part of, and one I'll do everything to prevent.

The snow crunched under my boots as I approached the front gate. The guards, playing 'grab ass' and passing their time, careful to not be lulled by the monotony of the night. They jolted upright the moment they saw me. No words were needed. They knew better. They opened the gates without hesitation.

"Michael... didn't expect you so late," one of them muttered, his voice uncertain.

I didn't bother replying.

Just kept walking.

The compound felt emptier than usual. The late-night crew was likely scattered—some half-drunk in Gamla Staden, others hunting for unsuspecting prey. The usual chaos of their existence humming somewhere beyond these walls. Jericho was the exception from them. I don't think he ever slept. It was like sleep was beneath him or maybe he didn't need it at all. Probably the gift of being the only true Everborn. Another tragic irony for the rest of us. He was gifted immortality while the rest of us lived as long as time allowed us.

So, he says, but my suspicions have been mounting over the years. The contents of this mysterious shipment he wants me to retrieve alongside the diary has something to do with him. I can feel it in my bones and there are cracks starting to form in his facade.

I made my way straight to his office, rehearsing the words in my head. The less-than-satisfying report I was about to give him felt like hot coals on my tongue. I knocked twice, then walked in without waiting for a response. There he was, sitting at his desk, hunched over a large map, his attention fixed like the world beyond it didn't exist. The sight of him so composed, so unbothered, irritated me more than I cared to admit.

"Sir," I said, respectful though every word tasted bitter.

Jericho didn't look up.

His eyes stayed glued to the map, he spoke with his voice drier than Sahara.

"I'm assuming the diary is in your possession, yes?"

I hesitated, my lips pressing together before I answered.

"My men couldn't locate it, but we know who has it." The confession tasted salty rolling off my tongue.

Silence.

Not even the raise of an eyebrow. Just the scratch of his pen against some paper, indifferent and cold.

I pushed on.

"It's the girl from Quality View Hotel—Natalie. Her advisor, Albin, was captured earlier and..."

My words stalled, the next sentence coiling on my tongue like a snake deciding whether to strike.

I weighed my options. *How much should I tell him?*

Jericho kept things from me all the time—little pieces of truth hidden behind that smug, unreadable face.

"...he didn't have any information for us at this time," I finished, masking the lie with a shrug, my voice smooth as glass.

Again silence.

It stretched thin, wrapping around the room like a constrictor with a stranglehold on its prey. I lost track of how long I stood there, the boulder of his indifference rolling over me with each passing second. If this was anyone else, I would have slit his throat already. But patience is what I told myself—though my patience was unraveling thread by thread.

Just as I shifted to leave, his voice drifted through the room—calm, unaffected.

"Make sure you retrieve the package when the ship comes in."

No glance. No acknowledgment. Just words tossed over his shoulder like I was an afterthought.

I didn't respond. Didn't waste my breath. I simply tilted my hat in silent agreement and walked out, the door clicking shut behind me.

Making my way to my room, I called an emergency meeting with my trusted crew. They followed me, not Jericho, but he was too far removed to noticed it. We gathered to discuss the mission at hand and what was at stake.

The attack from Natalie and the Night Walkers was 'need know to' information and right now no one other than me needed to know.

"Once we get the package, your days of playing small will be over," I started. "Tell anyone about this," I warned, my voice low and final, "and it'll be your last breath."

The next day, my men scoped the area and prepared the equipment that was needed for the docks. Meanwhile, I met with Morison to lay out the plan. Of course, I couldn't trust him—not with how close he was to Jericho. I only told him what he needed to know and decided I'd employ Leo to keep a watchful eye on him.

"You've been leaving your shop unattended a lot lately," I said, casually probing. His behavior over the past few days had been off, and I wasn't sure if Jericho had put him up to something—or if Morison had his own agenda.

"I've been going for walks," he replied smoothly. "The Nordic breeze feels good against my skin. Why do you ask?"

Lies.

Something about the pitch in his voice, the stiffness in his posture, the subtle shifting in his eyes—it was all off. But I played along. He wouldn't be a factor for much longer. When the time came to pick sides, he'd either stand with me or with Jericho. If he chose wrong, it'd be the last mistake he ever made. We all had choices to make soon.

"Sure," I said simply, rising from the table.

Outside, my two top men were harassing an old man, probably late on his rent.

"We've already given you an extra week, old man!" one of them snapped, a grin stretching across his face as if this was sport.

I glanced at the man—frail, trembling, his pride crumbling under the weight of debt. Some of the local boutiques in our territory were strategically selected as hideouts in case things ever went south. They also posed as places of employment for our educated Everborns like our Advokat.

This was my personal side hustle. Jericho knew nothing of this, and the owners of the establishments knew what we were. They paid a premium to my men—in exchange we used their facilities and didn't hunt them or their family.

I looked at the old man and felt nothing for him.

I shrugged.

"You've got one more week," I muttered. "Then," I paused and saw the terror in his eyes. "Well then you know what happens."

Out of the corner of my eye, I caught Leo walking up.

Damn it.

He had a knack for showing up at the wrong time.

"Leo," I called out with a smirk. "How are you, mate?"

The look on his face said it all—disappointment, maybe even disgust—as he glanced at the scene unfolding in front of him.

The old man was shoved aside, dismissed like trash.

I checked my watch, excitement buzzing just beneath the surface. It was feeding time. Once a month, we held a large, family-style gathering at Morison's. Hunters would collect the best humans they could find and coax them into having a drink. Some came willingly. Others were dragged. Either way we never had a shortage.

Morison would harvest the bodies and line them up around the bar like an all you can eat buffet.

The process of the harvest was simple. Seduced each catch with our eyes. Undress them with our voice. Make love to their other three senses. Then, with a careful slice to the wrist, let the blood flow like honey—slow, thick, warm, and inviting. The heart would keep beating as death introduced himself, slow and unforgiving.

We walked into Morison's transformed bar—now nothing more than a buffet of the fallen. Black trash bags and shower curtains covered the furniture, sealing away the room's former charm. In the back, a wood-burning stove blazed, a fire hungry to consume the discarded once we were done.

Trays of fruits, vegetables, and cheeses sat sliced and waiting, ready to be paired with the richness of blood. The scent clung to everything—dominant and inescapable. Blood dripped steadily, like a leaky faucet, from the wrists and necks of cold, pale bodies.

The sight stirred something primal inside me.

I glanced at Leo, and he was losing the battle of his internal struggle. His senses were wide awake, and he wouldn't be able to deny the forbidden fruit—not when its gift wrapped and served on a silver platter.

I grabbed the woman closest to me, her ocean-blue eyes storming with fear. My thumb traced her lips before trailing down to her chest, fingers pressing into the soft curve of her breast. A busty woman like this could feed a small Everborn family, I mused.

But she was mine.

I sank my teeth into her, her warmth coating my mouth as I drained her dry, all the while watching Leo from the corner of my eye slowly giving in to temptation.

Leaning in, I wiped the blood from my lips and whispered, "You'll enjoy it more than you think. Trust me."

And trust me he did, his hesitation fading with each pull. I had him now, wrapped around my finger like a little brother.

"Welcome to the fraternity," I muttered to myself, amused.

Leo was one of us, a trophy I would proudly display.

About an hour later, the feeding frenzy was over, the cleanup done, and Leo's transformation nearly complete.

I rallied the troops, ensuring they were motivated for the mission ahead. Everything had to go flawlessly and once Natalie attacked, I would slip out under the chaos with the suitcases.

As the group filed out of the room, I pulled Leo aside. "Keep an eye on Morison," I told him, watching for his reaction. Much to his chagrin, he complied.

The stage was set. All that was left, was for us to show up at the docks as expected and watch the pages unfold.

As the others prepared for battle, I smirked to myself internally. This was payback for all those years of keeping me in the dark. My symbolic middle finger to Jericho.

When we approached the docks, I pulled a small radio from my pocket, alerting the team that the ship was fast approaching. Leo and I made our way down to the crew members, two of my men posing as cops, while Leo and I played the part of the Swedish Coast Guard.

After a few unpleasant exchanges, we boarded the ship, slipping into the cargo hold, where the suitcases were waiting. I didn't know what to expect, but before we could open them, a sudden scream ripped through the night, carrying over the Baltic Sea like a death knell.

The ship lurched under my feet as more screams followed an explosion.

Let the show begin.

We rushed out, only to be met with carnage. The crew members lay scattered across the deck—cold, stiff, their bodies already beginning to rot. But it was the captain that caught my attention.

Time froze.

His body was carved up in a way I recognized instantly. The careful cuts, the bite mark—they weren't random.

They were Morison's handiwork.

Just like that, everything changed.

A sharp breath left me as realization cut through my fury. Surely Jericho couldn't have put him up to this. He was moving at his own accord. A backstabber and liar who smiled in my face hours earlier. Morison, who knew almost every detail of tonight's plan would be two steps ahead of me.

I was already late.

Shit.

Then, the shadows moved.

From the darkness, Night Walkers poured in; more than I had accounted for. The tides had turned.

We were outmatched.

Leo lunged into battle, tearing through them with an unnatural ferocity. I did the same but more or less toying with my opponent. I enjoyed the delicate dance of hand-to-hand combat. But from the corner of my eye, I watched Leo rip a man's throat out, then snap the neck of another.

He was fast.

Efficient.

Powerful.

And for the first time, I saw him as something more than just an outsider.

He mirrored me, and that alone rocked my foundation.

Jericho was strong, but he wasn't a fighter, not anymore. He relied on physiological warfare. He knew the threat of him caused more damage than physical pain could. But Leo fought like a warrior, like a force of nature that couldn't be contained.

And I felt something frightening—an unspoken pull toward him.

Suddenly my vision blurred.

Legs weak.

Blackness.

CHAPTER TWENTY-FIVE

PRIDE COMETH BEFORE THE FALL

A white light in the proverbial "end of the tunnel" shined brighter with each passing second. My heart labored with each pump, the rhythm syncing with the beeping of the device near my bed. A slow, creeping ache settled at the front of my skull, dull at first, then pulsing with intensity. The echoing sounds humming a haunting melody in my ear.

Beep.

Beep.

I glanced down—a hospital bed.

Wires ran from my arms, my body trapped between the sterile weight of recovery, and embarrassment.

My eyelids shifted back and forth, reluctant to remain open, as the fog in my mind slowly lifted. The subtle rise and fall of my chest came into focus.

Then—a shadow.

A menacing figure loomed over me, fuzzy and unrecognizable at first. My breath caught in my throat. As my vision cleared, the shape took form.

Jericho.

His face wore the usual look of dissatisfaction—cold, removed, uninterested. A presence that woke me from my dream-like state.

I forced myself upright, wiping the sleep from my eyes; then feeling the bandage wrapped tightly around my head. My limbs felt heavy, unfamiliar, slow. Confusion thickened in my mind, but reality cut through the haze with brutal force. I was in a compromised position, in Jericho's presence, and at his mercy.

My mind was a battlefield; thoughts clashing, wavering between fighting, or surrendering to death. A voice deep within whispered that I should fear for my life. But as Jericho's hollowed eyes bore down on me, I couldn't bring myself to feel anything but emptiness. In that moment death was the easier choice.

"Drink this," he said, nearly shoving a coffee mug of warm, fresh blood into my hand.

Cautiously, I raised the mug to my lips. This could be poisoned, but a part of me still believed Jericho had enough respect or sense of honor to do the deed the traditional way.

I downed the liquid, letting the blood tangle with my own, rejuvenating my senses and restoring my muscles like a magical elixir. I closed my eyes tightly, waiting for my body to drop.

Nothing.

"I'm not here to destroy you, Michael."

He took the mug from my hands, resting it on the nearby nightstand before lowering himself onto the foot of my bed.

I straightened up, already feeling better than I had moments before.

Jericho met my gaze, his voice devoid of emotion.

"You've already done that to yourself."

Was he here to gloat? Deliver a message? I could not tell. His offhand comment left me on edge, uncertainty gnawing at my thoughts.

I started to speak.

"The docks—"

"Are no longer your concern." Jericho cut me off without hesitation.

I swallowed hard. The lump in my throat tasted like a copper penny.

"You had one objective. And yet, you let a traitor and a girl with daddy issues best you."

He shook his head, barely holding in his fury.

"We were outnumbered," I snapped, but even as I said it, the words felt worthless.

"I don't care."

Jericho rose from the bed, stepping closer until his face was inches from mine; our nose close enough to touch.

"Your men lost faith in you. I've lost faith in you."

I would like to believe that after all these years I would be immune to his insults, yet his words cut deeper than I imagined they would.

"But all is not lost," he started. "It seems there's someone else more capable." His gaze shifted to the window as he peered into the distance. It was almost as if he was recalling a memory, then he turned his attention back to me. "And I've figured it out, Michael—you are not who I thought."

He casually strolled out of the room, letting the door close behind him. The metal latch clicked into place—a sound of finality.

I shuffled out of bed, noting how my injury was already fading as I made my way to the window. Hand resting on the glass, I watched as snowflakes drifted from the sky, slowly floating to the ground. Taking all the time they needed in their short existence of life.

Morison used to always say, 'There's a message in nature if one looks closely.' Now his words met nothing.

My fingers curled into a fist, knuckles turning yellow. Fog from my breath clouded the glass. Even as an Everborn, life was short-lived. And playing second fiddle? That was nothing but wasted existence.

My sorrow burned hot. Then self-loathing turned to rage.

I was on the outs, and I needed to gain Jericho's favor once again.

My fist slammed against the windowpane. The thick glass vibrated, white paint chipping off the wall from the force.

It was time to find out what Jericho was up to once and for all. The bottom was crowded but the top was not. It was time I had a seat at the table beside him—or I would sit alone.

I threw on my clothes and stormed toward the common hall where Jericho's office was.

When I entered, all eyes were on me; some filled with pity, others indistinguishable. A few of my loyal men approached, searching my face for weakness. I barely acknowledged them. My mission was clear: Jericho.

I no longer cared about the thoughts of others.

Let them stare.

Let the rumors be whispered.

In time, every tongue shall confess, I am the leader of the Everborns. And on that day every knee shall bow until their knees bled.

At the end of the long hallway, I spotted him stepping into the elevator just as the doors slid shut.

I stormed forward, no hesitation in my steps.

I caught the next elevator and time felt as if it was playing games with me.

By the time I reached the last floor below my shirt was soaked. The bandage on my head warm and wet from sweat.

I snatched it off.

Stumbling out of the elevator, I made my way toward the lab. I expected to find Jericho waiting, but instead, I was met with silence. The lights were on but No Jericho.

No one.

I scanned the room, my body tense, my mind sharp. I took a slow, deep breath to relax my anger—counted to ten—listened. The quiet stretched, but then, low murmurs surfaced down the hall. I tiptoed forward, following the whispers, and I moved with the grace and precision of a cat burglar.

It was Jericho and someone else.

I edged closer, peering around the corner, careful not to be seen. The scientist beside him was one of his lapdogs—one of the many marked by Jericho, making him untouchable to the rest of us. He had the kind of voice that made my hands itch, the kind of face that begged to be punched.

Then, something unexpected happened.

Jericho moved his hand in a subtle but practiced motion, and the stone wall before them shifted. A section of it cracked open, revealing a secret passage.

I held my breath.

How long has this been here? But more importantly where does it lead?

Jericho and his puppet stepped through, and the wall sealed shut behind them, swallowing their secret whole.

I hesitated for only a moment before following.

I waited, mentally replaying Jericho's movements before mimicking them. A soft hiss filled the air as the stone released. The air inside was different—heavier, like it had been undisturbed for years. My brows scrunched as I slipped through the opening, careful to mask my presence.

The deeper I went, the clearer their voices became. Still muffled, but enough to make out a few words.

Shipment.

City Docks.

The boy.

Everborn.

The words meant nothing alone—zero context.

Ahead, a metal grate came into view, casting thin slats of light into the dim passage. I moved quietly, crouching low, shielding my sight from the glare. Below me, in the center of the hidden room, stood Jericho, the scientist, and what looked like a large animal cage.

Raspy and exhausted, an unknown voice spoke—a woman's voice, a blend of a Swedish accent and a Southern drawl.

I caught her mid-sentence.

"Your plans are futile." She coughed.

Jericho, smug as ever, replied, "You wish that were the case, Susanne. But the reality is, your time is almost over."

Susanne?

I sifted through my memory—no one by that name had ever been mentioned among the Everborns. Jericho was hiding a mysterious stranger in his secret lab.

My pulse quickened.

I pressed my ear closer to the grate just as a mouse scurried past.

"...he will unite the two worlds. It's his destiny, and you cannot stop that."

Jericho's voice sharpened with sudden intensity. His hands wrapped around the bars of the cage, leaning in like an officer questioning a suspect.

"I've figured out your secret!"

The woman used what energy she had to spit on the ground, then laugh in Jericho's face. "No, you haven't." She croaked.

"Once I create my army, the Night Walkers will be wiped out, and the Everborns will achieve true immortality."

My breath caught in my throat. Immortality was a foreign gift that only Jericho possessed. This lab of his held a deep dark secret and that was that immortality could be created. But how?

I clenched my hands into fists, rubbing them against my shirt to steady myself.

The echoing sounds of footsteps startled me, but I remained quiet.

Jericho and the scientist were heading toward the stairs, making their way back to the exit. I moved fast, slipping away before they could see me. At the far end of the hallway, I pressed myself into the shadows, blending into the dark and staying vigilant.

Just before disappearing up the stairs, Jericho leaned toward the scientist and whispered, "I'll get Leo to find the diary and the cases. When he brings me the serum, be ready to start the transfusions."

Susanne, the diary, the suitcases—an unholy trinity.

Individually, they meant nothing to me. But to Jericho, they were everything. And they were the very reason I've been running around town on foolish missions.

I waited for Jericho and his minion to disappear before making my way back to the hidden lab. An enemy of my enemy is a friend of mine. Susanne—the prisoner—might have knowledge that could help me achieve my rightful place on the throne. If she did her reward would be freedom.

I stepped inside, flicking the power switch. The hum of the overhead lights crackled to life.

From the cage, a sudden movement.

"Back already?" a voice called out.

I stayed silent, my gaze sweeping across the room.

Medical supplies.

Paperwork.

Test files.

The scent of dried blood clung to the air.

I recognized one of the Night Walkers I hunted down weeks ago. He was here. A shell of youth, decayed, and dried. The rest of the captured Night Walkers were stacked in cages, their bodies limp, their faces frozen in time.

I exhaled sharply.

For some time, this had been right under our noses, and I never asked what he needed them for. Jericho—the man I once thought stood for our people—was just another politician with a secret agenda.

My eyes darted toward the ceiling, scanning for cameras, before cautiously making my way to the cage.

Underneath the torn rags, the woman standing inside was younger than I expected. She was frail but not broken. Her wrists and ankles shackled, but the way she carried herself, even in captivity, was unnerving. A beautiful wild lioness, a danger, if turned loose. Jericho had her enslaved for a reason.

She stepped forward, the dim light catching the wild strands of hair, that formed matted locks that covered her face.

She saw me.

She froze.

A breath hitched in her throat as she stumbled back, bracing on the bars behind her.

I narrowed my eyes.

"Who are you?"

She said nothing. Just stared.

A single tear traced down her cheek, catching the glow of the lights above.

My chest tightened.

"Who are you?" I demanded again, stepping closer.

She didn't move. Didn't speak. Just shook her head as if willing herself to deny something she didn't want to accept.

"Michael," she whispered.

The way she said my name sounded familiar.

Something twisted inside me.

"How do you know me?" I asked.

Nothing.

I stepped even closer, my voice sharper now.

"Answer me, woman!"

This time, she did.

Slowly, she raised a trembling hand, brushing hair from her face, revealing her eyes.

I knew I have seen those eyes from somewhere.

She stepped forward.

Just enough so that nothing but the bars separated us.

And then—

"I'm your mother."

CHAPTER TWENTY-SIX

MY BROTHER'S KEEPER

My gaze drifted from hers as I fought to catch my next breath. My mind flashed back to a time when her voice sounded familiar. At the same time the words felt foreign, like a bad joke I wasn't in on. I took a step back from the cage, the knots in my stomach fighting for first place. Then, without another word, I turned toward the door.

"Michael, wait!" she cried. "It's true."

I froze mid-stride. Just for a moment. Then, fury took over.

I spun back around, charging the cage, my hands slamming against the cold metal bars.

"You're no mother of mine!"

Her face didn't flinch at my anger. She only stepped closer, pressing against the bars like she could reach through and make me believe.

"Michael, we don't have much time. Let's talk."

I hesitated.

Not because I believed her, but because something about her eyes—those eyes—disarmed me. They stood for safety and love, yet I was certain that I have never seen this woman before in my life. And yet, the familiarity pulled at me, like a name I couldn't remember from a dream of a perfect woman—one I had never met, yet somehow always known. A fleeting presence just out of reach.

My mind was playing tricks on me.

"My mother abandoned me when I was a child," I said, my voice cutting through the stillness. I released the bars, stepping back, pacing. The words came sharper, harsher. "Traded me for a fix before she overdosed. Jericho found me alone—cold, frightened—nothing but a baby. The only parent I've ever known."

She gripped the bars taking the place where my hands were, her knuckles white. Her laugh came bitter, hollow.

"Is that the lie they've been feeding you?" She exhaled, shaking her head as she slowly sank to the cement floor. "You have no idea, my son."

"Stop calling me that," I snapped.

She met my gaze, her eyes locking onto mine.

"Michael, you know it to be true."

She let the words fall from her lips like a secret only she knew.

A sharp breath left my chest. My back straightened, shoulders squaring.

This woman was the prisoner, not me.

"What I know, Susanne," I spat, letting malice coat my words, "is that Jericho took care of me."

She didn't flinch. Not even a blink.

Like a warrior who has seen many battles in her lifetime. That calmness, unshaken, unmoved, infuriated me more.

"Don't be foolish, Michael."

Her voice was still strained with exhaustion, but her words cried with truth. Her focus drilled into me; probing, evaluating.

"You were discarded the second you failed at the docks."

Something shifted inside me. My head tilted to the side.

How much does she know about the docks?

I stayed silent, letting her speak.

"The only reason you're still alive..." she leaned forward, gripping the bars, "...is because, in some twisted way, he does look at you like a son. Just not the one he genuinely wanted."

My lips curled, and my voice faltered.

"Meaning?"

Silence.

I peered into the four corners of the lab afraid of being watched. Time felt as if it was running out, like the seconds were working against me. I glanced up at the grate, searching for the telltale movement of a shadow, or a presence. But there was nothing.

My focus snapped back to her.

"What do you mean?" I pressed again.

She exhaled, slow and measured, as if the words themselves were a burden.

"You're one of his lieutenants, so I'm sure you know about the prophecy," she muttered, her tone laced with bitterness, like the taste of the words soured her tongue.

"But like all things, details of the future can be blurry," she continued.

I looked at my watch and exhaled sharply, my foot tapping against the cold cement floor. I had been down here too long. My temples throbbed, a dull ache pulsing behind my eyes. I needed another drink of blood—needed to leave before I was seen.

"Get to the point, woman!" I demanded.

She studied me carefully, her eyes tracing the tension in my face, the way my shoulders stiffened.

"You're injured," she saw.

I swallowed hard. The warmth of my own breath felt thick in my throat.

"Get to your point," I repeated, though the words came slower now, uneven.

She didn't move; she held my gaze with an expression—one that only a mother could give. Something in her patience made her restless. She knew of unspoken truths that I wasn't ready to digest yet.

Suddenly, the room felt smaller. The walls pressed in, and my breath caught in my chest. My knees threatened to buckle under my weight, a strange, unwelcome sensation rushing through me like the first shot of a strong London gin.

I fought to push it down.

Could she be lying?

Perhaps.

But if she wasn't—if even a fragment of what she was saying was true—then the life I thought I knew was nothing more than a well-crafted lie. And for the first time, I felt alone.

Just like Leo.

His name hit me.

Leo.

Could Leo be the boy the prophecy spoke of?

Impossible.

He knew nothing of our laws, our customs, our traditions. He wasn't battle tested like I was. He didn't know the history of our wars, the price of our sacrifices.

A chill crept down my spine.

The sound of Susanne's voice broke through the budding storm in my mind.

"You should leave, Michael. Go, and never let Jericho know you were down here."

I clenched my fists, grounding myself back to the present.

"Why not?"

She didn't answer, but she didn't have to. I already knew. I had seen too much. The lab, his plans, her. If Jericho knew I had been down here, he wouldn't hesitate, and he would have my head.

I pressed her for more, but she only gave me fragments—enough to leave my mind in a mess, not enough to satisfy. Five minutes passed, filled with words I wasn't ready to acknowledge, truths I wasn't ready to accept.

I turned, leaving with more questions than answers.

By the time I reached the main lobby, my head was still spinning. The elevator doors slid open, and I stepped out swiftly, moving before anyone had the chance to notice. As I made my way to my room, I diverted my direction and headed to Leo's, reflecting on the madness that was circulating floors beneath us. Nothing made sense. It was like trading bad dreams for great nightmares, and I was stuck in the middle—purgatory.

I knocked on Leo's door, taking deep breaths and giving myself time to steady my nerves while I waited. I could storm in, leave no prisoners, and force the truth out of him, but that wouldn't be strategic. Not yet. I was still stuck on this compound, and Leo could be of use to me later—he still owed me a favor. My efforts were better spent testing the waters, seeing what lies would curse his lips.

I knocked again, my fist falling heavier this time.

What the hell is he doing?

Finally, the door swung open, and there he was—frantic, out of sorts, clearly not expecting me. His eyes widened, suspicion invading in his voice.

"Mike?"

I bit my lip.

Without delay, I wanted to rip his throat out for calling me that. He knew I hated nicknames. He did it on purpose.

I corrected him swiftly.

"I told you, mate." I pushed past him, giving him no time to react. "It's Michael."

My gaze swept the room, and then I saw an oddly familiar decanter sitting on the table.

Damn.

Jericho had already gotten to him.

I picked it up, turning it in my hands. The deep red liquid clung to the glass, thick as cough syrup.

"I see you've had your fill of the kool-aid. Amazing what the blood does for you, isn't it?"

I set the decanter down, watching him closely, searching for guilt, any sign of deceit.

Leo let the door swing shut behind him.

"I was starving," he admitted, his voice casual, but I could hear the unease underneath. "What can I say? I'm not exactly used to these methods."

I smirked. "Your methods." I leaned back against the table, arms crossed. "You mean middle-aged men who hate their marriages? And farm animals, of course. Hardly a dignified approach. I think I'll stick to tradition, mate." I rolled a toothpick between my teeth, waiting for a reaction.

He exhaled sharply.

"What do you want, Michael?"

I studied him. The anger I held for him was tangled with something else—gratitude. My fury could be misplaced. This man did save my life. But now, he was being talked about as if he was the second coming of the messiah and that was the problem.

I played along.

"First, I want to say thank you for getting me out of there the other night." I watched his face carefully. "I understand some of my men wanted to leave me behind." I shook my head in disbelief, letting my voice drop just. "They've already been dealt with. It's hard to find true loyalty these days, Leo."

He hesitated, and for a second, I thought he might say something. Instead, he shifted gears.

"I don't know if you've heard yet, but Morison was behind the attack."

I nodded, pretending to process the information before letting him know that I knew since that night at the docks.

Leo's lips twitched. "Why didn't you say anything?"

I turned back to the window, pulling the curtain aside just.

"Because our friend will get what's coming to him." I let the words settle before shifting my gaze back to Leo. "Speaking of which, I saw you and Jericho talking earlier," I said smoothly, lying to see what he says. "What did he want?"

His shoulders tensed. Just, but I caught it.

I already knew the answer. But I wanted to hear his version.

Pacing the room now, he went on about Morison. A nervous habit, or was he just trying to seem casual? He was keeping something from me. The diary came to mind, maybe Susanne.

"Nothing else?" I pressed.

I studied him. He was working hard to keep his story intact.

Fine.

Let him think he fooled me.

I started toward the door, stopping just before I stepped out. I gave him one final warning. A word is enough for the wise, but I knew Leo was in too deep to take heed of my words. I gave him a friendly pat on the shoulder, my grip lingering for just a second longer than necessary.

"See you soon, mate."

I stepped out, closing the door behind me.

As I strolled down the hallway, my movements were casual, but my mind was anything but. I needed to know what Leo was up to. He seemed like he was headed somewhere. I walked down and around the corner, far enough to be unseen.

I listened, waiting.

And then—

Leo's door creaked open.

His boots tapped against the marble floor.

I smiled to myself.

It was time.

He was heading toward the front doors, jacket in hand, his expression unreadable but his stride had purpose.

Something inside me settled.

The path forward was clear.

I knew what had to be done.

For my legacy.

For the legacy of our kind.

Am I my brother's keeper?

CHAPTER TWENTY-SEVEN

THEM

My lips curled into a slow grin, my eyes glowing with anticipation. My breath chased the wind like a boy on his first hunt—eager, reckless, exhilarated.

Through the front gates he went, leaving behind determined footprints in the snow-covered path. I stalked him from a distance like a cat, licking my lips as the unsuspecting prey landed squarely within my crosshairs.

Leo was big game.

And the hunt was on.

"Listen closely," I commanded the guards at the gate. "If Leo comes back here without me, I want you to keep your eyes on him."

Without waiting for a response, I motioned for them to open the gate. They obeyed without hesitation.

Over my shoulder, I called back, "Tonight's the night, boys."

Then, I stepped out into the cold, embracing the slow descent of snowflakes as they melted against my skin.

I made my way to Gustav Adolf Torg, stopping at a nearby café for an espresso. From the window, I watched Leo linger, his movements uncertain.

Rethinking whatever reckless mission he was on. From the outside looking in, he was nothing but a child drowning in waters too deep.

But to me he was a threat to my future.

The way he moved, the direction he was heading, it was obvious: Hyllie Blvd.

But why?

The espresso was bitter against my tongue, its sharpness fueling the quiet storm brewing within me. I tightened my grip around the mug, my fury growing as I thought through the possibilities.

If Leo was heading to Natalie—if he was aligning with her—the consequences would be catastrophic. And if Morison was still alive, his life would be mine, provided the Night Walkers hadn't already torn him apart.

The noise in the coffee house was deafening. Cups clinking, voices overlapping, chairs scraping against the floor—it all grated against my heightened senses, more than it ever had before. I clenched my jaw, forcing myself to tune it out. The espresso lingered on my tongue, but it wasn't the coffee that soured my mood.

It was the realization of the options that I had to choose from.

Stepping back into the crisp midday air, I breathe slowly, steam pulling from my lips. Across the street, Leo was making his way toward the intersection that led directly into Night Walker territory.

I took a shortcut, slipping through the alley where we first met. The memory struck me like an old wound—Leo, standing over a man he had just killed, hungry, sloppy, and completely unaware of the world he had just stepped into.

I could have—should have—killed him that night.

Yet, despite his presence, something about him had moved me. Beneath his guarded expression, I had seen something good. Something loyal in him.

I trailed behind him, keeping my pace slow, calculated. A couple hundred yards ahead, Leo slipped behind a building adjacent to the Quality View Hotel. My instincts were right. He was leading me straight to Natalie.

Too many passes.

Too missed opportunities but this was my chance to get Natalie.

Death was coming.

I rounded the taller building beside them, keeping to the shadows. Scaling the side, I crouched just behind a ledge, where I could both see and hear him. Then, a black blur streaked across my vision.

It was her.

I tensed, ready to strike if she had spotted me first. But from her calm laid back approach, it was clear she thought they were alone.

I leaned in, listening.

To my amazement, Leo greeted her not with open arms—but with a warrior's spirit. His grip lifted her from the ground, her body struggling, her breath cut short.

Good.

Then she spoke.

"He's draining Night Walkers of their blood."

The world beneath me stilled. My fingers dug into the brick wall, steadying my pulse. Natalie knows about the lab. About the Night Walkers. But does she know about Susanne? About Leo? About me?

Leo's actions had me fooled at first. His movements suggested he was one of us—an Everborn by nature. His stance, the way he lifted her effortlessly, the sheer power in his grasp—he was built for this. But his eyes told a different tale. The way they softened when she struggled. The way hesitation snuck up on him. He didn't have the heart to do what needed to be done.

Samson and Delilah.

A fool in love.

The thought alone made me want to end them both right then and there until Natalie uttered two more words.

"Jericho's army."

The phrase pinged back and forth in my ears.

How long had she known? How many others?

How is it that I only learned about Jericho's army a few hours ago?

Everyone knew more than me. It was a bitter realization, one that stoked the fire in my veins. I was still processing her words when—footsteps.

I turned sharply.

A Night Walker.

"What are you doing on this side of town Michael?" His stance was sharp, calculating the steps between us before making a move.

I glanced back down to Leo and Natalie making a quick note of where they were. I didn't want to lose sight of them, but I had to dispose of the threat in front of me—quietly. I turned back to him, lips shifting into a smirk.

"You know, mate, it's not proper form to sneak up on people."

The Night Walker chuckled, unconcerned. "So you say."

"So say me," I laughed.

"Right."

I exhaled through my nose, slow and steady. I had to be quiet. I had to keep my cover.

Without a sound, I lunged.

He swung—fast, he was trained—but I was faster. I moved fluidly, dodging his attack before wrapping an arm around his neck. His body twisted in protest, but my grip was iron.

I held him there.

Held him still.

Until the air left his lungs.

Until the fight drained from his limbs.

Until he was nothing more to me than dead weight.

I lowered his lifeless body to the ground and quickly took my position again, looking down on the pair. They were still talking although something in Natalie had shifted.

She sensed trouble.

I licked the blood from my knuckles, savoring the taste, before jumping down onto the other side of the ledge. My landing was soundless, effortless.

I strolled toward them, casual as ever.

"Everything good here, mate?"

Natalie wasted no time—she sprinted away the moment she saw me, vanishing into the night. Leo, on the other hand, just stood there, staring at me like he'd seen a ghost.

"How did you know I was here?" His voice had a tint of accusation.

I kept my smirk in place, strolling closer, my eyes following toward the direction Natalie had disappeared, watching her head to the hotel.

"Figured I'd check in," I said smoothly, focusing back on him. "My men said they saw you leave in a hurry. Thought I'd make sure you didn't need any help with... whatever this is."

I felt the heat radiating off his skin, the hesitation bubbling, and the doubt creeping in. He knew I was up to something.

He spoke up, "Jericho is creating an army."

Playing along, I repeated under my breath, "An army?" Feigning doubt, playing the role of the distraught bystander. Play a fool to fool the fool.

I kept my head down, my steps heavy with manufactured frustration as we made our way back to the compound. I stomped, mumbled under my breath, and kept my gaze ahead—passive, like a hormone raging teenager. Let Leo think I was lost in thought, distraught by what we had just learned.

Leo didn't say much either. I couldn't tell what was running through his mind, but it didn't matter. One way or another, I was leading him straight back to where I needed him.

This ends tonight.

As we approached the gates of Jericho's compound, my eyes met those of the two guards. A subtle exchange, a look of acknowledgment. They knew nothing of the details, but they didn't need to. Their loyalty was to me, not Jericho.

I picked up my pace, brushing past Leo as if my mind were elsewhere.

"Enjoy your day, mate," I tossed over my shoulder. "I've got some pressing issues to attend to."

And I did.

The final pieces were falling into place. Leo was going to play a vital role in ensuring my victory whether he realized it or not.

I approached one of my men in the lobby, leaning in close.

"Spread word to the others," I whispered, my voice low but firm. "Meet in my room in ten minutes."

He stared at me for a moment; his thoughts filled with unspoken questions. I met his gaze, giving him a quick wink—the only answer he needed.

Back in my room, I poured myself a shot of cold blood from the freezer. The occasion called for it. I let the liquid sit on my tongue for a moment before swallowing, feeling it coat my throat like liquid fire.

Two knocks at the door.

Pause.

One.

Pause.

Two again.

The signal.

I opened the door, and one by one, the men loyal to the cause filed in. They didn't know the details yet, but they had already made their choice—they had chosen me over Jericho.

I let the door close behind them and began my speech.

"Men, I have reason to believe that those entrusted with our survival have once again lied to us."

I let the words settle and watched the reaction on their faces. Waiting for the slightest reluctance—expecting for another traitor I'll have to knock down.

"For over a century, Jericho has kept secrets from us. He preaches about being the one true Everborn, but what if I told you that his power—his so-called divinity—is nothing more than a science project?"

A murmur rippled through the room. Uncertainty. Suspicion. Doubt.

I paced the room slowly, letting the silence stretch just long enough to pull them in. Have their hearts, control their minds. Jericho taught me that. And now it would be the very thing to take him down.

"He's building an army," I continued, my voice calm but loaded with purpose. "Not just to fight the Night Walkers... but to fight me...to fight you."

A few voices rose at once.

"What do you mean a secret army?"

"Why would he lie about this?"

I raised my hand, silencing them instantly.

"Brothers, right now, beneath your feet, lies an entire army of manufactured Everborns, true Everborns. Ones he has created himself!"

The air in the room disappeared.

"His power was never divine. It was built in a lab."

The room tensed. Their jaws clenched. They had suspected Jericho was hiding something for years. But now they had solid reason to follow me.

I let out a slow breath, glancing at each of them. They were ready.

Now, I just had to play my final hand.

"Jericho has led us astray. And if we do nothing, we will be nothing. But tonight, we reclaim our future and take back the power."

Suddenly, the compound alarm blared through the halls, cutting my monologue short. A sharp, piercing sound sent the entire place into a frenzy. My radio, sitting on the desk nearby, crackled with static before Jericho's voice cut through.

"Lock the compound down. No one leaves."

I was amused but unimpressed.

"Everyone act normal and get into position," I commanded, my tone calm and controlled.

As the room cleared, a smirk swept over my lips.

It can only be for Leo, I thought.

I strolled to the kitchen, grabbed an apple, and rolled it between my fingers before pressing a knife to its skin, peeling it in a slow, deliberate motion.

Then, making my way to the door, I leaned lazily against the frame, watching the chaos unfold around me.

Guards scrambled. Orders were shouted. Footsteps pounded against the marble floors.

I took a bite of the apple.

Unbothered. Waiting to see how this would play out.

Ding.

The elevator chimed as it reached the main lobby, drawing my attention.

Leo stepped out.

His attention was spread around the room, his movements—careful, cautious. I knew that look well. It was the look of someone who saw something they weren't supposed to. His posture was rigid, his breath uneven. I didn't need to guess where he had been. He had gone down to the lab.

The fire drill wasn't just a coincidence.

Jericho wouldn't let what was hidden beneath these floors become exposed.

Leo's gaze met mine, and in that instant, it was written all over his face—shock, dread, and the silent killer of regret.

Approaching me, he tried to mask it, but I spent too many years reading people to miss the way his fingers twitched, the slight hitch in his step. He was panicking and looking for a lifeline.

I tested his commitment to the lie I knew he would tell.

"Where've you been, mate?"

I sliced off a piece of my apple, placing it on my tongue, savoring the taste of what would soon be victory.

Leo's throat bobbed as he swallowed, his expression carefully neutral.

"I was walking the compound."

A lie.

But I expected nothing less.

I studied him, keeping my composure. He was unraveling right in front of me. His chest rose and fell irregularly. His eyes were lying—not enough for an amateur to notice, but enough for me. I could see it now he was wondering if I knew.

Behind him, the compound buzzed with movement. Guards reinforced doors, secured windows. The alarm had put the entire place on lockdown.

Leo didn't notice that my men were getting into position too. They had been waiting for this moment.

For my command.

I led him outside, playing it cool.

"Just checking in on the front gates," I said. He didn't question it.

My men were waiting.

After a few moments of questions that he did not properly answer, my patience ran its course. My men seized him, forcing him onto his knees like a man awaiting execution. He fought, but we had him tightly pinned.

I stepped forward, watching him struggle against their grip.

"Don't play games with me," I snapped, my words slicing through the night air like a blade. "What did you find in that lab?"

Leo clenched his jaw, his silence telling me everything.

I nodded toward one of my men.

Boom.

A brutal hit landed across his jaw, snapping his head to the side.

I hovered over him, my shadow draping across his face like a death sentence. The compound behind us was alive with movement, voices growing louder. Jericho would be here soon.

A lapse in judgment had guilt scraping at my insides but I needed to know the truth. I needed to know if Leo spoke to Susanne.

What am I doing? I thought.

I shook it off.

"Mate," I said, voice quieter, almost pleading. "Tell me what's down there."

He didn't react.

That pissed me off.

I crouched, lowering my voice. "We can work this out."

His lip parted, blood staining his teeth.

"I don't know what you're talking about."

I sighed, disappointed more than angry. Time was running out and if he wouldn't listen to reason maybe pain would get him to talk.

I nodded to my men again.

Crack.

Another hit across his face.

The door to the compound opened. The sound of footsteps and flashlights cut through the air.

Jericho.

I clenched my fists looking back to see the group approaching.

I leaned closer to Leo, voice barely above a whisper.

"Tell me, mate. Is she down there?"

His pupils dilated, a flicker of recognition flashing across his face.

And then, Jericho's voice thundered through the silence.

Damn it.

Too late.

I whispered the only thing I could.

"You know her too, mate."

His eyes widened.

Before I could process his reaction, pain exploded in my skull. My head snapped back, his head slamming into my face with enough force to rattle my vision.

Blood dripped down my chin.

By the time I came to, he had already taken out my men.

The fight was now on.

Leo and I collided like animals in the wild.

Fist to jaw.

Elbow to ribs.

We moved like mirror images, anticipating each strike, countering each blow. Our fight wasn't a brawl—it was a deadly, choreographed dance.

And Jericho watched.

He was enjoying this.

I saw Leo falter for just a second.

He was out of breath, just like me.

Then, he spoke.

"Jericho's lying to you," he said between sharp breaths. "The woman in the cage—"

My blood ran colder than the snow we were standing on.

The woman in the cage. His words brought me back to reality.

He knows.

My jaw locked. My pulse pounded in my ears.

A memory. Am I my brother's keeper?

I needed him to shut up.

He didn't know I already knew.

If he kept talking, he'd ruin everything.

I lunged, this time not to strike but to pin him down—to whisper my plan in his ear, to get him on my side before it was too late.

He needed to know the truth.

And then a loud spark and pop stopped caught my attention.

I froze in place.

The power line had snapped.

Darkness swallowed the compound whole.

And Leo's shadow was gone.

LEO

CHAPTER TWENTY-EIGHT

FRIENDS IN UNFAMILIAR PLACES

"No smoking in here, please."

She waved a hand frantically, trying to clear the smoke from her space while rolling the window down.

I stared at her, silent, my mind a web of tangled thoughts. Without a word, I turned toward the window beside me, watching the buildings and trees zip past as we sped toward a hidden outpost.

Bringing the cigarette to my lips, I took two short drags, the burn in my chest dulling the turmoil within. The moon hung high above, pale, and watchful, casting its cold glow over the road ahead.

I fought back the sting in my eyes, flicking the dimly lit cigarette out the window.

"As you wish, your majesty."

Natalie sat up straighter, waving the smoke away with a flick of her wrist.

"Cut the bullshit, all right?" Her voice was quiet but firm. She exhaled, settling back into her seat. "I know you're upset, but I need you to get your bearings under you."

I let out a slow breath, weighing my next words thoughtfully.

"How—" I paused, calculating the odds. "Did you find me? How did you know to come?" The pieces of the puzzle were still unclear, but deep down, I was grateful.

Natalie and her men had caused the blackout at Jericho's compound. They came in unexpectedly reminding me of the Cavalry. When the lights went out, they moved in like thieves in the night, slipping me out while everyone's attention was diverted—mine included.

"I had a hunch."

Natalie crossed her legs, resting her hand lightly on her thigh. Our eyes met for a moment before she bit her lip, then absentmindedly twirled a lock of her hair around her finger.

"When Michael interrupted our little powwow, I knew he had to know more than he was letting on," she continued, her voice sharper now. "That's when I ran back to my men. We needed to follow your trail."

I scoffed.

"So, you stalked me—like an animal. Like Michael."

She let out a dry laugh.

"Yeah. Just think, if we hadn't, your head would be floating in the Baltic, halfway to Germany by now."

I huffed, looking away.

"I guess that means I owe you—"

"Enough!"

The voice came from the shadows of the car, sharp and familiar.

Morison.

I tensed.

"Let's just get to the outpost and work out the details," he added, his tone unreadable.

I stole a glance at him, still uneasy sitting across from the very man who had betrayed his own kind. You can't trust someone like that. A man who will side with whoever benefits him the most. And when the time comes to switch teams again, he'll eagerly trade jerseys.

"Tell me, Morison," I leaned in closer; my voice soiled with venom. "When you decided to betray your group, what hurt the most? The fact that you're a dead man as soon as Jericho sees you. Or the fact that history will forever remember you as a traitor?"

Morison's expression remained unreadable, but his fingers curled where they rested. A restrained reaction, but a reaction, nonetheless.

Beside him, Natalie inhaled through her nose, slow and deliberate. Her lips pressed into a thin line—exasperation, calculation, maybe even a silent warning. She didn't fully trust Morison either, I could tell, but she has grown to trust him enough to work alongside him and keep the peace...for now anyway.

"Pull around the back," she ordered the driver, her voice leveling the tension before Morison could respond. "We're here."

She paused and held my gaze as she stepped out of the car, something unspoken passing between us.

Enough for now Leo.

We entered the outpost and were immediately greeted by a group of Night Walkers. One took Natalie's jacket without hesitation, while another extended a steadying hand as she eased into the leather seat facing the small gathering. She commanded the room without words, her presence alone shaping the energy around her.

The atmosphere gripped me.

These men were followers, but not like the Everborns. There was no brute force keeping them in line, no unspoken fear binding them to obedience. Here, they followed from a place of admiration and respect. Out of loyalty. It was a stark contrast to the world on the other side of the city.

Who was she, really?

Morison made his way toward a bar nestled in the corner, a choice of liquor bottles lining the countertop. Naturally, he gravitated there, a usual place of comfort. He wasn't exactly one of them, but he moved with the ease of a man who had adapted. I watched his hands carefully as he mixed cocktails, wondering if the act was a habit or a tactic.

Then there was me.

I leaned against the far wall, taking in the scene, still unsure of my place in it. A few eyes made their way to my direction, momentary glances, no signs of shock that I was here. Others barely acknowledged my presence, as if I were just another piece of furniture in the room. I could have been another pattern on the wallpaper for all they cared.

Should I speak, or keep my wandering thoughts to myself?

A familiar knot rolled around in my chest. The same restlessness that had followed me since the moment I set foot in this world. Searching for a place of belonging.

A steady voice interrupted my thoughts—soft, yet confident and pulled me back.

"...The next step is to rescue Susanne," Natalie said, her voice smooth, unwavering.

I snapped to attention.

She motioned toward Morison, who acknowledged her with the lift of his glass, as she went on.

"That's where Morison comes in." She paused just long enough for effect.

Then, her gaze landed on me.

"And Leo."

The sound of my own name startled me, as if it had no place here. A second wind surged through me, shaking off the lingering fog of exhaustion.

What does she mean, Leo?

I straightened from the wall, both feet planting firmly on the ground, my posture shifting instinctively as the attention of the room turned toward me. Watching. Waiting. They turned their backs and returned their focus back to Natalie as she rose with quiet authority.

Before she could utter another word, I processed her earlier claim. She was planning a rescue mission.

"Morison knows the layout of Jericho's compound in and out."

My teeth pressed into my bottom lip, curling as I exhaled.

She continued, "He has assured me that we can get in."

The room didn't take kindly to that statement. Their composed silence cracked, giving way to hushed murmurs, then full on dissent. The displeasure was felt, rumbling through the group like a slow building storm.

It was like watching the creation of an angry town mob. On a witch hunt and Morison was the target.

But he kept his head down, pretending to be occupied with the bottles at the bar, but I caught the subtle shift in his shoulders, the way he tensed ever so slightly. He knew what they thought of him. He knew his position here was the bottom rung of a rusty ladder.

Poor bastard.

Natalie, however, remained still, her hands resting on the small of her lower back. She let them air their frustrations. No protests came from her, no attempt to silence them. She was letting them have their moment.

Until finally she spoke.

"Leo arguably is our best fighter," she announced, her voice slicing through the discord. "Some of you have had the unpleasant fortune of finding that out firsthand."

A few heads turned in my direction, not a lot but enough to feel the air shifting.

Unconsciously, I shouted across the room.

"So, I'm here as a soldier." I felt like an old towel. Worn, used, and abused. I let the words settle before continuing, slower this time, more deliberate. "For you now."

I turned toward Morison—the other outsider—making my way to the bar to drown out my misery.

Before I could take another step, Natalie's voice rang out, firm and absolute, leaving no room for interpretation. I looked back.

"Yes—yes, you are."

My stride faltered.

My stomach twisted.

She didn't stop there.

"You are here for many things, Leo. And one of them is to fight. Make no mistake of that fact!"

I cocked my head, caught between disbelief and something I could not name. She did not soften the truth. She did not try to dress it up or cushion the blow.

For a few passing seconds, I did not know how to react.

Without a word, I turned my attention back toward Morison, reaching for a cocktail on the table, letting the weight of her words settle in my chest.

Behind me, I heard her dismiss the room, and the quiet shuffle of boots on hardwood followed as the gathering dispersed.

Then, slow, methodical steps.

I could feel her eyes burning a hole through my back. Watching, studying, wanting answers I didn't have.

Her small, delicate hand grabbed my shoulder and redirected my focus.

"Follow me," she demanded.

She turned toward the back door, leading the way without waiting for a response.

I hesitated; I caught the mesmerizing, movements of her hips swaying as she walked away.

Without another word, I set the drink down and followed her like a lost puppy. I was caught in the trail of her scent, her perfume roping me in.

Ironically, Michael was right, I needed to stay sharp.

I swallowed my thoughts and regained focus, while walking out the back door unsure of what hell was waiting for me on the other side.

CHAPTER TWENTY-NINE

FEAR OF THE UNKNOWN

The sky stretched vast and black, the only illumination coming from the distant shimmer of stars and the headlights of the vehicle we arrived in slicing through the darkness. Loose gravel rolled beneath my boots, shifting unpredictably with each sluggish step forward. I pushed through the night, mental exhaustion settling deep in my bones.

And there she was.

Standing beneath the pale glow of the moon, she was a vision of stillness, unmoving, unreadable. Her expression gave nothing away, but the way she held herself—a quiet, simmering authority—reminded me of an angry mother waiting for a child to approach, prepared to deliver a lesson I wouldn't soon forget.

She didn't speak.

Didn't move.

She just waited.

Patience—something I admittedly needed in the moment.

I braced myself, expecting the sharp edge of her words, a well-deserved reprimand. But when I reached her, she surprised me.

She held out her hand.

"Hand me one of your Winstons."

My momentum stalled for a moment, searching her face for a tell—was this a test?

Her fingers fluttered impatiently, urging me to hurry.

I patted my chest pocket, then quickly shifted to my pants, fishing out a small red box. I plucked two cigarettes free—one for her, one for me.

She took the stick between her lips, her mouth a soft contrast to the sharp, unreadable expression in her eyes. Rose colored and plump.

I retrieved my lighter, flicking it once. A small flame performing the Waltz before us.

She leaned in.

Inhaled deep.

A thick cloud of smoke twisted like a tornado before settling in the cool night air.

"You don't strike me as a smoker," I muttered, leaning back against the car, lighting my own cigarette, savoring the moment like a fiend chasing his next hit.

"I'm not," she said. "But you're really working my nerves."

Silence.

Then, the smallest breath of laughter slipped from her lips.

I joined in.

"Fate," she started, her voice steady. "It's a funny thing, you know?"

I didn't answer, unsure of where she was leading this conversation.

"I tell you to stay away after freeing you. Of course, you don't listen. You kill some of my men. And then, I rescue you again." She took a slow drag of her cigarette before letting it fall to the gravel, grinding the ember out beneath the sharp heel of her boot. "But here you are."

"But here I am," I echoed.

"Right where you're supposed to be. Fate."

I hesitated, rolling the last bit of my cigarette between my fingers before flicking it off into the darkness. I couldn't help but think what would have happened if I had never gone back to Morison's after Fox Retreat Hill? Would

I be here right now? I probably never would have heard of Michael, Jericho, Everborns and Night Walkers again.

The thought lingered, unwelcome.

"So, are you going to tell me a little about yourself?" I shifted the conversation, testing the waters while digging for clarity. Natalie was more than she presented, and I could see it in the way the men in the room followed her lead without doubt. There was something about her presence, something powerful yet humble.

Trying not to sound flirtatious, I murmured, "Let's start with your favorite color, perhaps?"

She flashed an innocent smile, a hint of amusement in her eyes, before rising from the hood of the car. Instead of answering, she started pacing, her movements slow while recounting a deep buried memory.

"Many years ago, there was a battle on Fox Retreat Hill," she began.

I cut in.

"The attack on the Everborns while they slept?"

She stopped mid-step. Her head spun quickly. Even in the low light, I could see the fury rising in her cheeks, burning red hot, like embers catching air.

"That's the nasty tale that's spin around," she said, her voice laced with something unspoken. Then, as if the memory itself fueled her, she started walking again—this time with purpose, each step striking the earth like a challenge.

"But it's not the full truth."

She lifted her gaze to the sky, her expression, lost somewhere in the past. I watched her in silence, letting her words settle in my mind. Up until now, I had only heard the story from one side.

How much of what I knew was just propaganda?

Her lips parted, and this time, her voice was steady.

"At that time, the two factions were segregated. The Night Walkers ruled our world, and the Everborns were treated as low-class citizens. We are pure blood. Their blood was soiled. Tainted."

I held her gaze, listening, absorbing.

"The Everborns didn't accept it. Rightfully so. There were rumblings. Whispers of resistance. Some Everborns went into the city, taking the lives of humans and leaving their bodies to be discovered." Her jaw clenched. "Naturally, the city reacted with a witch hunt. The Everborns' actions put all of us at risk."

I frowned.

"But why? Why were the Night Walkers so afraid of humans discovering the truth?"

Her demeanor shifted. For the first time since we started talking, she looked uncertain. She was calculating each word before speaking it aloud, as if saying it would make it real.

Finally, she exhaled sharply.

"They were afraid because of science."

I frowned, my lips parting.

"What?"

She hesitated again, glancing away for a split second before meeting my eyes. This time, when she spoke, her voice was lower, quieter—a dirty little secret she slipped through her lips.

"The fear isn't that humans will find out about us," she clarified. "It's what they will do once they understand the power of science. What happens when they realize they can create us—bend nature to their will?" Her words hung between us, heavy with fear that was unspoken.

I didn't move. My mind raced, trying to wiggle through the maze that was hiding the meaning behind what she was saying.

"The Everborns were never supposed to exist, Leo," she whispered.

A cold chill slid down my spine.

"They are an experiment," she finished, her voice barely above a breath. "One that should have never happened. They were created by a woman who was forced. Her biggest sin was love."

I stumbled back, leaning against the car as I lit another cigarette. The tragedy of one woman's love had created years of bloodshed.

Natalie's voice carried it—the anger, the sorrow. The way her words stuttered, the crackle between syllables. Frustration and pity in the same breath. I saw something I hadn't before—not just determination, not just strength but a burden of some sort.

And in that moment, I had the urge to hold her.

To do something, anything to take that weight from her shoulders.

But instead, I pushed forward. I had to dig deeper.

“Do you know why they were created?” My voice was low, neutral.

She turned to face me, inhaling deeply, her chest expanding like a balloon before she let the breath go in a long-controlled exhale.

“There was a man named Henrik,” she started. “He wanted to build an army—the same army Jericho is trying to create—to fight against the ones who cursed him.”

Henrik.

The name snapped something loose in my head. A conversation from before. A memory rushing forward.

Without thinking, the words flew from my mouth.

“The boy who was sold to the Children of the Moon—the one who was marked?”

Natalie’s gaze locked onto mine. A flicker of surprise, followed by clarity.

“You’ve heard the story?”

I nodded once.

“A less-than-reliable source told me,” I murmured, while recalling Jericho’s story in my head.

I examined her further, “you speak with the weight of a leader carrying the lives of her people,” I pressed. “Why is this so important to you?”

She walked over, leaning one shoulder against the car door, her fingers absently spinning the silver ring on her pointer finger. Her gaze drifted downward, settling on the crest engraved into the metal. For a moment, her expression softened, as if recalling a fond memory.

“This ring is the only thing I have left from a father I never knew.” She slid it off her finger and handed it to me.

I held it up under the moonlight, examining the intricate details. The crest—it was familiar. I was sure I had seen it before, but I couldn’t place where or when or even if it was a dream.

“I was told he fought on Fox Retreat Hill and died in battle. My mother died giving birth.”

The ring was solid and heavy. The silver was polished to a glow, reflecting my questioning grin back at me. I turned it over between my fingers, tracing the intricate crest. Something about it tugged at the edges of my memory, but I could not quite place it.

Carefully, I reached for her hand and slid the ring back onto her finger. Her skin was warm beneath mine, but she didn't pull away immediately. A quiet inspection of my hands holding hers followed, her posture softening—swept away in the moment.

Suddenly a switch had flipped, she snatched her hand back, reminded of my filthy Everborn status.

I smirked.

"Both of my parents were Night Walkers," she said, voice measured. "But only my mother sat on the council. She was selected for her intelligence, her bravery, her blood purity level. That's why I'm in line for a seat one day."

I frowned, rolling the image of the crest through my mind again. I knew it. I had seen it before. The thought of it wouldn't escape my mind.

Instead of chasing the memory, I asked the obvious.

"You have the ring of your father, but do you have any stories, portraits, or things of your mother?"

The question struck a nerve. Suspicion replaced the nostalgic glow from moments before. The woman I encountered in the alley my second day had returned—the one who had slashed my cheek before even knowing my name.

She ignored the question entirely.

Instead, she shifted the conversation with a forceful precision.

"The only reason you're here and not dead," she said firmly, "is because of the prophecy—the one that speaks of an individual who would either unite us or destroy us."

I shrugged, showing disinterest.

"And you assume that's me?"

Her tone sharpened.

"Yes. And so does Jericho. And possibly Michael."

I scoffed.

"What makes you think that?"

She reached into the inner pocket of her coat, retrieving a small notebook. Holding it up between two fingers and at eye level.

"This."

It was the diary.

The same one Michael had been searching for.

"But only Susanne knows the rest of the story," she added.

The diary—nothing more than a ragged old notebook—had been the cause of so much drama since I arrived in Malmö. Seeing it in person now felt surreal, like gazing upon an ancient relic, the Holy Chalice even. My mind drifted to the man who lost his life in that abandoned, dank house on the outskirts of town.

”A man lost his life over that, you know," I said, watching as she slowly tucked it back into her jacket. ”He was protecting you."

Her eyes sharpened.

"You saw him?"

I thought nothing of her question, assuming it was casual curiosity.

"Yeah," I said, voice neutral. "I was standing outside of an abandoned house, keeping watch for Michael, but close enough to hear bits and pieces of his interrogation."

She was quiet for a moment, then, in a tone that was suddenly too careful, she asked, "What did he look like?"

Before I could even form an answer, she was on me—her hands clutching my collar, her breath hot and urgent against my face.

"What was his name?" she demanded. "Did you hear his name?"

I blinked, caught off guard by the sudden shift. Her grip wasn't tight, but her desperation was suffocating. I inhaled slowly, prying her hands off me with gentle restraint.

"My mind's been through a lot," I muttered, thinking back to that night. "So much has happened in a short time so things are blurry." I closed my eyes for a beat, forcing myself to sift through the haze of memories.

The cries.

The scent of blood in the air.

The presence of death clinging to the walls.

Then, a name surfaced.

"Calvin, I believe. Why?"

Her whole body stiffened.

The reaction was immediate. Her knees buckled. The strength she carried so well, the composure she kept shattered in an instant.

I barely caught her before she hit the ground.

Her breathing was uneven, irregular. Her hands trembled, clenching into fists against my chest.

Her voice cracked, barely above a whisper.

"Albin," she choked out. "His name was Albin."

The chill of the night settled deeper, and Natalie needed warmth; needed rest.

"We should get you back inside." I gestured toward the entrance, guiding her through.

She was in a trance, in another world, when she said to herself, "I'm going to kill Michael."

Morison was already moving toward us, balancing three coffee mugs in his hands. Instinctively, I shook my head, a silent warning. Not now. This wasn't the time for conversation, especially with the man who had once been an enemy, now turned questionable ally.

I helped Natalie down into a leather chair nearby. With a snap of my fingers, one of her men fetched a blanket, draping it over her shoulders.

The room was quieter now. Most of the gathering had cleared out, leaving behind only the occasional murmur of whispered conversations and the steady shuffle of playing cards.

Natalie's face was flushed—whether from the cold, anger, or exhaustion, I could not tell. Her expression was distant, and she was checked out. She was no longer useful in this moment. She needed rest. But the mission couldn't wait, time was of the essence, it needed to be planned.

I drew a slow, steadied breath as the world around me began to mold, my senses sharpening with each second.

The fire burned hotter.

The scent of charred wood filled my lungs.

The candlelights flared brighter, the crackle of logs louder, and the hum of blood rushing to my head—familiar.

A moment I had lived before.

Michael.

When he had been knocked unconscious, I stepped forward. Took the lead without thinking—it was the natural order of things.

And now, fate was pulling me into that role once again.

The scattered pieces of information, like cards laid bare on a table, snapped into focus:

Susanne.

The diary.

Henrik.

The boy.

I thought harder.

The woman in the cage.

Michael.

The time had come.

No matter how far I tried to push against it, I always ended up here.

At the center.

At the helm.

Natalie was out of commission, and Morison knew the ins and outs of the compound. I would have to work with him for now.

We had no more time to waste.

The mission had to begin.

The time was now.

CHAPTER THIRTY

TROJAN HORSE

Between the window curtains, the sun peeked through, eager to start the day anew while most of the Night Walkers were winding down, preparing for sleep. Their world worked on a complex system—some worked day jobs, keeping a facade for the unaware public. Others tended farms, breeding animals purely for blood consumption, carefully managing their instincts to avoid giving in to their predatory nature. Then there were the night workers, like Natalie at the hotel. I learned that her role wasn't just a job—it was for her protection, though it was obvious she rarely followed the rules.

The Night Walkers had laws that mirrored the common world, governing themselves within the constraints of their hidden existence. Their very nature revolved around blending in, a complete contradiction to the Everborns, who embraced what they were without shame. The more I observed, the less mystique they held. Strip away the secrecy, and they were just another group of people trying to survive.

Ordinary.

Almost boring.

Natalie had passed out in the chair shortly after I laid her down, exhaustion finally catching up to her. I, on the other hand, couldn't sleep. Instead, I spent hours gathering details, absorbing what I could about their unique world. By the time the sun reached its peak, I swallowed my pride and approached Morison.

"Give me a shot of your best," I said, tapping the bar, my voice low but engaged.

He studied me for a second before a slow smirk formed, the kind that hinted at amusement rather than surprise.

"I was wondering when you were going to come talk to me."

He slid a shot glass toward me—Jameson Irish Whiskey. Lifting another in his own hand, he raised it.

"Skål."

"Skål," I nodded.

The whiskey burned as it went down, sharp and lingering. I set the glass down, wiping my lips with the back of my hand, the warmth settling in my chest.

I met his gaze, with a question rolling off my tongue, fiery than the drink itself.

"Why did you do it?"

His glass hit the table with a subtle clink. His gaze drifted, his breathing shallow, and he was fishing for an answer buried deep within himself. Slowly, his eyes made their way to mine, and he finally spoke.

"For my own humanity—for our humanity," he said, gesturing toward the sleeping Night Walkers.

"Why do you care about your enemy?" I countered.

He exhaled slowly, his breath heavier now, still searching for the right words.

"Let's just say this isn't exactly what I signed up for."

I let the silence stretch between us, then let out a quiet chuckle, shaking my head.

Thinking of my own journey I replied, "I can relate to that."

His true intentions remained hidden, but the remorse behind his spectacles held an honesty I couldn't ignore. Shifting my weight in the bar seat, I exhaled and cut straight to the point.

"Natalie is exhausted, but I think it's time we talk about the search and rescue."

Morison didn't hesitate.

He reached under the bar and pulled out a rolled-up blueprint, smoothing out its worn edges across the counter. I noticed the area of the layout at once—Jericho's compound.

"I'm assuming these weren't just lying around at city hall somewhere?" I asked, knowing the compound was unknown to the mortal eye.

A silent smirk played on his lips as he glanced at me over the rim of his specs.

"No, of course not."

He pulled out a handful of pens, slid one in my direction, and then scattered a few colored tokens across the blueprint. "Pick a color," he said, voice laced with anticipation.

His hands twitched as he started making his own marks, humming under his breath like a man who had been waiting for this moment. There was a strange excitement in the way he moved—an old strategist finally stepping back into a role he knew too well.

"This is the entrance to the compound," he said, marking an X. "And here's the back." Another X.

I nodded, unimpressed.

"That's the obvious, yes," I said, waiting for him to bring it all in.

His grin widened as he leaned back, head tilting toward the ceiling as if a light bulb in his head went off.

Then, with absolute certainty, he declared, "The Greeks."

I raised a brow. "What about them?"

"The Battle of Troy," he said, slamming a fist on the table, causing the pens to rattle.

I exhaled. "Morison—"

"We need a Trojan Horse!"

I narrowed my eyes, my mind running through what he was suggesting. "A Trojan Horse?" I repeated slowly, testing the words.

"Yes," he said, smiling. "Think about it—you and Michael already used a version of this tactic when you disguised yourselves as Coast Guards. The men at the gates never leave their post. They won't recognize everyone who comes through the entrance."

I sat up.

"We send in two, maybe three, of our own men," he continued, tapping the front gate with his pen. "They walk right up, say the welcoming phrase, and they're in. Once night falls, they'll open the doors from the inside."

He leaned forward, the energy practically buzzing off him. "And that's when the real fun begins."

"I'm still confused on how we actually get inside."

Morison barely looked up, already moving pieces across the blueprint like this was just another game of strategy.

"Well, when night falls, our men will kill the two guards at the front." His tone was casual, dismissing their lives as effortlessly as he had once switched sides in this war. "They replace them, open the gate, call for backup."

He slid one of the colored tokens from the back gate to the front.

"One of their men will come up to the front—code yellow—while the rest of us enter through the back. There'll be one guard stationed there. We take him out quietly."

I processed the information. It sounded easy enough, but the plan was still missing a crucial part—the extraction.

"How do we get Susanne?" I asked, eyes locked onto his.

A quiet change settled over him, a sense of unease cracking through his confidence.

"That..." he exhaled, running a hand through his hair. "That's the hard part."

I said nothing, waiting for him to elaborate.

"Getting through the gates is easy," he admitted. "But getting inside the building?" He shook his head. "That's suicidal. We must draw them out—lure them into the open while we stay in the shadows, take them out one by one, two by two."

He paused, his fingers drumming lightly against the counter.

"Eventually, chaos is going to erupt." His gaze met mine, sharp and deliberate. "By then you should have already been in the building."

"Like I said, you're the best fighter we have," Natalie's voice cut in as she approached the table, brushing off the last traces of her nap. "And you've seen the lab before."

She appeared without warning and her energy was still off from before. Her shoulders were stiff, her stance unnaturally rigid, her voice dark, void of its usual control. The weight of Albin's death still clung to her, an unyielding ghost. Her last words the night before—I am going to kill Michael wasn't an idle threat.

It was her promise.

"Seen the lab, yes. But I've technically never been inside," I corrected, my voice even.

Morison's fingers drummed against the table, the sound mimicking the rhythm of galloping hooves. The repetitive noise grated against my heightened senses. My jaw tightened, the irritation pooling in my chest before my hand slammed down on his, stopping his movement in an instant.

He blinked at me, startled. Then, without protest, he muttered, "Sorry," before pulling his hand back.

He refocused, tapping the blueprint.

"The staircase down to the lab is at the far end of the hall." He slid a token across the map, marking the location. Then motioned toward the bolt cutter leaning in the corner of the room. "There's an old lock on the cage, break it, get Susanne, and make your way back up. Hopefully, the coast is clear by then."

"Hopefully," I repeated, voice laced with doubt. "The plan doesn't have many assurances. Just a bunch of hopeful ideas."

Natalie's voice sharpened.

"That's war, Leo. Nothing is certain."

She turned on her heel, summoning her driver with a simple flick of her wrist. As she reached the door, she glanced back at me, her expression dull.

"I guess it's time for you to meet the council. Let's go."

The car shot forward, tires spinning in place before gripping the road, kicking up dust and gravel as we sped away from the outpost. Natalie, Morison, and I were en route to the Night Walker Headquarters, which, wasn't far from the hotel where I had first met Natalie.

I felt nervous though I had no expectations for this meeting. I didn't know how the council would view me—or my supposed place in this prophecy. I fought to keep my mind fixed on the mission. Recover Susanne and get the rest of the details from her on how to stop Jericho.

I turned toward the window, but the sunlight was blinding—so unusually harsh that my corneas felt on fire.

"All these years, and you still can't control your heightened senses?" Natalie was less than impressed.

I muttered, "My senses never flared this high before—before all of this."

Morison gave me a firm, almost fatherly pat on the back.

"You'll get used to it. You're just overly excited right now."

"My hunger was the only thing I had to learn to control," I added, my voice quieter.

Natalie leaned in.

"How did you survive all these years alone?" Her curiosity seemed genuine. Then, she squinted, and she dug further, "You feed, but you feed like us. That's unusual."

Morison adjusted his seat, turning his body toward me, his curiosity piqued as well. "Yes, that's very much the trait of a Night Walker," he mused before glancing at Natalie. "No offense."

Her response was swift, sharp.

"It's not a trait. It's a preference."

Morison frowned.

"Why would anyone prefer to ignore their natural instincts?"

I raised my voice, putting an end to the back and forth before it could escalate.

"Because I don't like what I become when I lose control," I said.

Their bickering stopped and they both refocused on me. I was rubbing the temples of my head, massaging the looming headache before I could finish my explanation.

"Something didn't feel right when I fed. I just thought there had to be more," my voice laced with pain.

I had already told Morison my story before—the one about my foster parents, their deaths, and the emptiness that followed. I didn't repeat it now. Instead, I let the silence fill in the spaces between my words, letting Natalie form her own assumptions.

"Every day had no meaning," I finished. The words had lost their shape by the time they left my mouth. For years I didn't know if I was cursed by the devil himself or trapped in a nightmare with no ending. Now I'm currently wondering if ignorance was better.

I turned toward the window, the sun still too bright, and my reflection distorted by the glare of the sun. I snapped my head back once more, dragging my fingers through my hair. Then, something caught my eye.

Beneath the seat in front of me, barely visible in the dim lighting of the car, sat a familiar black suitcase.

My breath hitched.

I pointed.

"Is that from the docks?"

Morison hesitated.

"It is."

Something tightened in my jaw.

"Is anyone finally going to tell me what's in it?" My voice carried more frustration than curiosity. People had died for these cases.

Morison didn't answer right away. He exhaled through his nose, then finally admitted, "There are four large capsules with vials inside. Each suitcase holds four." He gestured toward the trunk. "The other three are in the back."

Natalie cut in before I could respond.

"The serums, when injected into the bloodstream, create an Everborn."

My head tilted.

"That's it? It's that easy?"

Morison shook his head.

"Not quite. Everborns for all intents and purposes are birth defects."

Natalie crossed her arms.

"There's more to it that Susanne conveniently left out of her diary."

Her voice was laced with frustration, though whether it was aimed at Susanne or the situation itself, I wasn't sure.

"Jericho has kept her alive this long for a reason. He's missing something that only she can provide."

I leaned back into the seat, processing her words.

"But isn't she supposedly immortal?" I asked.

Morison chimed in, "Technically she is but Jericho must know more to the story."

Silence filled the car as the unanswered truth settled between us.

I scratched my chin, my gaze gravitating toward the window again. The city had started to shift around us. The streets blurred into something more structured, more intentional. Then the car curved around a corporate like building, its glass panels sleek and sterile—unassuming to the human eye.

Natalie's fingers drummed against the armrest. Even she wasn't sure how this was going to play out. The council would either confirm if I was or was not the savior that they needed.

The pressure mounting on top of me as we inched closer to the headquarters.

We were here.

CHAPTER THIRTY-ONE

BURIED SECRETS

Opulence.

The only word fitting for such a place.

Jericho's compound was large, imposing, and far from modest, his was more of a haunting castle—but the Night Walkers' Headquarters was something else entirely. The very walls spoke of history, carved with intricate details that whispered of power, of a lineage that had long ruled from the shadows. Every corridor exuded elegance, a seamless blend of old-world grandeur and modern indulgence. They didn't just live—they lived well, flaunting their wealth, their status, their superiority. And like always, nose up, and eyes turned downward looking past the tainted blood—The Everborns.

The parking garage was silent except for the low hum of the car's engine cooling down. As we stepped out, the elevator doors slid open to reveal an older gentleman, his sharp gaze dancing between us.

"Natalie, you're back?" His voice was polite, but the hesitation was there—brief, almost imperceptible—his eyes pausing on Morison and me. "With guests?"

His words weren't a question, not really. More of a veiled challenge.

Natalie barely acknowledged him, her authority settling into her posture like a well-worn coat.

"Help my driver with the suitcases in the trunk," she said, her voice smooth, unwavering.

The man hesitated just a fraction too long before nodding.

"Of course."

Natalie was more than a general leading the charge. Her duality showed she could command a group of fighters with her presence alone. But here, she was royalty, and she held the beating hearts of the people in her hand. The cost of knowledge was heavy on her shoulders and perhaps too heavy of a cross to bear alone.

The grief of Albin's death still lingered in her movements, subtle but present. Morison noticed it too.

As we stepped into the elevator, the silence stretched between us. Then, Morison broke it.

"Albin," he started.

A slow, deep breath escaped my lungs. I placed a hand on his chest, stopping him from pressing the issue any further.

Morison didn't pull away.

Instead, his fingers wrapped gently around my wrist, moving it aside with quiet insistence. There was no malice in his eyes, only understanding.

"He must have been important to you," he continued.

Natalie kept her head forward, jabbing the button to take us to the top floor.

"He must have loved you deeply," Morison went on. "He risked everything going to Michael—"

Natalie's head snapped toward him.

"He was like family," she hissed, her tone sharp enough to cut stone.

The anger in her didn't deter Morison. If anything, he leaned in further. He remained calm, measured, like a mentor guiding a student toward a difficult truth.

"Care to tell us more?"

In that moment, I realized something. I had never really asked Natalie about Albin—who he was to her beyond being her protector. I had assumed his role, but Morison was right. He had to be more than just some assigned watchdog. He went to the enemy for help. Only love can make someone that reckless.

Natalie hesitated. The occasional creak of the elevator pulleys filled the silence. Then, finally, her lips parted, her voice lower now, raw with grief.

"Albin was with me since I was a child." A tear slipped down her cheek, but she made no move to wipe it away. "My parents weren't there, and he filled a void I didn't know I had. He was more like a father to me."

Her breath hitched, but she pushed through.

"He deserved more credit than I ever gave him," she admitted, voice cracking. "He kept me safe from the wrath of the council—took the brunt of their anger for me."

Her shoulders trembled. She tried to straighten her posture, to bury the emotions swelling inside her, but they spilled like a cup overflowing.

Her fists clenched, and without warning, she struck the elevator doors—once, twice, again. Each hit landed harder, leaving a dent square in the middle of the door, the dull clang echoing in the confined space.

Morison let it happen, standing still as the grief bled out of her in violent tremors. I was lost and had no idea what to do or say to ease her pain. Then, after a few moments, Morison stepped in, wrapping firm but steady arms around her.

She thrashed at first, her body stiff, the sobs coming in quiet, broken gasps. But when she realized he wasn't letting go, she stopped fighting.

Instead, she collapsed, his chest absorbing her. Her head rested there, as if she had found a place of comfort she didn't know she needed. Morison showed true compassion, and from that moment on, I saw a trusted ally with him.

The elevator came to a halt, its chime breaking the intimate silence before the doors slid open to a grand hallway. My anticipation was plastered across the polished marble floors, reflecting back at me as I stepped forward. The path ahead was illuminated—not just by light, but by the only power I felt I had left.

Hope.

Hope that the council would support the mission ahead. Hope that they could provide guidance; answers I desperately needed. Whether or not I was the key to the prophecy didn't matter to me. What mattered was ending this war and restoring balance between the two factions.

We stopped just in front of the council's chamber, huddled like Sveriges Fotboll team preparing for our opponent.

Natalie spoke first.

"When we go in there, follow my lead. Don't speak unless spoken to."

She would know best. I didn't argue. I simply nodded.

"Should I wait out here?" Morison asked.

"No," Natalie said, her voice softer now. "You standing with us will show the council that we are united in a common goal. It may sway their favor in our direction."

Her instructions were clear, and the importance of this moment made the front of my head throb. I rubbed my palms together, trying to rid them of the dampness, the burn of anticipation creeping up my skin as Natalie reached for the doors. A shift in air pressure greeted us—the force from within pushing against my face, thick and unwelcoming.

I braced myself.

One by one, we stepped inside.

The room swallowed us whole.

The light chatter inside died instantly. The air tightened, the presence of disapproval, intrigue, and quiet condemnation wrapped coiled around us like a serpent. It sucked the oxygen from the space, leaving nothing but expectation.

I felt like a child interrupting an adult conversation not meant for my ears.

The council members sat in their decadence, surrounded by other Night Walkers indulging in wine, fruit, and the spoils of power—their riches on full display. Their stares bore into me, sharp and dissecting, peeling me apart layer by layer.

The silence undressed me, slow and embarrassing—like the realization of sin entering the world.

My eyes were open.

"Natalie," a voice finally broke through. "We have been waiting for you."

Immediately, another voice cut through the room, commanding, ”Step forward—the three of you.” His tone carried the presence of authority, leaving no room for negotiation.

As we obeyed, he gave a slight nod, and three guards stepped forward, positioning themselves behind us.

His gaze remained cold, scrutinizing.

”You were granted permission to go to the docks, not to embark on an unsanctioned side quest.”

Natalie opened her mouth to respond, ”I understand, but—”

”Are you aware that Albin is dead?” he interrupted. News must have made its way up through the grapevine, but he gave her no chance to explain.

A ripple of whispers spread across the room.

Quiet gasps.

Muted conversations.

Shock and speculation ignited like a slow burning fire.

The council member's eyes burned with accusation as he leveled his gaze at Morison. ”No doubt, the man standing beside you is responsible.”

The murmurs soured, soiled with judgement, and quickly, all the blame landed on Morison.

”Seize him at once!” he commanded.

The guards moved instantly without missing a step.

Heavy hands fastened onto Morison's arms, twisting them behind his back. The sound of iron cuffs clicking into place echoed in the vast chamber as he struggled against their grip.

The echoes of the crowd gasping only ignited the tension. They were looking upon us like criminals.

My instincts told me to help, to fight, but the silent whisper and look from Natalie was enough to keep me still. Our backs were against the wall, and the council made it clear that this would not be a two-way conversation.

“I had nothing to do with Albin's death!” Morison protested, but his words were cut short as a gag was brutally shoved into his mouth.

The facade of the Night Walkers—the civility they wore like fine silk—was hanging on by thread. Their judgment had already been passed, their actions no different from Jericho's. The only difference was how elegantly they dressed their cruelty.

I sharpened my focus, preparing for anything.

"The other man beside you," the councilman's gaze shifted toward me, "who is he?"

Natalie paused.

She struggled to form the words. Her hesitation alone was enough for me to take action.

I stepped forward.

"My name is Leo."

The council leader straightened, has face was composed but not at ease. His lips parted—then he stopped short. Instead of speaking, he swallowed a deep breath, calculating his thoughts, and staring down at me like a problem that could bite back.

"You must not be from here," he said finally, his voice void of warmth. "You don't know our customs."

"I'm not of your world," I replied.

The room collectively gasped. Shock rippled across the chamber. I had struck a nerve.

Again.

Natalie shook her head subtly, a warning begging me to not push them.

One of the council members turned to the others.

"He speaks out of turn!"

They talked among themselves, their voices just low enough that I could not make out their words.

Then, another leader turned his attention back to me.

He asked, "Where do you come from?" His eyes examining me like he discovered an ancient artifact.

"Where I come from is no concern of yours," I said, my tone deliberate as disgust for their actions bubbled inside of me. "I'm only here to unite the clans."

Natalie found her voice and stepped forward, standing side by side with me. She raised her chin, her voice steady.

"I believe Leo could be the boy from the long-awaited prophecy."

That statement sent the room into chaos.

Voices layered over one another, sharp and rising. Some of them hissing words of an open rejection of me. Others debated, their gestures animated, fighting to have their stance heard. Fruits and trash were hauled our way while someone from the crowd yelled "blasphemy!"

The council leader lifted a hand, commanding silence.

"What evidence do you have for such a claim?" He demanded.

Natalie didn't flinch.

"The prophecy speaks of a child who will unite or destroy us," she held her voice steady. "Jericho believed, for years, that the boy could be Michael."

A pause.

She let the words sink in.

The she added, "but what if Jericho was wrong?"

Silence.

I could feel the idea shifting in their thoughts, the fear laced into their uncertainty.

The whispers grew quieter. One by one, members of the council glanced at each other, searching for answers.

Finally, the leader exhaled, deeply.

"Clear the chamber," he ordered.

A heavy pause.

Then, one by one, the others obeyed, leaving the room until only the three of us and the council remained.

The door closed with a low, echoing thud.

"Are you the boy she says you are?" One of the members asked. A glimmer of amusement swept over her face.

I shrug my shoulders, annoyed and growing tired of their interrogation.

"I am who they say I am."

"Yes," another replied sharply. "But who do you say you are?"

The question sat with me for a moment.

The truth was, I didn't know. I was playing a part—a role cast for me before I was even born. But that wasn't a story I could easily accept. Was the prophecy even real, or was it just another myth to keep those with no influence in check?

The bigger question was, what is our purpose?

They were right—Natalie had shown no evidence to back up her claim. If I truly was "the one," shouldn't I feel something? My only motivation was bridging the gap between the two factions—and that wasn't even my responsibility.

Still, I replied, "I am Leo. A lost soul with no past, a drifter looking for my place in this world."

The words flowed effortlessly, lifting the weight off my shoulders from the revelation. For the first time, I was honest with myself.

I wasn't a savior.

I wasn't a prophecy.

I was lost and I wanted nothing more than to find a home.

The council turned to one another, speaking in silence—telepathic, ancient, indistinguishable.

Then, the leader in the center stood tall. His voice was measured but absolute.

"We've been patiently waiting for this day."

The words sent a ripple of confusion between Natalie, Morison, and me. With a simple nod from the council leader, the guards released Morison from his restraints.

The leader's voice remained steady as he resumed, "There was once a boy, marked by a group of sisters known as the Children of the Moon." He paused, studying our reactions before continuing. "His name was Henrik."

Something about his tone shifted. He wasn't just recounting a prophecy—he was telling a history.

I listened carefully as he stepped out from behind the grand desk, closing the space between us.

"Henrik, the first true pureblood, haunted the night as he walked, was controlled by the sisters. Forced into servitude. Even made to lie with them—giving each one a child."

He let the words linger before moving forward.

"But eventually, Henrik grew weary of being their slave. He rebelled."

The room seemed to shrink as his voice deepened, the tale revealing itself like a long-buried truth.

"He walked among humans—lived as one of them, ate with them, took lovers among them. Searching for a woman who could be his equal, a wife of his choosing. But in time, he decided he was above them all."

The leader's expression darkened, his voice lowering as he delivered the final blow.

"Henrik did not just wish to be free. He wished to rule. He wanted to enslave the humans, and he wanted to kill the sisters."

The story was different from the way Jericho told it, but the essence stayed the same. Natalie and I exchanged a glance, both unsettled by their version of events, left in silence, unsure of what to say. Morison, however, remained unfazed. That struck me as odd.

I cut in, my voice steady.

"But the Everborns came from what?"

The leader clasped his hands together, long, slender fingers interlocking.

"Genetics played a part. For unknown reasons DNA determined if you were full blood or not. The woman he ran with was testing on full bloods, an abomination at best though not entirely her fault."

Natalie leaned in, her voice a whisper against my ear while keeping her gaze ahead. "Susanne was Henrik's slave after she fell in love. She couldn't break free."

The leader continued.

"That was when Puritas Sanguinis was formed." He gestured toward the group behind him. "When Henrik's plans were discovered, the sisters approached the Night Walkers and appointed seven to serve as leaders. Their purpose—our purpose—is to ensure our world stays hidden from human interference."

Morison, silent until now, finally spoke, his voice edged with defiance.

"And that's why you cast the Everborns aside? Like they were nothing?"

The leader shook his head.

"The Everborns followed Henrik and grew reckless," he hissed. "Henrik died, and Jericho took the throne—hellbent on fulfilling his vision."

Another council member scoffed from the shadows.

"A true travesty, honestly."

I pushed through the rising tension.

"What does the boy have to do with any of this?"

The leader exhaled slowly.

"Ah, yes. The boy." He met my eyes, his stare unblinking, voice sharp enough to cut. "The sisters only said the future was unclear."

A pause.

A shift.

"What I do know is that Leo's mere presence could set off a chain reaction."

The room went still.

"No one knows what comes next. Which is why it's best if you leave, Leo. Go back to where you came from. We have dealt with Jericho all these years and don't need you being the catalyst to our downfall."

He performed an about face and swiftly walked to his seat, leaving us with nothing but ambiguity. No meaningful answers—only the warning that the future was uncertain and that my presence alone can alter the present and future.

My chest burned with frustration.

This was the mighty council. The revered leaders spoken of like gods, entrusted with preserving balance. Yet, here they sat, cowering behind their own fears, afraid of the prophecy they were meant to uphold.

If fate had already been decided, then nothing here would stop what was meant to come to pass. Fate versus choice, whichever it was, the decision laid in my hands.

Without another word, I turned and made my way to the exit. Morison and Natalie followed in silence until Natalie stopped.

"My mother?" she asked suddenly.

The council leader, still settling into his chair, raised his brow.

"I beg your pardon?"

Natalie turned fully, cementing herself in place. I reached for her arm, my voice low.

"Leave it alone for now."

She blinked and desperation took a hold of her.

"I can't," she said. Then, jerking free from my grasp, she stepped forward. "You're not the only one who's lost, Leo."

With that, she approached the council's desk, back straight, chin high, the fire in her voice unwavering.

"Was my mother part of the original seven?" she asked, her tone steady. "It just dawned on me that I don't know much about her."

A hush fell over the room.

The council leader exchanged glances with his peers before whispering into the ear of another member.

More secrets.

He exhaled heavily, the weight of hidden truths clear in his stare.

"I was a generation after your mother," he admitted, his voice quieter now. "And she was a generation after the second." He leaned forward, meeting her eyes. "There are buried secrets passed from generation to generation—ones you would have uncovered eventually."

He paused, annoyed that she was forcing the truth out of him sooner than he intended.

"But since you seem so determined to break every rule we've set, I'll tell you this," he continued, his voice turning sharper. "She had a mindless love affair with some common Night Walker who got himself killed at Fox Retreat Hill." He smirked, clearly enjoying the decomposition of Natalie's composure. "When it was discovered that she was with child out of wedlock she was stripped of her title."

He hesitated.

"As a member of Puritas Sanguins her stain on the council was forbidden."

Morison shifted uneasily, his foot tapping against the marble floor, his heels shifting from side to side. Something about this revelation struck him differently.

The air was suffocating. I had the sickening feeling that whatever came next would land like a blow to the gut.

"Do you know what happens when you're starved of blood?" the councilman asked suddenly.

Natalie's breath skipped.

"I've never thought about it."

"You dry out," he answered, his words slow, deliberate. "Like a raisin under the sun."

The dark smirk on his face was unbearable, smug with the cruelty of it. He enjoyed this.

"It makes pulling the fangs out easier," he went on. "And then the sun does the rest—turning you to dust."

A heavy silence followed.

Then, with a casual push off the desk, he sank back into his chair, delivering the final blow.

Case closed.

Natalie's entire body trembled.

Rage.

Grief.

A storm on the verge of breaking.

She bent at the knees her stance shifting. I knew this posture.

She was about to transform.

Morison stood rigid, staring ahead, but his eyes were hollow. I had heard enough of his war stories to know what haunted him. The atrocities of the past, the ones written in history books, the ones he had witnessed firsthand.

And Natalie...she was seconds away from throwing herself at the council.

I had to stop her.

In a blur, I moved to her side, gripping her arm just before she could lunge.

The seven members of the council rose from their seats as one, patiently waiting, and expecting fully for us to strike.

I raised my free hand in surrender.

"No need."

The leader sneered, his lip curling.

"Leave at once."

The warning was final.

I didn't hesitate. I guided Natalie and Morison out of the hall, leaving the council behind. If I was lucky, I would never have to deal with them again.

As soon as we reached the corridor, I exhaled the breath I had been holding in.

"We need to gather your team and execute Morison's plan sooner rather than later," I said to the two of them.

Silence.

I turned to Morison.

"Morison" I screeched.

He snapped out of his thoughts, blinking as if shaking off a dream.

"Roger that," he said.

Then I turned to Natalie.

"Are you okay?"

She didn't answer at first. She was leading us now; her pace set with purpose.

"We're heading to the den," she finally said, voice void of hesitation. "And getting my men ready."

I thought of the council and their lack of leadership. Natalie's mother and the torment they put her through. Truly, there was no place that was safe.

Natalie cut through my daze without looking back.

"This war is so much bigger now."

CHAPTER THIRTY-TWO

OLD HIGH, NEW LOW

"This won't be easy," Natalie began, standing tall, her voice firm as she addressed the gathered Night Walkers. Some of the same men and women I had met at the outpost earlier stood among them, dressed in all black to mirror the Everborns, and their faces hardened with resolve.

"There will be blood," she continued. "And there's a chance some of us won't make it back."

Her words cast a blanket of uneasy truth over the room. It was never a guarantee that everyone would come home when crossing enemy lines. Still, the fact had to be stated. It was within those brutal, honest moments that you dug deep and found yourself. And in the end, the truth was always appreciated.

Morison and I lingered near the back wall, greeting the familiar faces as the crowd continued to gather. I leaned toward him, keeping my voice low.

"We've got a good turnout."

"We do," he murmured. "And we'll need every one of them. The second that alarm goes off; Jericho's henchmen will come pouring out in droves."

Just before I could answer, a memory flashed through my mind.

The terror.

The helplessness.

The sheer powerlessness I felt when the compound descended on me. My body tensed at the recollection, the unease settling deep in my chest.

Like a fool, I was entering the lion's den again, but only this time, I knew the lion was actually occupying the den—Jericho.

"When I have Susanne, then what?" I asked, my voice low and laced with uncertainty.

Before Morison could respond, the sound of applause and a war-like chant erupted across the room, cutting our conversation short. Natalie's speech had ended, and as she made her way toward us, her steps were powerful and deliberate. She had rallied the troops, and she intended to see this mission through. A scene I've known well.

"Gentlemen," she addressed us, her voice firm. "Let's go in honor."

She crossed her right hand over her chest, the motion precise and controlled. A silent pledge. The light caught the faint glow of her ring; the crest displayed like a proudly hung flag. There was something almost ritualistic about it, a gesture steeped in history.

The entire atmosphere mirrored the night at Morison's, before the docks, the moment before the storm. Back then, I had felt like I was doing the right thing, too. Now, there was no room for emotions.

This wasn't just about receiving precious cargo.

It was about saving a woman who might hold the key to stopping a never-ending war.

Peace was the goal.

"That's an interesting ring on your finger." Morison's voice filled with curiosity; his gaze fixed on Natalie's ring. "Mind me asking where you got it from?"

Natalie lifted her hand, examining the ring as if truly noticing it for the first time. Then, she slipped it off, rolling it between her fingers before sliding it into her pocket.

“I’ve had this old thing since I was a child,” she admitted. “I always thought it belonged to one of my parents, but” she paused. “Who knows if that’s true anymore.”

I glanced at my watch. The night was creeping forward.

“Shall we?” I said, stepping toward the door.

We stepped outside into the cold night.

An overcast of thick clouds hid the moon, blanketing the world in a muted darkness. The wind was quiet—unnaturally still. The only sounds were the steady rhythm of boots against the ground, almost synchronized, and the steady thump of my own heartbeat, breaking the silence like a distant war drum.

Instead of vehicles, we marched across the city, moving in coordinated clusters like an infantry unit. Each group weaving through different alleyways and side streets, adjusting their timing, always staying hidden in the shadows. Natalie emphasized unpredictability, while Morison focused on the logic behind our movements.

”This way, if we’re caught, we won’t all be together,” he pointed out.

When we finally regrouped just outside the compound, the massive structure loomed over us, its high gates casting long shadows. Despite its imposing presence, the layout had its flaws. Blind spots that went unnoticed, likely because no human ever ventured this far. Security had been designed to keep outsiders from discovering the compound, not to defend against an organized assault.

Crouching low, I fixed my gaze on the front gate. Two guards stood at their post, engaged in casual conversation, their attention drifting. It was time to send in the Trojan Horse.

I twirled my finger, then pointed toward the entrance. Two Night Walkers appeared from the bushes, dressed in the signature black suits of the Everborns, provided by Morison.

”You’re sure this is going to work?” I whispered.

”Patience,” Morison replied. ”Give it a moment.”

From our vantage point, we could only see their backs as they approached the gate. Hand gestures, forced laughter, an easy exchange of words, was all part of the act. After a brief pause, the guards waved them through.

Two minutes later, their bodies were being dragged outside the gate.

One of our men pried the radio off a fallen Everborn's hip before the other retrieved the bodies, hauling them into the cover of the trees.

He gave the hand signal, and the gate was ours.

Like a well-oiled recon troop, the first part of our group advanced toward the gate, taking their positions inside the walls. Natalie, Morison, and I led the rest of the team toward the back of the compound. The static of the radio crackled through the air, and as expected, one of the guards rushed toward the front.

Perfect timing.

"This is it," Natalie whispered.

Like a swarm of hornets, we jumped the gate, closing in on the remaining guard before he could react. He barely had time to register what was happening before he was nothing more than a cold, stiff body. Superstition says that when you die with your eyes open, it's a reckoning for all your sins. His dark eyes met mine, frozen wide in death, and for reasons I couldn't explain, I prayed for his soul.

"You're up," Morison said, nudging my back.

I gave him a silent confirmation, and just as I was about to move toward the building, a small hand wrapped around my arm. Natalie's grip was firm, and despite the layers between us, the warmth of her touch seeped through my jacket.

"Be careful," she said, her voice firm but personal.

My lip curled against my teeth, lost for words. Instead, I simply met her gaze and replied, "I will."

I double checked the radio on my hip.

Batteries still good.

Keeping low, I raced across the courtyard, my body pressed close to the shadows. When I reached the far end, I flattened my back against the brick wall, forcing steady breaths as a thin cloud of condensation formed in front of my face.

Muffled voices vibrated through the stone against my ear.

I waited.

This was a one-time deal.

Get in, get out, and don't get caught. Otherwise, I'd be facing the biggest fight of my life.

The voices eventually faded, their presence dissolving into the depths of the compound. I reached for the door. The old door was heavy like a boulder, and the hinges groaned as I pried it open just enough to slip through.

The change in temperature made me hesitate. I glanced back at the door, but no draft came through. Still, my senses were on high alert, paranoia creeping in with every step.

I moved carefully—rolling from heel to toe, distributing my weight evenly to keep my footsteps silent. Slow and steady as I found my pace. Even my breathing felt too loud in the dead stillness. When a mouse scurried past, my throat clenched, and I nearly choked on my own spit.

I wiped the sweat from my forehead and pressed forward.

The building's layout wasn't intricately designed; five hallways leading to a central lobby, duplicated on each floor. The corridors housed everything from living quarters to training gyms, and other basic amenities but I had lucked out. This was the storage wing, a graveyard of lost and discarded items.

And yet, something felt off.

The air was thick, humid.

The stone walls, slick with dew and moss, made the space feel damp despite the cold outside. My fingertips briefly brushed against the surface, jerking my hand back and using my jacket as a napkin.

Light from the central lobby bled through the end of the hall.

Voices grew louder.

Shit.

I dropped to a crouch, pressing myself behind an overturned school desk. The main lobby was too open of a space, and I knew I wouldn't make it to the elevator unseen.

I needed a plan.

Fast.

The steady flashing red dot on the radio caught my eye. I snatched it off my belt loop, considering my options. If I could tune into the Everborn frequency,

I might gain an advantage. But using it came with a risk—if my voice was heard, the entire mission could come undone.

I peeked around the desk.

Three soldiers; two men walked past the hallway but the third started heading my way. Fighting this early into the mission would only complicate things. If I could avoid unnecessary bloodshed, I would. The death toll on both sides was starting to press against my conscience.

I kept my sights on him while I pressed a hand against the wall behind me, tracing it and slowly retreating until I felt the opening of a nearby door.

He was distracted, so I slipped inside.

The room was cold and dark, filled with old furniture stacked against the walls, providing enough cover to observe him. He paused just outside, patting his jacket in search of something before pulling out a carton of cigarettes.

A smoker.

Of course, and he would be heading to the back exit. But once he saw there were no guards stationed, his antennas would rise.

I reached for my radio to alert Natalie—

My fingers met empty space.

Time stopped.

My breath stalled as looked down to my belt loop then quickly back to the hallway.

The Everborn knelt beside the desk I had been hiding behind, and in his grip was my radio. Just like that, I would have to do what I must in order to keep this mission alive.

I slipped out of my jacket and into the hallway. He spotted me immediately. The dim lights and shadows obscured parts of my face, but he saw enough to confirm.

"Leo?" his voice stuttered with fear.

I didn't answer.

My focus was on the subtle shift in his stance, the almost imperceptible movement of his heel preparing to step back. He was about to make a run for it. My senses flared, instincts zooming in. It was as if I saw his decision before, he even committed to it.

Before a sound could leave his lips, I was in front of him. One leather gloved hand clamped over his mouth, the other twisting and pinning his arm to his side.

He thrashed, trying to scream, but my grip was tight. His lips split against the pressure of my palm, blood seeping between my fingers. I dragged him backward into the room, quietly shutting the door behind us.

I gave him the honor of a quick and painless death.

"Sorry, min kompis," I whispered before snapping his neck with a sharp, quick twist.

His body slumped, and I lowered him to the ground gently. The radio, still clutched in his stiffening fingers, had already begun to cool.

The deed was done, and there was no turning back. Once the seal is broken, the next kill comes easier.

And easier.

And before you know it, you're counting down, waiting for the next day to start your streak over.

I tiptoed back to the wall, gauging my opportunity. The muffled chatter had vanished, leaving only the sound of my own breathing. I peered around the corner, scanning the four intersecting hallways.

Clear.

Without hesitation, I moved swiftly toward the elevator, keeping my profile low. My pulse hammered in my ears as I glanced up at the floor indicator above the doors.

I pressed the button.

Descending.

The glowing numbers ticked down, each one tightening the grip around my chest. My leg trembled like a jackhammer, the silence around me deafening.

One floor to go.

Then—Michael's voice.

My stomach twisted.

His words carried through one of the corridors, sharp and irritated, but I couldn't pinpoint which one he was coming from.

The ding of the elevator arriving nearly made me flinch. My hands shot up, ready to attack if someone was on the other side.

The doors slid open.

Empty.

I exhaled, stepping inside just as Michael's voice grew louder.

"Just keep Jericho occupied," he ordered.

Damnit.

His voice was too close.

I repeatedly stabbed the button for the lab, hoping the doors would close faster. I pressed myself against the wall as flat as I could.

Then I heard nothing.

Michael had stopped mid-sentence.

A breath hung in my throat.

"What happened?" The other voice said.

Michael's voice low. "Nothing. I just thought I—"

The doors sealed shut.

The elevator began on its journey.

Michael's voice faded, swallowed by the distance. But the damage was done. Whether he saw me or not didn't matter. He wouldn't stop until he knew for sure.

The race was now on.

My reflection shined off the stainless-steel elevator doors. The man staring back at me wasn't the same one who had arrived in this city. For better or worse, that version of me was dead. I had to accept that, and find clarity, or I wouldn't make it out of this compound alive.

I studied my reflection, running a hand through my hair before reaching into my front pocket. Pulling out a carton of Winstons, I lit one up and took a slow drag. The elevator filled with thick ribbons of smoke, the scent of tobacco burning through my lungs. The taste was different this time, and the bitterness did nothing for me.

I took another drag, but nothing.

My old high was suddenly my new low.

The double doors slid open.

The man in the reflection disappeared with them.

I let the cigarette slip from my grip, the ember still glowing as it hit the floor. Then, with the heel of my boot, I crushed it into my past.

Onward to Susanne.

The corridor was suffocating. The narrowed stoned walls stone walls trapped the heat, offering no ventilation. Dim mining lamps hung from the ceiling every few feet, flickering shadows across the damp rock. Water dripped steadily, tracing slow paths down the stone before pooling somewhere unseen, the soft plinking sound barely audible over my own breath.

The main lab was now in sight.

I crept forward, scanning the empty room. It looked exactly the same as before—untouched, frozen in time. Running a finger along one of the desks, I rubbed the dust between my fingertips. Nothing had moved. It was clear now that the main lab was nothing more than a ruse.

I turned toward the rock wall, standing motionless as I dug deep into my memory. I had watched one of the scientists enter and exit before.

Think, Leo.

Damn it.

I had forgotten the pattern.

My thumb pressed against the small button on my radio. I needed to ask Morison, but the static in response confirmed what I already suspected—there was no signal down here.

Another oversight.

Anxiety prickled in my chest, tightening like a vice.

I had to figure it out myself.

Taking a deep breath, I ran my hands over the stone, tracing over the surface in slow, methodical motions, trying the first pattern that came to mind.

Nothing.

My pulse ticked faster. I tried another sequence, smoothing my palms over the rock in deliberate strokes.

Then the sweet release of pressurized air.

A hiss echoed through the corridor as the hidden door cracked open. I took one last glance down the hallway, ensuring I wasn't being followed, before stepping through.

One way in.

One way out.

The moment I entered, the silence wrapped tightly against my ears. The secret lab was still unlike the time Jericho was down here. I leaped over the grated floor where I had once crouched, listening to Jericho's every word. Now, I stood in the place I had only watched from the shadows.

The door leading deeper into the lab was already unlocked.

My pulse quickened.

I stepped onto the metal staircase, the clanking of my boots against the steel deafening in the heavy silence. The deeper I went, the stronger the stench became—a sickening blend of medical chemicals and rotting flesh. I raised a hand to my mouth, swallowing back the bile that threatened to rise.

I made my way past a large silver examination table. Blood, long dried and blackened, was splattered across its surface. The bodies I had seen before were gone. Surgical tools soaked in blue, fluorescent liquid sat in metal trays, their jagged edges catching the dim light.

A clipboard sat on the table. I picked it up, flipping through the pages. A list of names, none of them familiar. I scanned the document twice. No mention of me. No mention of the name I was looking for—Natalie.

I set it down, my jaw tight.

The soft beep of my watch snapped me back. Another hour had passed. I had no more time to waste.

At the back of the lab stood the cage.

Its thick metal bars loomed before me, strong enough to hold a lion. I approached cautiously, the echo of my footsteps bouncing off the walls.

The sound of chains dragging against the floor sent a chill down my spine.

She knew someone was here.

With my voice just above a whisper, I called out, "Susanne."

The rattling stopped.

I stepped closer.

"Susanne," I repeated, my fingers now close enough to graze the bars.

From the shadows, she turned to face me. Her head tilted, watching.

Silent.

The dim light illuminated her face, and I faltered.

Her eyes.

I've seen them before.

They shone even through the tangle of her matted hair, even beneath the filth and rags she was draped in. They belonged to someone I knew.

Michael.

My words lodged in my throat.

"Are you Susanne?" My voice barely held.

She studied me for a long moment.

Then, a slow smile spread across her lips.

"So, the prophecy was blurry indeed."

CHAPTER THIRTY-THREE

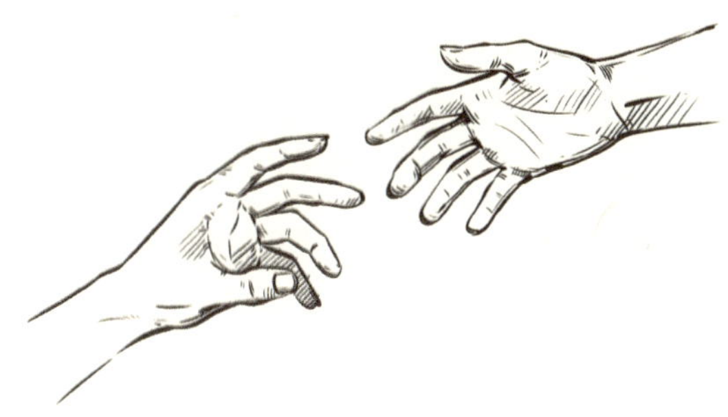

JOHN 15:13

My knees buckled.

I heard the word 'prophecy' uttered countless times. But something about the way she said it, the certainty in her voice.

I paused.

For a moment, I believed her.

A breath later, I forced myself to move.

"Prophecy or not, we have to go."

I reached for the bolt cutters at my side, running my fingers along the cage's lock, feeling for any hidden wires that could trigger an alarm.

Nothing.

I raised the bolt cutter to the padlock's clasp. It was old, its once dark silver now dulled and tarnished. Heavy, inverted triangular in shape, with a serpent coiled around two crossed roses molded in the center. The keyhole was unusually placed underneath.

I pressed the cutter's teeth firmly against the clasp and inhaled deeply. Then, like a beast flexing its strength, I squeezed with everything I had.

Clack!

The lock thudded onto the ground, the vibration echoing through the lab. My breath skipped, ears straining.

Nothing.

No alarms.

No sounds of rushing footsteps.

The gate's hinges screeched as I pushed it open. Susanne stood still, silent, her gaze fixed on me—not with fear, but something else. It was like she was studying me in way that a professor studied their craft.

I stepped inside the cage slowly, hands raised to show I meant no harm.

”You never answered my question. Are you—”

”Yes, I am Susanne,” she cut in. ”I just hate my association with the name.”

My nose twitched at the bitterness in her voice.

”I'm getting you out of here,” I said.

I moved closer to break the shackles binding her, and the stench hit me like a brick wall. The sharp ammonia burned my nostrils, my eyes watering as my stomach churned. She had been living in her own waste; her rags permanently stained with filth. But there was no need to say anything. She knew her condition.

With her ankles and wrists finally free, it was time to go.

“I'm assuming you have a way out of here?” she asked.

We made our way to the door, but she was dragging behind me, her pace sluggish. At this rate, running wouldn't be an option. I turned to her, my voice flat.

“Sort of.”

She nodded as if that answer was good enough. A small smile cracked from her lips as she pushed her matted hair from her face.

“Didn't want to have to but I guess we'll be fighting our way out.” She stretched her arms, then arched her back, rolling her shoulders. “It's been a while since I've had freedom of movement.”

She winked at me, and I quickly recalculated our escape. But before I could say anything, she moved past me, taking the lead.

“Hey! How do you know where you're going?” I called after her, picking up my pace.

She didn't slow down. Instead, her stride lengthened, her footing steady as she climbed the stairs, exiting into the corridor of the main lab. Her gaze swept the area—not with caution, but with familiarity. Like she was searching for something specific.

"You've read my diary, haven't you?" she asked, finally stopping in front of the elevator. "The one they stole from me?"

I paused.

"I haven't but Natalie—"

She turned, her expression hard to read.

"Who do you think built this place?"

Her voice wasn't just confident—it carried the weight of dark truths hidden under pride and cracking under the strain of regret.

I didn't push for more answers. This was hers once. That much was clear. But somewhere along the way, she became a prisoner in the very place she built.

She wasn't just a woman with answers.

She was the answer.

I studied her in silence, watching as she stayed poised, unshaken beneath the weight of it all.

The elevator arrived with a low chime, and Susanne stepped inside without hesitation. I followed, but something about the way she carried herself unsettled me. It was as if she was saving me and not the other way around.

"We should be careful going up to the main lobby," I said.

She turned her head, offering me a smile before looking forward again. A quiet hum escaped her lips before she finally replied, dismissive, almost amused.

"Yeah...we should."

My stomach knotted.

I counted the numbers on the elevator panel, watching as the numbers lit up.

Lab... Basement... Main Lobby...

The doors slid open.

Blinding lights... a wall of bodies.

Michael stood in the center, flanked by a group of Everborns. They were waiting for us.

The radio on my hip crackled with sudden static.

The signal was back.

"Leo, are you there?" Natalie's voice cut through, urgent, desperate.

My fist tightened.

Michael's frown quickly turned into a smile, raising his hands to a slow, mocking applause.

"I knew it," he said, voice dripping with satisfaction.

Theatrical, smug, and triumphant. He was enjoying this moment.

"My eyes never deceive me, mate."

Just then, my head snapped to the side. A stiff breeze flew past me and knocked me off balance, my cheek stinging like a small paper cut. Before I could react, I turned back toward Michael—only to find Susanne had already taken down two of his men and shoved him out of the way.

The gums around my fangs itched.

My vision sharpened, instincts firing on all cylinders. Blood rushed through my veins like wildfire. I leaped from the elevator, catching the first Everborn charging at Susanne. I flipped him over my shoulder, then drove my heel into his chest, twist and pinned him to the ground.

I caught sight of Michael retreating through the madness, but before I could pursue, another Everborn blindsided me.

A fist crashed into my jaw. I barely flinched before returning the favor, my knuckles meeting bone with a satisfying crack.

Natalie's voice crackled over the radio. "Get Susanne out of there! Now!"

I scanned the lobby, searching for Susanne in the midst of the brawl. She had just let an Everborn slip from her grip, his body crumpling lifelessly to the floor.

She wiped her lips, unbothered.

Another opponent rushed her.

She slipped his first punch, ducked the next, then seized him by the throat. She pressed her index and middle finger into the side of his neck with precision. When she yanked them out, his blood squirted like a fountain. Then she sank her teeth into him, right where she drilled the two holes. She took a few deep gulps of his blood, then shoved his limp body aside.

Another fighter came at her.

She wasted no time.

Grabbing him by the arms, she wrenched them back and drove her knee into his spine. A sickening crack echoed across the room. His body folded in on itself like a beach chair, collapsing to the ground.

Susanne wasn't just fighting. She was butchering them.

Her expression remained unfazed, and her eyes were now hollow and darkened. There was no hesitation. No remorse. Only cold, brutal, vengeful violence.

Hell, hath no fury like a woman scorned. The pain she had endured for years had taken its final form; manifesting into a tornado of emotions wrapped into one powerful being.

Now, I understood why they had shackled her.

Susanne wasn't just a prisoner.

She was a monster.

We made it to the exit where I initially entered. I was longing for the breeze of the cool air but instead we were immediately met by a brutal battle taking place. The smell of metallic blood was in the air. Groans, and the sound of war cries drowned out the sound of the leaves blowing in the wind.

Susanne didn't miss a beat.

She leaped into action, continuing her onslaught. I scanned the battlefield, searching for Natalie. She was in the back, holding her own against two Everborns.

I *have to get to her,* I thought.

I reached behind my waistband, retrieved the knife Michael once gave me. I slid it out the sheath and there was no turning back. I tore through the courtyard, dodging and countering every attack that came my way, taking lives where necessary, sparing those I could. Natalie was a formidable fighter, but when our eyes met, something in her shifted. A smirk of relief flashed across her face then amazement when she saw Susanne.

Morison appeared instantly—his body hitting the ground with a loud thud.

He was slowly making his way to his knees, so I didn't slow down.

I moved in, delivering a crushing blow to the nearest enemy while Natalie drove a brutal kick into another's face. We worked in sync, a practiced rhythm of survival.

Finally, I buried the knife into the chest of an Everborn, before thrusting it into his gut. Rage took over me. I screamed, loud and primal as I drove the blade deeper.

I pulled out, then reentered his gut once.

Twice.

Three times.

Then I ripped the blade upward, splitting him open to the belly button. His lifeless body collapsed beneath my feet, entrails spilling like a butchered pig.

I scanned the battlefield.

The fight was escalating fast. We had Susanne, but the longer we stayed, the more forces Jericho would send.

"Morison. Natalie," I called, still focused on our surroundings. "We have Susanne, we need to go."

Silence.

"Morison?" I called out again.

A sound broke through the chaos. A wet, choking gasp. A sound I grew accustomed to hearing but didn't want to face it at this moment.

I turned.

Natalie was on her knees, cradling Morison in her arms. Blood soaked through her fingers, pooling beneath them.

"He saved me," she whispered.

Morison coughed, his breath shallow, blood bubbling at his lips. With a trembling hand, he reached into his jacket, pulling out a small, worn handkerchief.

"A long time ago," his voice rasped, barely above the loud fighting around us. "I met a beautiful woman named Nadia."

Natalie's brows furrowed.

He exhaled slowly, blinking as if trying to focus. He wasn't just talking anymore.

These were his confessions.

"Before the battle at Fox Retreat Hill," he murmured, "I was nothing more than a low-ranking soldier. Sent to infiltrate Jericho's operation. But things don't always go as planned. I got stuck under Jericho's watch. The council never came for me. They left me there to rot."

His grip on the handkerchief tightened.

"The Night Walkers attacked," he continued. "And by then...I no longer trusted the council. But Jericho—he had a vision. A plan to make sure we never had to hide. That we would never be seen as lesser again. So, I followed him. I thought I was doing the right thing. But somewhere along the journey I lost my way."

He swallowed hard, looking down at the handkerchief. "But I held onto this." He brought it to his nose, inhaling weakly.

Jericho's voice rang out from the field.

"Is that my old friend, Morison?" His tone was mocking, smug. He stood a few meters away, Michael beside him. "Finally come back to face punishment like a man, yea?"

Natalie flinched at his words.

Morison's breath stifled. His face twisted in pain but not just from his wounds.

"Nadia was... such a wonderful woman," he whispered. His hand trembled, gripping Natalie's sleeve. "But our love had to be kept a secret."

The words hit like a hammer to the chest.

I felt it before I even fully understood it. Images of Morison's shop and his collected antiques flashed to my mind. But more importantly I remembered where I saw Natalie's crest before.

Morison unraveled the handkerchief and in the center was the very same crest on Natalie's ring.

A family coat of arms.

Natalie's strength buckled. She looked upon Morison differently now.

"I never knew," Morison rasped. His voice was failing now. "The Night Walkers left me to die. The council erased me from history. I never knew she was pregnant. I would have come back for you."

His grip on her arm slackened.

"I never knew, Natalie."

His breath rattled.

"I'm sorry."

His body went limp.

Natalie gently laid him down and slowly rose to her feet. Her eyes brimmed with tears, but behind them stirred a storm of anger, confusion, and a thirst to avenge her father.

Susanne knelt beside Morison, her voice soft with gratitude.

“Greater love has no man than this,” she whispered.

Then, as she closed his eyes, she finished.

“That a man lay down his life for his friends.”

CHAPTER THIRTY-FOUR

THE EVERBORN

Over the wall, into the streets, and down dark alleyways. We weaved between old buildings, roundabouts, and hidden Night Walker routes, moving like shadows through the veins of the city.

Never take the same route twice.

Morison taught me that early on.

My chest burned from the cold air slicing through my lungs, each inhale sharp and punishing. The rapid exchange of breath mirrored the pounding in my ears.

We were on the run.

I risked a glance over my shoulder.

Nothing.

No figures lurking in the darkness. No hurried footsteps. No pursuit.

Had I imagined it? Or had Michael simply let us go?

The shame, guilt, anger, and sorrow from what had just happened burned inside me, a whirlwind I couldn't yet process. Everything after Morison's final words happened fast. There had been no time to grieve and there was no time to waste.

Susanne was the mission all along, if we failed to get her to safety, Morison's death would have been for nothing.

Fighting our way out was no longer a possibility. We were outnumbered, overmatched. Retreat and live long enough to regroup. That had been my first instinct. I grabbed Natalie and Susanne; we scaled the compound wall and ignored the venomous insults Michael and Jericho hurled at our backs.

Pick your battles.

Another one of Morison's teachings, etched into my mind.

This time, it meant something.

His absence didn't feel real. I felt caught between a nightmare and reality, unable to tell the two apart.

I looked at Natalie. Her face was unreadable. Her eyes were dry. Not a tear, not a drop of emotion. But her movements were clear. Robotic but calculated.

She had flipped a switch. And I wasn't sure if she'd ever turn it back on.

But one man's death had breathed life into another's soul.

As the night wore on, Susanne was transforming before me. The battered woman I had freed from the cage was fading, replaced by a woman that was stronger—a woman glowing with renewed energy. Her skin no longer clung to her bones, color returning to her face. Her eyes, once dark, now burned with intensity. And with every stride she took, she stood taller.

She caught me staring.

"Blood rejuvenates me faster than most," she said.

"How did you survive all these years?" I asked, unable to ignore the way her youthful beauty was slowly returning.

She leaned against the brick wall, smirking.

"Jericho kept me on the edge of life," she said, her voice disturbingly casual. "Gave me just enough to keep breathing. Just enough to have the energy to beg for death on some nights."

There was something haunting about the way she spoke plainly, raw, and unfiltered. She didn't flinch. She didn't soften the horror of it. Every syllable carried the burden of terror. An eerie calmness that sent a chill through me.

I couldn't imagine it. Didn't want to.

I turned to Natalie and offered my hand, pulling her to her feet.

"We have to get back to HQ."

"I don't trust the council," Natalie said.

"Yes, but don't we need the vials?" I countered.

Before she could answer, Susanne stepped between us, a new spark in her eye.

"Are these vials filled with a green, fluorescent liquid?" she asked.

Natalie hesitated before nodding.

Susanne's demeanor changed abruptly.

"You need to take me to where you have them."

We picked up our pace. Paranoia was heavy on my mind. The sounds of eerie laughing, Michael's voice, Jericho's eyes, stalking me at every turn and every blind spot. Even though we were deep in Night Walker territory, I could not shake the feeling of being watched.

When we reached Natalie's building, she motioned toward the stairwell.

"Not the elevator. Someone will see us coming."

We took the emergency exit, climbing in silence. The hall outside her apartment was empty. We slipped inside quickly, waiting as Natalie retrieved the suitcases.

Susanne's gaze lingered on her.

"I wish I had her bravery when I was younger," she said.

I looked at Susanne, stunned at her confession.

"You seem pretty brave to me."

She exhaled, shaking her head.

"It wasn't always like that. There was a time when fear and love clouded my judgment. A time when I cowered in the darkness."

"What did you do to make Jericho enslave you?"

Susanne angled her head towards me while considering the question. Natalie walked in, two cases in hand, and broke the strange stillness that suffocated the room.

"It wasn't necessarily what I did," Susanne said firmly. "It was who I became."

Natalie placed the suitcases on the dining room table. The silver latches popped open. "There are two more in my room, but they're all the same."

Susanne took a deep breath and hesitated, as if afraid to touch the vials. Finally, she wiggled one free from the foam casing and held it between her fingers, lifting it, and examining the contents thoughtfully.

"Ah, yes," she said under her breath "So, he's managed to recreate the serum."

"What do you mean?" I asked.

Susanne placed the vial back into the suitcase, then glanced at Natalie, tilting her head toward the kitchen.

"Fika?"

Natalie stiffened, her expression irritable.

"You want coffee? Right now?"

"Is fika no longer customary in Sweden?" Susanne mused. "I know I've been gone a while, but—"

"Cut the bullshit, lady!" Natalie snapped, her composure finally cracking. She pulled out the black notebook and shoved it toward Susanne's face. "Are you the Susanne who wrote this or not?"

Susanne reached for it, but Natalie quickly pulled it back.

"You'll get this after you talk," she said, storming off to the kitchen to make coffee.

Susanne watched her go, a small smile tugging at the corner of her lips.

"See what I mean?" she said, glancing at me. "Her bravery."

I subtly licked my dry lips. I was stuck and I was caught between a rock and a hard place. Natalie's anger was valid, and time was slipping away. But if Susanne truly had the answers we needed, we had no choice but to play this at her pace.

"She's still processing Morison's death," I whispered to Susanne. "She also lost another father figure not too long ago."

Susanne returned her attention to Natalie. Admiring her from a far. But it wasn't the kind of admiration I expected. It wasn't the admiration of a legend recognizing another.

It was an assessment.

"Tragic," she murmured. "But her pain will be useful one day."

I squinted.

Her tone and phrasing reminded me of Jericho. Cold. Calculated. Maybe, after all these years, she had picked up on his way of operating, his way of playing chess.

Natalie returned, carrying a silver tray with three coffee cups. She set them down with more force than necessary.

"Shall we begin?"

Susanne inhaled, savoring the aroma before taking a sip. She let the liquid sit on her tongue for a long moment. Then, without a word, she cracked her fingers, sat down, and crossed her legs. Her gaze dropped to the carpet, distant.

"Those vials," she said, "They're called Compound Green x9 and are used to create an Everborn."

Natalie and I exchanged looks, but Susanne continued, her voice quiet, almost detached.

"Jericho kept me alive all these years because my blood is required to activate the serum."

Silence hung in the air.

"So why hasn't he done that yet?" Natalie asked, her tone suddenly even, controlled.

Susanne smiled.

"To answer that my dear," she said, "we must start from the beginning."

I braced myself for the secrets she was about to unleash—the kind that had been lost to history.

I sat down, wrapping my fingers around the coffee mug. The warmth seeped through the clay, easing my mind for just a few seconds.

She began.

“When I came to Malmö, I was a young, naïve girl.”

Natalie rolled her eyes. She had told me before how much she disliked Susanne’s ignorance when she first arrived.

“On a work study,” Susanne continued, “learning from some of the brightest minds Harvard Medical could give you access to.”

She raised the mug to her lips, finishing the last sip of coffee.

“I thought I was going to change the world...” Her voice stuttered. “And I did. Just not in the way I ever imagined.”

She paused, taking a beat to process her own journey and her downfall.

"I was ordinary. Nothing special. Just another scientist, too busy with clinicals and working on an experimental drug to cure cancer," she admitted.

"Is that where the vials come from?" I asked.

"Not quite," she corrected. "Locked in that cage for years, I had time to think. At first, I thought meeting Henrik was a coincidence, but later, I realized I was chosen."

I pressed my lips together. Her story sounded familiar.

I had been a pawn for Michael.

Morison was a pawn for Jericho before me.

Susanne was a pawn for Henrik.

All of us stalked like prey while they kept a watchful eye on us.

A vicious cycle.

It made me wonder was fate real. Or was it just an obstructed destination, shaped by the hands of those who knew how to manipulate it.

"The night Henrik told me what he was, I was terrified," Susanne admitted. "But he assured me that if I ever tried to leave, he'd find me."

She exhaled, shaking her head.

"And I saw him in action enough times to know his threats were honest."

Natalie muttered under her breath, "He sounds like a real Prince Charming."

Susanne chuckled.

"Believe it or not, he had his ways. But the constant push-pull, the love bombing—it was too much to overcome."

Her gaze flicked toward Natalie's coat pocket.

"The diary. How far did you read?"

Natalie held it up.

"Up to the part where you planned to kill Henrik."

"Ah, yes. The grand finale."

Susanne nodded, recalling the details.

"As you know," she said, facing Natalie now, "I conducted numerous experiments. And one day, I discovered the serum that would transform Henrik into a god-like being. One who could rule this world and walk the earth for eternity."

She sighed.

"But of course, I didn't think he or anyone deserved that power."

"So how did you become an Everborn?" Natalie demanded.

Susanne shrugged.

"Well, it was either me or him. And the only way I was going to defeat him was to become something stronger. Thus, the first Everborn was created."

"I'm not following," I said. "You killed Henrik because you became an Everborn. But you said the serum alone doesn't do the trick. What am I missing?"

Susanne smiled.

"See, I knew Henrik was planning to kill me that day," she said. "Which was perfect."

Natalie scoffed.

"Knowing someone wants to kill you is hardly what I'd call perfect."

Susanne's grin widened.

"I injected myself with the serum beforehand."

She leaned forward. "But it's not the serum alone that does it. It's the bite."

"The bite?" I echoed.

"Specifically, the DNA from his saliva," she clarified. "The DNA activates the serum. Once in my system, the combination morphs and binds to the genes. The transformation takes place instantly—painfully, I might add."

Susanne reached into the suitcase, pulling out another vial.

"Jericho and his minion Luca have finally figured out how to make the serum."

Natalie's posture darkened as realization struck.

"And they must have experimented on the missing Night Walkers before getting it right."

Her voice was edged with both curiosity and agitation.

She stood abruptly; her gaze fixed on Susanne.

"Kind of like you," she added. "Guess history repeats itself." She exhaled sharply. "I need a breather."

Without another word, she quietly slipped out of the apartment.

Susanne remained silent, but her smirk lingered.

"Anyway," she said, turning toward me. "He hasn't killed me because he's the puppet master of games. He told me long ago that I'd live to see Henrik's vision come true. He worships that man, Henrik, a Night Walker ironically a martyr for the Everborns."

I frowned.

"Then where did the other Everborns come from?"

Susanne's gaze darkened.

"They were born. Birth defects of Henrik's habitual incest. Some are pure blood—Night Walkers, some are not—Everborns. Only two pure bloods can make another Night Walker which is why the council has strict laws about relationships outside of their kind."

I stiffened. The weight of her words settled over me.

"I, on the other hand, carry none of their weaknesses," she continued. "Because I was the only one manufactured."

"And Jericho?"

Susanne tilted her head, as if deciding how much to share.

"The night I killed Henrik; I made two vials of the serum before fully committing to my decision." She exhaled, almost amused that she figured out a though crossword puzzle. "Jericho must have found the second vial that night and injected himself."

She glanced at me.

"He was already pure blooded, so he didn't need the assistance of being bit to death. But that's where he lacks knowledge."

I scratched my chin, trying to piece it all together—the past, the present. My mind tangled in a deep web of betrayals, deceit, and power.

My eyes drifted to the label on the vial.

"The serum," I murmured. "Lecce, Italy?"

Susanne frowned, as if the name itself was unlocking something buried.

"That's a good question," she said slowly, piecing the puzzle together herself.

She took a moment, considering.

"I had a mate I worked with that year from the Puglia region of Southern Italy," she admitted. "Lecce has an international university there, but I'm not sure of the connection."

The room went black.

A second later, emergency red lights flared to life, flashing in rapid pulses.

Then came the alarms.

Deafening. Overwhelming.

The high-pitched ringing tore through my skull, leaving me disoriented.

"The hell is that?" Susanne shouted, pressing her hands against her ears.

"I don't know," I said, forcing my thoughts to focus.

I looked toward the door, expecting Natalie to return but she was still gone.

Panic surged through me.

"We need to find Natalie before anyone realizes we're here," I said.

Susanne had moved to the window, pulling the curtain aside just enough to peer out.

She went still.

Then, slowly, she turned back to me.

There was no panic in her eyes. Just a slow, sinking awareness.

"I found her," she whispered.

CHAPTER THIRTY-FIVE

ROMULUS & REMUS

The room collapsed in on me. Getting smaller with each passing second. My knees buckled as I fought to find my footing through the confusion and wave of nausea. The alarm, loud and grating, only worsened the disorientation, sending sharp pulses through my skull.

I forced myself to focus. My mouth felt dry, but the words finally came out.

"What do you mean you found her?"

I knew the answer before Susanne spoke. Deep down, I knew she was in trouble. And nothing good would come from this.

Susanne released the corner of the curtain, her expression unreadable.

"It seems Michael had followed us after all," she mused.

Time to go.

I barely got the words out before she was already moving, steps hurried toward the door.

We stepped into the hallway.

Empty.

My eyes swept the area, searching for any sign of movement. No frantic shuffling of feet. No screaming. No soldiers.

Something was wrong.

I grabbed Susanne's arm, nodding toward the staircase.

"There." I pointed. "We'll take the stairs down to the lobby."

She barely glanced in the direction I was pointing.

"Stairs or lobby it doesn't matter. They know we're coming."

Her tone was indifferent. Almost eager for someone who spent years locked up. She was ready for a fight.

I, on the other hand, understood that killing one—maybe two people would end all of this.

I looked up and said, "I'm still trying to figure out who the good guys are."

Susanne scoffed, pressing the button for the elevator instead.

"Good is a matter of perspective, Leo. What angle are you looking from?"

Ding.

The elevator doors slid open, swallowing us whole.

She leaned against the wall, arms crossed.

"A baby is being born the same time a man is murdered. Yin and Yang. Survival for one person sometimes means death for another."

She paused and kept her attention forward to the door.

"Always remember that Leo," she finished.

I studied her carefully.

"Are you saying there are no good guys?"

She tilted her head, amusement in her smile.

"I'm saying life belongs only to those bold enough to shape it."

My shoulder raised in an upward motion.

"My intentions were futile then."

I swallowed the thought like a bitter pill, accepting that nothing in this world was as it seemed. Even Susanne, once a helpless captive, was beginning to resemble the very people who had enslaved her.

The elevator doors slid open.

As we stepped out, she continued, "Many wars have been fought on the backs of good intentions."

The lobby was as empty as the halls above, but a cold draft crept through the room, wrapping around me like unseen hands.

I remained vigilant, bracing for an ambush, every shadow a threat, every slight of movement a warning. My fists clenched, my body coiled, ready.

But nothing.

The front door stood open, and the wind poured in, sharp as needles against my skin. It howled like a lone wolf singing beneath the full moon.

Each step I took on the cold marble floor was measured and steadied like war drums before battle.

This was it.

I wasn't an Everborn.

I wasn't a Night Walker.

It was time to stop suppressing my instincts and embrace the man that I am.

As we neared the entrance, Michael stood front and center, a knife pressed to Natalie's throat.

My fingers curled into fists, so tight my nails bit into my palms.

Behind him, a sea of Everborns stood at attention, their presence looming, unwavering. At their feet—Night Walkers.

Michael's voice rang out, smooth and commanding.

"For years, we have lived under Night Walker rule." He turned, addressing the crowd. "One to unite or destroy. That is the prophecy. Tonight, I will fulfill our destiny and make us one."

The crowd roared.

I leaned toward Susanne, keeping my attention on Michael.

"If he's the boy, then the future was already written."

She exhaled deeply.

"The future is blurry, Leo. That's what the sisters told me the night before I created the serum."

"You were visited by the Children of the Moon?" My pulse quickened. "Then the prophecy is real?"

Susanne shook her head, then reached for my hand.

"The diary doesn't have all my thoughts. There's more."

My attention was diverted to Michael as lifted the knife from Natalie's throat, raising his hands in mock surrender as he stepped forward.

"No lives need to be lost, Leo. Just give me Susanne." His voice was calm. "Please," his tone almost persuasive.

"I can't do that, Michael."

Firm.

Final.

Michael paused and his disappointment left him speechless for what felt an eternity.

After some seconds he responded plainly.

"Okay then."

And then I saw it.

Before it even happened.

I lunged.

I was moving before Michael's blade struck.

Before Natalie hit her knees.

My body collided with his, sending us both crashing to the ground.

A thunderous impact.

My blood burning like hell's inferno.

Natalie rolled out of the way, breath ragged.

Susanne was already in motion, launching herself into the fray, tearing through the first Everborn in reach.

The two factions collided like a violent storm, and the air filled with the sound of screams, war cries, and the scent of fresh blood.

Michael and I collided, locked in a violent tangle, rolling across the ground before breaking apart.

We stood just a few feet separating us now.

This time, I was the aggressor.

I flexed my fingers, crimson streaks lining my knuckles, and took a step forward.

"Let's finish what we started," I said, mocking his tone, my voice low and menacing.

Michael wiped blood from his mouth, his familiar smirk creeping across his face.

"I'm happy to see you're finally embracing what you are, mate."

We began to circle each other, the world narrowing down to just the two of us.

For a brief moment, everything else faded.

Then—his hands lowered just.

I struck.

Crack!

My fist met his jaw, clean and sharp.

He dodged my next blow and countered with a brutal strike to my ribs.

A sharp jolt shot up my spine.

I swung again—missed by inches.

We clashed, our hands locking, each of us forcing our weight against the other before breaking apart again.

Michael exhaled, shaking his head.

"I've done this for far too long, mate."

My breath was shallow. My stance low, predatory.

The fight was shaping up exactly like the last one.

We knew each other's moves. Mirrored in a way that made my stomach turn.

I went for a leg sweep. He leaped over it.

He swung, but this time, I saw it coming—countered with precision.

He was growing tired. But he was relentless.

Our eyes met and something about his gaze unsettled me.

I recognized them again as visions of the past flashed through my mind.

Not just in the way you recognize a person's face, but in a way that ran deeper. It was like looking into something familiar. Something I'd known all along. The way his eyes gleamed under the moonlight was the same way Susanne's had when I first saw her.

Their structure. Their color.

Something inside me twisted.

He reminded me of her, and she reminded me of him.

What the hell does that mean?

We paused, breathing hard as neither one of us had an advantage.

Then Susanne's voice broke through.

"End this foolishness, Michael."

Michael straightened, his smile vanishing into a harden look. Grief and anger displayed behind his exterior.

"Don't address me like you know me, woman," he demanded.

Susanne took a step forward.

"Susanne, don't," I warned. "There's no reasoning with him."

Michael laughed, cold, sharp.

"No reasoning?" He echoed. "If only you knew...brother."

My pulse thundered in my ears.

Susanne's voice rose.

"Michael, you will destroy everything."

"No," he snapped. "I will build something great. Something big. Bigger than Rome!"

The fighting around us was losing momentum.

Natalie's hand landed on my shoulder.

"HQ is being overrun. This place isn't safe anymore."

Susanne took another step toward Michael, her voice quieter now.

"It's true, Michael. You are the boy in the prophecy."

She hesitated.

From the shadows, another voice emerged.

"And so is Leo."

I turned just as Jericho stepped into view.

"I couldn't let you two have all the fun." He smirked, standing next to Michael. "Susanne, I figured it all out." His eyes flicked toward me. "How did you do it?"

The action paused like the universe was giving us a moment to breathe.

The world waited on Susanne. On her confession. She exhaled slowly, her voice steady.

"Coincidence or fate, but my water broke the night Henrik came to take my life. Hell, it was probably stress that did it."

Her words sent a cold wave through me. Disgust. Confusion. Horror.

"You were pregnant when he tried to kill you?" My voice was hoarse.

"I was," she admitted.

Then she turned to Michael, motioning toward him.

"Jericho took Michael when they came for me."

My heart stilled, missing its next beat.

Michael's eyes. Susanne's eyes. It all made sense.

She turned, looking back in my direction while she addressed me. Her final words.

Something in my body shifted. The predator inside me shrank, replaced by something worse.

"But before they arrived, I hid the quieter of the two in a cabinet, with a letter for my assistant. Her and her husband were also from Dallas."

The words barely left my lips.

"My foster parents?" I asked

"You had twins," Natalie added.

Michael moved before I could react.

He grabbed Susanne, yanking her close, his knife flashing under her chin.

"Yes, she did!" His voice was sharp, venomous. "That's right, brother—meet Mommy!"

I blinked.

The words blurred in my head, struggling to process.

Susanne used the strength she had left and drove her elbow into Michael's gut. The blow knocked the wind from his lungs, and he stumbled backward gasping to catch his breath.

Before I could blink, he bolted toward the back of the building and without hesitation, I chased after him.

Behind us, Jericho's voice rang out, sharp and commanding.

"Stay with the others!" he shouted as he took off after us.

Susanne and Natalie followed, their footsteps close behind.

I rounded the back of the building, heart pounding, eyes darting through the shadows. But Michael was hiding and lurking somewhere in the dark.

"Come out and talk to me, brother!" I shouted into the stillness.

Silence stretched until a figure stepped into the center of the clearing.

Michael.

"How does it feel, Leo?" he called out. "Knowing the prophecy speaks of a boy but come to find out it could be either of us?"

Jericho was the first to arrive, panting from the chase, his coat flaring behind him, a shadow trying to keep up.

"Michael. Stand down."

But Michael didn't hesitate. His face was blank, too calm.

He stepped forward and, without notice, wrapped a hand around Jericho's throat with deliberate ease. It wasn't the first time he'd imagined doing it. This scene had played in his head countless times.

"You're not in charge anymore," he said, a horrifying humor in his voice.

Jericho's eyes widened, not from fear, but from the quiet acceptance that his days on the throne were over.

They acknowledged the power transfer between each other, and the tragic history of displeasure passed between them.

Secrets.

Lies.

Failures.

Wins.

It all lived in the narrow space between Michael and Jericho.

He turned to me next and behind his now black eyes, there was nothing. No semblance of humanity. No conflict. Just void.

"It's time to cash in on that favor you owe me, Leo."

Before I could react—

Snap.

The sound cracked through the air like two light sticks in the dark.

Jericho's body jerked. His legs folded beneath him. But Michael didn't let him fall.

Instead, he bit down.

Fangs tore through Jericho's throat, blood spraying in pulses as his body convulsed in Michael's arms.

Michael drank deep. For him, it was no longer about power.

It was personal.

With no wasted motion, he carved into Jericho's chest with his knife and cut out his heart.

When it was over, he let the body drop as if it didn't matter anymore. Jericho was discarded meat for the buzzards.

He held Jericho's cold heart in his hand, admiring his new prized trophy.

Michael lifted his head, and thick-rich blood ran down his chin and jaw, soaking into the collar of his shirt.

He reached down, tore a strip from Jericho's shirt, and slowly wiped his mouth clean.

I was silent.

Then he looked up and smiled.

I barely had time to process it when the movement from around the corner caught my eye.

We were surrounded.

Everborns flooded into the space, forming a tight circle around us.

Michael took a single step forward.

"This man," he declared, pointing to me, "has murdered our fearless leader!"

A roar erupted from the crowd, and they surged forward. Their eyes wild, fangs bared.

I braced for my end.

But just as they descended, Michael stepped to my side.

He raised a hand.

The mob froze.

Michael was framing me and was orchestrating the entire story from the beginning.

"Stand with me." His lips curled. "Let us rule as brothers are meant to."

He paused, letting the moment stretch.

Then he looked at Jericho's body starting to rot and his smile faded.

He leaned in close, his cheek against mine, and whispered in my ear "or suffer the same fate."

Susanne stepped forward, her eyes fixed on Michael. The look she gave him wasn't hatred.

It was pity.

A sorrowful acknowledgment of just how far he had fallen and how dark his path had become.

Michael tensed, stepping back as she spoke.

"Congratulations, Michael," she said. "You have united the two. But this was never the way."

"Seize her!" he roared.

Time slowed.

But before anyone could react, Susanne looked at me and gave me her final words.

"Puglia," she whispered.

And in a blink—she vanished.

Gone.

No trace.

No wind.

No blur. Just...gone.

Only Michael and I knew what that meant. Only he and I could move like that. But even for us, she had slipped away too fast. She was stronger, quicker, and more viscous than us, but tonight she finally made her escape after all these years. If I survived the night, I had a sinking feeling this wouldn't be the last time I saw her.

The silence that followed was tangible. Everyone stared at the empty space where she'd stood, waiting for an explanation that wouldn't come.

But nothing.

From the back a voice cut called out. Calm. Smooth. Deliberate.

"Excuse me... if you would."

Heads turned.

From the shadows appeared the leader of the Night Walker council, moving with unnerving grace.

He walked toward Michael as if strolling through a dinner party, not a battlefield. In his gloved hands, he carried two familiar black suitcases.

The ones from Natalie's room.

Michael didn't flinch.

Natalie stiffened beside me.

"What is this?" she blurted.

The council leader smiled faintly, his posture relaxed, his tone casual.

"It seems Michael and I have more in common than I originally thought."

"You can't be serious," Natalie pressed.

The surviving Night Walkers were on their knees, their bodies battered, beaten, defeated.

He turned to them but could not stomach what he saw—so he did what he always did; lifted his chin and turned his nose up.

"You are all free." He paused. "Long as you do not plan to rebel. No more Night Walkers. No more Everborns. We are one now," the council leader said.

The words rang out, hollow and absolute as he placed the suitcases at Michael's feet.

I moved to strike, but a force wrenched me back. Strong arms locked around me, pinning me down.

I fought against their grip, but they held firm.

The council leader turned back to Michael, his expression neutral.

"Killing him will only make him a martyr. It will give the remaining survivors something to fight for." He gathered his thoughts. "May I suggest exile instead?"

Michael stared at me, his lips curling into something between amusement and calculation.

"Exile it is."

His gaze locked onto mine, a slow smirk playing at the corners of his mouth.

"Take your love interest with you."

"You son of a bitch!" Natalie shouted.

The council leader barely looked at us, his voice calm, detached.

"Nothing personal. It's just politics."

The world was at a standstill.

A single snowflake landed on my nose the same time my life flashed before me. Each memory running like a film on loop. Details so vivid I could taste the blood from my first kill. That night I turned was the only time I ever truly begged for the death. The agony made me cry to the moon, but my vision was now clear. The moon perfect in all its flaws, guiding me like a beacon on my journey; a journey nothing more than a cumulation of choices. Fate, destiny, and even a prophecy, is man made, and anything man made can be manipulated.

The snow began to fall faster.

I lifted my head, inhaled the cool air, and tasted the damp on my tongue.

The thick clouds separated and the light from the full moon shone bright. A reminder that I was never alone, and like a big brother it always had my back.

I lowered my head, and my eyes met Michael's.

He made his choice.

I adapted his smirk; it slowly formed across my face.

And I made mine.

EPILOGUE

My ears twitched.

A low, rhythmic thudding echoed in the distance. I couldn't tell if it was my heartbeat or just another dream.

The knocking continued.

I shot up from the bed, my sheets soaked through with sweat.

Not again.

I wiped my forehead with the back of my hand, but it was no use, my skin was clammy, my body still caught in the lingering haze of sleep. Sunlight forced its way through the curtains, bright and unrelenting. I jerked my head back, squinting as my eyes struggled to adjust.

Reaching for the gold pocket watch on the nightstand, I clicked the top button.

21:49.

For fuck's sake.

From behind the door, a hesitant voice called out.

"Sir?"

I exhaled sharply.

"Just come in already."

The door squealed open, and a frail, thin man stepped inside, closing it behind him.

"What do you want, mate?"

He swallowed, his posture stiff.

"I wanted to inform you, sir... Puritas Sanguinis is here."

I dragged a hand down my face.

"All seven of them?"

"Yes, sir."

Sliding to the edge of the bed, I slipped my feet into my slippers and threw on my robe. A smirk tugged at the corner of my lips.

"Perfect."

The man shifted uncomfortably.

"Shall I let them know you'll be down shortly?"

I adjusted the robe over my shoulders and gestured toward the window.

"Yes. And close my curtains. I hate this time of year."

"Yes, sir, I understand." He tugged the curtains shut, pressing them tightly together. "The days in a Swedish summer are very long."

He turned toward the door, moving carefully right until I stopped him.

"Luca."

He stiffened.

"Any progress?"

A pause too long. My frustration bubbled beneath my skin. He knows not keep me waiting.

"Getting close, sir."

I lifted the pocket watch to eye level, clicking the button and pointed to the hand ticking.

"Time's ticking, mate."

Luca gave a silent nod and slipped out of the room.

I got dressed quickly and made my way to the courtyard where the council was waiting.

"The great Puritas Sanguinis," I said, arms stretched open, a wide grin on my face. "Thank you for meeting with me."

The leader of the council stepped forward, cautious.

"Forgive me for asking, sir, but is there a reason we were summoned at this hour?"

I reached over my shoulder and snapped my fingers, motioning to my guards.

"Yes. I have a present for you all."

A few moments later, a group of Everborns filed into the courtyard, carrying the gifts in question. The council remained still, but their silence shifted.

The leader's eyes widened. He took a step back.

"What is this?" His voice was firm but questioning.

"A coffin." I smiled cheerfully. "One for each of you."

The coffins were laid out across the grass, their polished surfaces almost blinding under the late sunlight. The locks popped open with sharp metallic snaps. My men stepped behind each council member.

I motioned toward the coffins, still grinning.

"Step in. I hear they're comfortable."

The leader's head snapped toward me.

"I think not! Why would we do that?" His tone hardened.

I reached into my pocket, pulled out a cigarette, and rested it between my lips.

"You, of all people, should understand..."

I struck a match, igniting the tip. A slow inhale, a brief pause and then I let the smoke release into the humid summer air.

"Nothing is personal."

I winked.

The council barely had time to react before my men kicked the backs of their knees, sending them crashing to the ground.

Screams.

Struggles.

Nails clawing at the dirt.

Ropes secured their hands and feet.

I stepped forward and they were being lowered into their coffins. Smiling and looming over the leader's coffin. Slowly, I blew a cloud of smoke into his face.

"You didn't hold up your end of the deal."

A flicker of panic crossed his face.

"Wait—" His breath stalled. "You said—"

"I know what I said."

The coffins slammed shut.

I took one last drag from my cigarette before tossing it on the dirt.

"It's just politics."

Screams of terror faded as the coffins were hoisted and carried away. I didn't look back. I didn't care. Their deaths would be slow, agonizing, and absolute. No one would dare break a deal with me again.

I strolled toward my office, calm, collected. The air was warm; the scent of fresh bloomed flowers filled my nostrils.

I closed the door behind me, eyes immediately drawn to Jericho's old, faded map, with little red dots on the wall. I traced a path from one city to the next, frustrated. I stared at it for a long moment, thoughts swirling until my senses itched.

Something was off.

I turned sharply, fangs bared, hands raised ready to attack.

I hesitated.

A man sat at my desk, feet crossed, arms relaxed, flanked by two sheepdogs seated on either side of him. He was young, tan-skinned, with a thick black beard hanging a few inches from his chin. He wore a white linen suit and carried a creepy, cheerful smile.

"Who are you?" My voice was steady, but my mind raced.

The man didn't flinch. His voice was calm and even.

"My name is Anthony. Who are you?"

Casual.

Unbothered.

As if he truly didn't know.

My jaw tightened.

"I've never seen you before."

Anthony simply shrugged.

"Well, that's because I'm from Lecce. Lecce, Italy."

The words sent a shock of something through me that I didn't like. I studied him, pacing the room, but he didn't move.

"How did you find this compound?"

Anthony rose from the chair.

"Sorry, I'm running late." He adjusted his cuffs, then slipped on a vanilla-colored fedora. "I need to speak with Jericho. Do you know where he is?"

I chuckled darkly, shaking my head.

"Jericho is no longer of service. Let's just say he's retired."

Anthony smile faded, his eyes darkening.

He looked disappointed.

He sighed, slipping his hands into his pockets.

"That's too bad."

He turned toward the door.

I stepped in front of him, blocking his path.

"And why is that?"

He met my gaze, but he offered nothing but a smug expression.

"Because his debt is now yours," he said like it was nothing, like he was casually talking about the weather. "Now, excuse me."

My mind spun.

What in the world could Jericho possibly owe anyone. The details didn't make sense, and the presence of this new guy was making my skin crawl.

I lunged, grabbing Anthony by the shoulder, spinning him back toward me but the second I touched him, my back was pinned against the wall.

Feet suspended.

Vision blurring.

I struggled to breathe.

His grip tightened around my throat like collar, his strength stronger than I ever felt.

He couldn't be an Everborn.

I would have known him.

He was not a Night Walker either.

Anthony held me there effortlessly, watching me struggle.

His voice was quieter now. Sharp and menacing.

"Stupido...arrogante...bambino."

My body fought against his grip, but it was like trying to bend steel. He released me, letting me drop like a used rag doll.

He knelt beside me as I clutched my throat, trying to calm the crushing pain, my face flushed with horror. His gaze met mine and his eyes flashed red briefly before fading back to normal.

He leaned in, his voice low, reciting a warning.

Then, just before walking away, he said—

"Did you really think you were the only ones?"

THE END

*From the beginning this time...**Book 2 – Secrets Buried***

ABOUT THE AUTHOR...

Born in Brooklyn, NY in May 1989, Nixon spent his childhood and early teens moving throughout the East Coast of the United States, constantly adapting to new cities, schools, and cultures. As a first-generation American, he was exposed to a wide range of perspectives that deeply influenced his storytelling. *"Writing has always been my creative outlet, but early on I was discouraged from pursuing it. Instead, I turned to music, writing and recording songs throughout my teens and early twenties."*

In 2010, after being dismissed from Anna Maria College due to lack of tuition funds and a brief period of homelessness, he joined the U.S. Army as a Scout in the 82nd Airborne Division. His military service introduced him to people and places that would later shape his writing. After the Army, he lived an unconventional life as a cowboy, working on ranches across the U.S. and exploring small-town America. Before pivoting to a corporate career, he once again faced homelessness—eventually finding his start at a Big Four bank in August 2018.

Despite climbing the corporate ladder, a series of personal and professional challenges left him unemployed for 18 months. In November 2024, he traveled to Malmö, Sweden, and shortly after, the inspiration for The Everborn Chronicles was born. His work is rooted in dark, introspective storytelling, layered mystery, and interconnected plots driven by complex characters. He specializes in grounded, character-driven fiction rooted in the real world, layered with myth and supernatural tension.

Beyond The Everborn Chronicles, the author is also working on The Choices We Make: A Short Story Collection—a literary project inspired by his journey through struggle, trauma, and triumph. The collection explores real-life hardships, quiet horrors, and the power of choice. In addition to writing, he is developing the screenplay for a TV adaptation. He is also the founder of House of NIXON, a veteran-owned creative studio and storytelling press dedicated to building bold, cinematic narratives across mediums and platforms.

While he continues to divide his time between the United States and Europe, he currently spends most of his year in Malmö, Sweden, where he's exploring the city's creative scene and its ties to Copenhagen's film culture. His recent work has begun to reflect the visual restraint and psychological depth found in Nordic Noir.

www.ingramcontent.com/pod-product-compliance
Lightning Source LLC
Chambersburg PA
CBHW030553310726
48979CB00011B/2138/J

* 9 7 9 8 2 1 8 7 5 4 6 1 7 *